PENGUIN BOOKS

New Penguin Parallel Texts: Short Stor

Ernst Zillekens was born and educated in Germany. He read
English and Latin at Bonn University and was awarded a D.Phil.
in English Literature. He taught German at Oxford and at
Charterhouse, where he ran the Modern Languages Department
for eighteen years and where he is currently the Senior Librarian.

NEW PENGUIN PARALLEL TEXTS

Short Stories in German

Edited and translated by Ernst Zillekens

PENGUIN BOOKS

PENGUIN BOOKS

Published by the Penguin Group
Penguin Books Ltd, 80 Strand, London WC2R ORL, England
Penguin Putnam Inc., 375 Hudson Street, New York, New York 10014, USA
Penguin Books Australia Ltd, 250 Camberwell Road, Camberwell, Victoria 3124, Australia
Penguin Books Canada Ltd, 10 Alcorn Avenue, Toronto, Ontario, Canada M4V 3B2
Penguin Books India (P) Ltd, 11 Community Centre, Panchsheel Park, New Delhi – 110 017, India
Penguin Books (NZ) Ltd, Cnr Rosedale and Airborne Roads, Albany, Auckland, New Zealand
Penguin Books (South Africa) (Pty) Ltd, 24 Sturdee Avenue, Rosebank 2196, South Africa

Penguin Books Ltd, Registered Offices: 80 Strand, London WC2R ORL, England

www.penguin.com

First published 2003

024

Set in 10/12.5 pt PostScript Monotype Baskerville
Typeset by Rowland Phototypesetting Ltd, Bury St Edmunds, Suffolk
Printed in England by Clays Ltd, St Ives plc

ISBN-13: 978-0-140-26542-2

www.greenpenguin.co.uk

In memory of my mother,
Liselotte Zillekens

Contents

Introduction

Any selection is necessarily eclectic and offers a personal view of the stories which have been chosen. The present selection is therefore by definition not an objective survey of this particular genre in German during the past twenty-five years. My aim in assembling this volume of *German Parallel Texts* has been to include a variety of themes and a range of different approaches to storytelling. I shy away from using the term 'short story', as it does not always do justice to 'Erzählung' in German, where the raw material of the narrative can be more extensive than in the traditional British or American short story, and where bigger issues may be confronted.

In Birgit Vanderbeke's 'Das Muschelessen', the only case where I have included an excerpt, the narrative evolves from one event – an evening meal – at which a mother and her two children are present, but not the father, the actual focus of the story. The plot is minimal, as the only event is a conversation over a dinner where the main dish – the mussels – is not consumed. The time-span of the narrative is one evening, with some brief flashbacks to previous events in the course of the conversation. What emerges is the progressive questioning of the authoritarian father figure, who has been striving to mould his entire family in his own image, that of a matter-of-fact, analytical scientist. His destructive influence, particularly on his wife, whose artistic gifts he has systematically suppressed, are gradually exposed. The brief excerpt in this volume contains all these elements.

Dieter Wellershoff also centres his narrative around a meal in 'In Erwartung der Gäste', this time an imminent dinner party, which has a comparable function as a catalyst. In this instance it triggers off a process of reflection by the central character about her affair with the husband of one of her guests and the role of the wife in their

relationship. While Birgit Vanderbeke strips away taboos, Dieter Wellershoff penetrates levels of deception and self-delusion.

Gabriele Wohmann pursues similar goals in her satirical story 'Bessere Zeiten', where she deftly exposes the delusions an elderly couple harbours about the use of cars. They are the perpetrators of all the foibles they find fault with in other drivers they are observing. The way in which she constructs this story underlines the importance of delusion in this context: as a reader you only realize at the end of the story that the couple is actually sitting in a car.

In 'Lascia' by Judith Hermann love has given way to wordless loathing, but in the course of the story a journey with a stranger resolves the atmosphere of enmity between the former lovers, who achieve a new *modus vivendi*, where possibilities are reopened, even that of a future together. The journey reveals the hostility between the two lovers as a form of delusion, as a state of emotional turmoil which has destroyed all sense of perspective.

A sense of perspective is crucial to Georg Klein's 'Chicago/ Baracken'. In this instance it is the perspective of the past, the past of Hitler's Germany. The reader encounters it on foreign soil in the shape of the character of Mr Arno, who is a German émigré living in Chicago. He has made it his life's work to produce a definitive translation of Hitler's *Mein Kampf* as a warning against fascism. The story calls into question whether such a warning can be created effectively in several ways. The narrator, the husband of an avant-garde percussionist, is completely detached from the past which his father had to struggle to come to terms with, because he has no direct link with it. His wife views the past with detachment; it is no problem to her that someone might be dealing in Hitler memorabilia. And Arno himself is caught in a contradiction. It is perfectly acceptable for him to earn money by selling Nazi memorabilia – and fake memorabilia at that, as the pistols he sells are actually 'souvenirs' from the former DDR – whilst endeavouring to produce a warning against fascism in his free time. Furthermore, his perception of the skills required of a philologist to produce an effective translation is such that he loses himself in minutiae that turn his plans to produce a comprehensive new translation of Hitler's book into a

quixotic adventure. Two different aspects of Germany's past are brought together here, but the more immediate one of the DDR is not dealt with. It is overshadowed by what preceded it – the war – and what followed it – German unification, which has produced a new future for the country, as the conclusion of the story suggests.

In Christoph Hein's 'Grossvater und die Bestimmer' the character of the grandfather is overshadowed by the past in a different way. He has spent his life as a man of principle, as a Christian committed to honesty and dedication to duty. As an experienced farm manager he constantly brings these qualities to bear. But he is not prepared to compromise his personal beliefs when it is expected of him by the newly established Communist regime in the DDR, where the allegiance of a party secretary in a machine factory is deemed a more crucial qualification for the position of manager of a big farming estate than the many years of experience and excellent results the grandfather has to offer.

While Christoph Hein illustrates how life in the early days of the DDR was characterized by a destruction of true values, Jurek Becker reveals the oppressive nature of the STASI, the secret service in the DDR, in his story 'Der Verdächtige'. In this satirical story the narrator takes his own personality to the point of self-obliteration to exorcize all suspicion of having been unfaithful to the ruling ideology, only to realize that all his endeavours have been in vain. Ironically, it is the total futility of his own efforts which sets him free from the consequences of any suspicions at the end.

Siegfried Lenz's story revolves round a conflict of a different kind: that between critic and writer, how the qualities the author perceives in his writing may not be shared by a critic. Here it leads a writer to pay a visit to a critic's weekend retreat to demand satisfaction for the terrible injustice he feels the critic did him by dismissing one of his stories because he had been singularly bored. He is hoping that the critic might be suitably chastened when he has heard his latest story. When in the absence of his foe he reads it to the critic's wife, his failure to engage the reader is exposed by the ease with which his listener can complete the narrative.

Different narrative techniques are used in these stories, ranging

from third-person narrative in 'Die Zuhörerin oder Eine absichtsvolle Wegbeschreibung', 'Bessere Zeiten' and in 'In Erwartung der
Gäste', where it is interspersed with a first-person viewpoint, creating
a stream-of-consciousness effect, to first-person narrative. 'Lascia' is
told from the perspective of the girlfriend, 'Grossvater und die
Bestimmer' from the point of view of one of the grandfather's grand-
sons. This results in a distance from the events of the narrative, as
the child does not fully comprehend the significance of the events
which unfold before him. This is also true to a degree for another
first-person narrative, namely 'Das Muschelessen', where the son of
the family is the narrator. 'Chicago/Baracken' is told by the husband of the percussionist, whose role in the narrative is purely passive. 'Der Verdächtige' is also a first-person narrative, one that takes
the form of a personal confession.

None of the stories chosen have complex plots; their concision
helps to intensify the message they set out to convey. All details are
relevant to the narrative. The narrative time ranges from a short
break in 'Bessere Zeiten' to a few days in 'Grossvater und die
Bestimmer'. The venues are also restricted almost entirely to one
place. While I do not claim that these are the most successful stories
published in the last thirty years, all these factors help to turn these
stories into highly effective narratives. The difficulty of finding an
objective yardstick against which to measure the quality of fiction is
illustrated very well in Siegfried Lenz's story, where the story within
the story illustrates the difficulties of creating a successful plot line.
One particularly interesting aspect of the stories is the use of irony, of
which there is quite a variety of examples in this collection, be it dra-
matic irony in 'Das Muschelessen', where the mother finds her out-
of-tune violin broken in the wardrobe one day, or verbal irony at the
end of Siegfried Lenz's story, where the critic's wife presents her
visitor with some poppy-seed cake, adding that it is her husband's
favourite cake (he is not her visitor's favourite person) and that
poppy-seed aids and strengthens both patience and memory, two
areas in which the visitor has shown deficiencies.

The earliest of the stories in this collection is Jurek Becker's 'Der
Verdächtige?', which was published in 1980 and is reproduced here

in the original spelling. (The new spelling is used in this volume only when it is used in the German source from which the story has been taken.) The most recent story is 'Lascia' by Judith Hermann, which was published in 2002. None of the stories chosen has been published in English before. In my translations I tried to remain close to the original, attempting where possible to recreate some of the flavour of the German.

I would like to thank my friend Margaret Jacob, Emeritus Fellow of St Hugh's College, Oxford, for her excellent advice on my translations; my friend Andrew Thomson for his meticulous proof-reading; and my editor, David Watson, for his thoughtful improvements.

The Listener, or a Description of a Route with a Hidden Motive

SIEGFRIED LENZ

Die Zuhörerin oder Eine absichtsvolle Wegbeschreibung

Eine erzählte Laudatio,[1] vorgetragen zum achtzigsten Geburtstag von Teofila Reich-Ranicky[2]

Die Frau des Kritikers war allein zu Haus, in der massiven Hütte am Zürichsee, die nur über einen Privatweg zu erreichen war und die deshalb die benötigte Ungestörtheit während eines Kurzurlaubs versprach. Beim Zubereiten des Tees fühlte sie sich beobachtet, und aufblickend entdeckte sie ein fremdes Gesicht hinter einem Fenster, ein noch junges Gesicht, das einen harten, entschlossenen Ausdruck probierte. Sie öffnete die Tür; ohne Gruß, ohne eine Erklärung schob der Fremde sie zur Seite, trat in die Hütte und lauschte ins Innere, und da er kein Geräusch hörte, fragte er – und in seiner Stimme lag eine vorsichtige Drohung –: Wo ist er?

Statt zu antworten, bot die Frau des Kritikers dem Fremden einen Platz an, lächelte freundlich, musterte die abgegriffene Ledermappe,[3] schlug dem Fremden vor, den feuchten Mantel abzulegen, und als der, widerwillig und nach einigem Zögern, darauf einging, fragte sie, ob der Besucher vielleicht Schriftsteller sei. Der zeigte sich nicht überrascht, verdrossen[4] nannte er seinen Namen – Beat Wrobel –, nannte den Ort seiner Herkunft – Baden-Baden – und bestätigte, dass er Schriftsteller und eilig hierhergekommen sei, um Wiedergutmachung[5] zu fordern für die tiefste Verletzung, die er je erfahren habe.

Die Frau des Kritikers nickte teilnahmsvoll und bot dem Besucher Tee an. Bevor der trank, wollte er wissen, wann die Frau des Kritikers ihren Mann zurückerwarte, das konnte sie nicht sagen, da ihr Mann mit einem Freund von Max Frisch verabredet war, der dafür bekannt war, so lustvoll über eigene Pläne zu sprechen, dass ein Ende nicht abzusehen war. Der Besucher nippte

The Listener, or a Description of a Route with a Hidden Motive

A narrative tribute delivered on the eightieth birthday of Teofila Reich-Ranicky

The critic's wife was alone at home, in the huge cabin on Lake Zurich, which could only be reached along a private path and which therefore ensured that, as was necessary during a short break, they would not be disturbed. While she was making tea she felt as if she was being watched and when she looked up she saw a strange face at one of the windows, a young-looking face trying to adopt a hard, determined expression. She opened the door; without a greeting, without an explanation, the stranger pushed her aside, stepped into the hut and listened inside and when he heard no sound he asked – and there was a cautious threat in his voice – Where is he?

Instead of answering, the critic's wife offered the stranger a seat with a friendly smile, cast an eye over the well-worn briefcase and suggested the stranger should take off his damp coat, and when he reluctantly and with some hesitation went along with her suggestion, she asked whether the visitor might be a writer. He showed no surprise, grudgingly he gave his name – Beat Wrobel – gave the place where he came from – Baden-Baden – and confirmed that he was a writer and had rushed here to demand satisfaction for the greatest offence he had ever suffered.

The critic's wife smiled sympathetically and offered the visitor some tea. Before he took a sip he wanted to know when the critic's wife was expecting her husband to return. She could not say, as her husband had arranged to meet a friend of Max Frisch's who was well known for talking about his own plans so enthusiastically that one could not predict when the meeting

am Tee, blickte auf seine Uhr, musterte grüblerisch die Frau des
Kritikers, und vor ihrem erkennbaren Wohlwollen verharrte er
eine Weile in Unentschiedenheit.

Dann aber, von Erbitterung belebt, sprang er auf, und gegen die
Eingangstür sprechend, fragte er anklägerisch: Darf er das? Darf
ein Kritiker sich damit begnügen, den Inhalt eines Buches wieder-
zugeben, ohne auf die Struktur, den Konflikt, die Psychologie der
Personen einzugehen? Darf er, als Ergebnis seiner Lektüre, ledig-
lich feststellen, er habe sich einzigartig gelangweilt?[6] Und darf er
schließlich einem Autor vorhalten, dass auch ein Buch über die
Langeweile um nichts in der Welt langweilig sein dürfte?

Freundliches Opfer fremder Zeit

In einer Art nachzitternder Erbitterung wandte er sich der Frau des
Kritikers zu: Darf er das? Die Frau des Kritikers ermunterte ihn,
einen Schluck Tee zu nehmen, dies sei ein Earl Grey, eine Teesorte,
die durch einen folgenreichen Unfall auf See entstanden sei, tief im
Bauch eines Teeseglers, beim Sturm. Mit einer Nagelschere schnitt
sie eine Zigarette in drei Teile, zwängte ein Drittel in eine
Hornspitze und begann zu rauchen. Sie schien nicht verblüfft, als
der Besucher seine Ledermappe öffnete, ein Manuskript hervorholte
und – die Reihenfolge der Seiten überprüfend – die Abwesenheit des
Kritikers bedauerte, da er vorgehabt habe, ihm eine mitgebrachte
Erzählung vorzulesen, nicht zuletzt, um ihn zur Zurücknahme seines
verletzenden Urteils zu bewegen. Nach allem, was ihm zugefügt
worden war, glaubte er ein Recht auf das Zeitopfer zu haben. Die
Frau des Kritikers nickte, deutete einladend auf die Schnittchen mit
Lachsschinken und Geflügelsalat und sagte, dass die Schnittchen
eigentlich ihrem Mann zugedacht waren, falls er nach später
Heimkehr noch Hunger haben sollte. Der Besucher biss in ein
Schnittchen, legte es abrupt auf den Teller, und als habe der erste
Bissen ihn unerwartet inspiriert, musterte er plötzlich die Frau des
Kritikers, freimütig forschend, sondern abwägend, und dann sagte er
mit einer Stimme, die keinen Widerspruch duldete: Sie werden mir
zuhören, Sie! Ich werde Ihnen meinen Text vorlesen, und Sie

might end. The visitor took a sip of tea, glanced at his watch and sized up the critic's wife pensively and for a while he remained indecisive in the face of her obvious good will.

But then, animated by anger, he leapt up and, talking in the direction of the front door, he asked accusingly: Can he really do this? How can a critic make do with relaying the plot of a book without referring to the structure, the conflict, the psychology of the characters? How can he as a result of his reading merely note that he had been exceptionally bored? And finally how can he reproach an author that a book about boredom must under no circumstances be boring?

A friendly sacrifice of a stranger's time

In a kind of after-quiver of bitterness he turned to the critic's wife: Can he really do this? The critic's wife encouraged him to have a little more tea; it was Earl Grey, a blend of tea that had come about as a result of a momentous accident at sea during a storm, deep in the hull of a tea schooner. She cut a cigarette into three parts with a pair of nail scissors, squeezed one third into a cigarette holder and began to smoke. She did not seem surprised when the visitor opened his leather case, took out a manuscript and – checking the order of the pages – expressed his regret at the critic's absence, as he had intended to read him the story he had brought along, not least in order to make him take back his hurtful verdict. After the way he had been wronged he thought he had a right to claim the sacrifice of some time. The critic's wife nodded and pointed invitingly at the smoked salmon sandwiches and the chicken salad and said that the sandwiches had really been intended for her husband, in case he should still feel hungry if he returned late. The visitor bit into a sandwich, put it abruptly down on his plate and, as if the first bite had unexpectedly inspired him, he suddenly examined the critic's wife in an openly inquisitive but nonetheless calculating manner and then said in a voice which would not countenance any objection, You will listen to me, yes, you. I will read

werden mir zuhören! Die Erzählung heißt: Wegbeschreibung –
haben Sie verstanden? Die Frau des Kritikers nickte freundlich:
Bitte, sagte sie zuvorkommend, lesen Sie, ich werde bemüht sein,
Ihnen zu folgen. Und der Besucher las.

Gefährliche Wege durch die Gefahr

„In Hamburg, zur Mittagsstunde, ging ein alter Mann suchend
durch Grünanlagen, und als er eine Bank entdeckte, beschleunigte
er seine Schritte. Auf der Bank saß ein tadellos gekleideter Mann in
mittleren Jahren und blätterte in einem Aktenordner und machte
hier und da knappe Notizen. Der alte Mann sprach ihn an, entschul-
digte sich für die Störung und fragte, auf welchem Weg er wohl zum
Hauptgebäude der Baldovia-Versicherung komme, man habe ihm
gesagt, vom Ost-Eingang des Hauptbahnhofs sei es nicht allzu weit.
Beim Namen der Versicherung Baldovia hob der Mann auf der
Bank den Kopf, mit schnellem Blick taxierte er den Fragesteller,
klappte den Aktenordner zu, beriet sich einen Augenblick mit sich
selbst und empfahl dann dem Alten, die Grünanlagen nach dem
zweiten Rosenbeet zu verlassen, auf die Ringstraße hinzugehen und
dieser zu folgen bis zu einem weitläufigen Verkehrsknotenpunkt.
Hier, meinte er, müsse man achtgeben, es sei einer der gefähr-
lichsten Plätze der Stadt, drei viel befahrene Straßen schnitten sich
da, und obwohl ein Wald von Ampeln einen sichereren Weg garant-
ieren sollte, müsste man dort um sein Leben rennen."

Gut, sagte der alte Mann, über eine Kreuzung, und wie weiter.
Dann gehen Sie an der Tankstelle vorbei, sagte der Mann auf der
Bank, es ist ein zeitgemäßer, ganz auf Selbstbedienung eingerichteter
Laden, der übrigens allwöchentlich überfallen wird, zwei Pächter
wurden bereits erschossen. Obwohl das allerdings gegen Mitternacht
geschehen ist, tut man gut daran, beim Passieren auf der Hut zu sein."

Der Besucher unterbrach seine Lesung, musterte prüfend die
Frau des Kritikers, die aufmerksam, nichts als aufmerksam
zuhörte, und fragte leise: Lese ich verständlich genug? Mehr als
dies, sagte sie, und mit einer ermunternden Geste: Bitte, lesen Sie
weiter.

you my script and you will listen. The story is called 'Description of a Route' – is that clear? The critic's wife gave a friendly nod: Please, she said encouragingly, read, I will try to follow you. And the visitor read.

Perilous paths through danger

'In Hamburg one lunchtime an old man was walking through a park for something and when he saw a bench he quickened his step. On the bench sat an immaculately dressed middle-aged man who was going through a file, making the odd brief note here and there. The old man addressed him, apologized for disturbing him and asked how he could best get to the main building of the Baldovia Insurance Company; he had been told that it was not too far from the east entrance of the main station. When he heard the name Baldovia Insurance the man on the bench lifted his head, summed up the questioner with a swift glance, closed his file, thought to himself for a moment and recommended that the old man should leave the park after the second rose bed, turn into the ring road and walk along it up to a large road junction. Here, he said, one had to be careful, it was one of the most dangerous spots in town; three busy roads met there, and although there was a forest of traffic lights that ought to guarantee one's safety one still had to run for one's life.

Fine, said the old man, so across a traffic junction and then? Then you walk past a petrol station, said the man on the bench, it is a completely self-service modern place, which is robbed every week by the by, two tenants have already been shot. But although that had happened at about midnight, one is well advised to be on one's guard when going past.'

The visitor interrupted his reading, looked quizzically at the critic's wife, who was listening attentively, and never less than attentively, and asked her quietly, Am I reading clearly enough? More than enough, she said, and with an encouraging gesture she added, Please read on.

Und offenbar erfreut über die Ermunterung, setzte der Besucher die „Wegbeschreibung" fort.

„Nach der Tankstelle, erfuhr also der alte Mann, kommen Sie auf Ihrem Weg zum Baldovia-Gebäude an einem Fisch-Restaurant vorbei, das vorübergehend geschlossen ist; man hat dort Barsche aus einem afrikanischen See zubereitet, die, statt mit Netzen, mit einem chemischen Betäubungsmittel gefischt worden waren. Wenn Sie sich dann konsequent links halten, werden Sie in einen Tunnel eintauchen, den unsere Junkies für sich entdeckt haben, die sind nicht maßlos, nie bitten sie um mehr als eine Mark; deshalb empfiehlt es sich, immer einige Markstücke in der Tasche zu haben. Und von der Brücke, die Sie danach erreichen, werden Sie in einiger Entfernung, hoch über einigen Lagerhallen, die mannshohen Buchstaben BALDOVIA erkennen, auf dem Dach des Hauptgebäudes."

Abermals unterbrach der Besucher seine Lesung, blickte erstaunt auf die Frau des Kritikers, die keinerlei Ungeduld oder Missmut erkennen ließ, sondern teilnahmsvoll und wie in der Erzählung verschlagen[7] etwas zu fragen hatte. Ob der alte Mann, so fragte sie, nicht noch einmal alle Markierungspunkte wiederholen sollte, also Kreuzung, Tankstelle, Fischrestaurant, Tunnel und schließlich die Brücke – das wäre doch nahe liegend. Der alte Mann, sagte der Besucher verblüfft, tut es tatsächlich, er vergewissert sich, indem er alle Markierungen wiederholt, doch Ihnen wollte ich diese Stelle ersparen. Lesen Sie, bat die Frau des Kritikers, und schon nach wenigen Sätzen glaubte sie, eine gewisse Lustlosigkeit herauszuhören – er las eiliger, las nunmehr monoton, und auch, nachdem er einen Schluck Tee getrunken hatte, änderte sich seine Tonart nicht. Ihre musterhafte Erwartung brachte ihn dazu, die genannten Wegmarkierungen nur noch runterzurappeln, aber dann fing er sich, kehrte zum Mann auf der Bank zurück und ließ diesen die Wegbeschreibung fortsetzen.

Dem suchenden alten Mann wurde empfohlen, die Lagerhallen rechts liegen zu lassen und auf eine unscheinbare Kirche zuzusteuern, eine Seemannskirche. „Haben Sie die passiert, kommen Sie auf den Lutherplatz, der bekannt ist für beinahe tägliche

And obviously delighted by the encouragement the visitor continued his 'Description of a Route'.

'After the petrol station, the old man was told, you will pass a fish restaurant on your way to the Baldovia building, which is closed for the time being; they served perch from an African lake there, which instead of having been caught in nets, had been anaesthetized chemically. If you then continue to keep to the left you will enter a tunnel which the town's junkies have made their home; they are not greedy, they only ask for a Mark, it is therefore advisable to always carry a few Mark coins in one's pocket. And from the bridge which you get to after that, you will be able to see in the distance, high above some warehouses, the man-high letters BALDOVIA on the roof of the main building.'

Again, the visitor interrupted his reading and looked in astonishment at the critic's wife, who was showing no sign of impatience or displeasure, but instead, being full of sympathy and deeply engaged in the story, had to ask a question. Wouldn't the old man, she asked, run through these landmarks again, that is the traffic junction, the petrol station, the fish restaurant, the tunnel and finally the bridge – that would seem obvious. The old man, said the visitor full of surprise, did indeed make sure by repeating all the landmarks, but I wanted to spare you this section. Please read on, said the critic's wife, but after only a few sentences she felt she could detect a certain lack of enthusiasm, he was reading more quickly, was now reading in a monotone, and even after he had a sip of tea he did not alter his tone. Her impeccable assumption made him simply rattle off the aforementioned landmarks, but then he regained his composure, returned to the man on the bench and had him continue the description of the route.

It was recommended to the inquiring old man that he should pass the warehouses on his right and head for an unassuming-looking church, a seamen's church. 'When you have passed that you will come to Luther Square, well known as the site of almost

Demonstrationen. Wer da hineingerät, muss Farbe bekennen, muss sich parteiisch verhalten, keinem wird es dort nachgesehen, meinungslos zu sein. Angesichts dieses Sachverhaltes sind Handgreiflichkeiten unvermeidbar, und weil das so ist, finden Sie am Rand des Lutherplatzes ein geräumiges Sanitätszelt mit geschultem Personal für erste Hilfe. Der angestrengte Gesichtsausdruck des alten Mannes verriet, dass er still für sich alle Ratschläge wiederholte, vielleicht auch schon die Risiken bedachte, die er laufen würde auf seinem Weg zum BALDOVIA-Gebäude.“

Zuhören ist Vorauseilen

Plötzlich, mitten in einem Satz, schob der Besucher die Seiten seines Manuskripts zusammen und legte es, anscheinend enttäuscht über sich selbst, auf den Tisch. Was ist, fragte die Frau des Kritikers, warum lesen Sie nicht weiter? Statt seine Unterbrechung zu begründen, schüttelte er den Kopf, steckte sich ein Drittel Zigarette an und wandte sich an seine Zuhörerin. Stockend fragte er: Sie müssen sicher oft zuhören, oder? Oh, sagte sie, ich tue es gern, ich tue sogar nichts lieber als dies, wer richtig zuhört, ist dem Erzählten immer schon voraus; Zuhören, wie ich es verstehe, ist vorauseilen, obwohl es nicht immer Freude macht.

Der Besucher dachte über ihr Bekenntnis nach und fragte: Dann wissen Sie vermutlich auch, worauf meine Erzählung hinausläuft? Sie haben es sehr früh angekündigt, sagte die Frau, vielleicht zu früh – wo einem bei einer einfachen Wegbeschreibung mit so vielen Gefahren gedroht wird, empfiehlt sich nichts mehr, als sofort eine Lebensversicherung abzuschließen. Ich bin sicher, dass der Mann auf der Bank, der mit dem Aktenordner, ein Profi war, ein Mitarbeiter der BALDOVIA auf Honorarbasis. Und wenn mich nicht alles täuscht, schlug er dem alten Mann vor, sich erst gar nicht auf den Weg zum Versicherungsgebäude zu machen; sondern die Antragsformulare gleich hier auf der Bank zu unterschreiben.

Der Besucher stand auf, unzufrieden mit sich selbst, zwängte er

daily demonstrations. Anyone who gets caught up in these has
to declare his colours, has to take sides, no one is allowed not to
have an opinion. In view of this state of affairs scuffles are inev-
itable, and because this is the case you will find a spacious
medical aid tent at the edge of Luther Square, where trained
staff offer first aid. The strained facial expression of the old man
showed that he was quietly repeating all the advice to himself,
and also was perhaps contemplating the risks he would have to
face on his way to the BALDOVIA building.'

Listening is rushing ahead

Suddenly in the middle of a sentence the visitor gathered the
pages of his manuscript together and put it on the table, appar-
ently disappointed with himself. What's the matter, asked the
critic's wife, why aren't you going on with your reading? Instead
of giving a reason for his interruption he shook his head, lit a third
of a cigarette and turned to his listener. Falteringly he asked, I am
sure you have to listen a lot, don't you? Oh, she said, I enjoy doing
it, there is nothing I enjoy doing more; when you listen properly
you are already ahead of the narrative. Listening, as I see it, is rush-
ing ahead, although that does not always give pleasure.

The visitor thought about her confession and asked:
Then you probably know where my story is heading? You
announced it early on, the lady said, perhaps too early –
when the simple description of a route contains the threat of
so many dangers then the most advisable thing to do is to
take out a life insurance policy. I am sure that the man on
the bench, the one with the file, was a professional who
worked for the BALDOVIA on a commission basis. And if I
am not altogether mistaken he suggested to the old man that
he did not even have to make his way to the insurance building, but that he could sign an application form there and
then on the bench instead.

The visitor got up, dissatisfied with himself, stuffed his

sein Manuskript in die Ledermappe, und ohne sie anzublicken, fragte er: Wenn Ihr Mann nach Hause kommt: werden Sie ihm von meinem Besuch erzählen? Sicher, sagte die Frau.

Sie haben wohl nichts dagegen, wenn ich jetzt gehe, oder? Ich kann Sie nicht aufhalten, sagte die Frau des Kritikers, aber ich möchte Ihnen noch etwas mitgeben auf den Weg. Dort, wo ich herkomme, ist es so, da erhält der Besucher etwas für den Heimweg.

Sie packte ein paar Stücke von dem selbst gebackenen Mohnkuchen ein. Sie sagte: Es ist der Lieblingskuchen meines Mannes. Mohn, fragte er, und sie darauf: Mohn, ja; wie ich gehört habe, befördert Mohn die Geduld und stärkt das Gedächtnis. Der Besucher nahm stumm das Geschenk an, und was sie nicht erwartet hätte. Er verabschiedete sich mit einer Verbeugung.

manuscript into his leather briefcase and, without looking at her, he asked, When your husband gets home, will you be telling him about my visit? Of course, said the lady.

You have no objections if I go now, do you? I can't stop you, said the critic's wife, but I would like to give you something for your journey. Where I come from it is customary to give something to the visitor for his journey home.

She wrapped up a few pieces of the home-made poppy-seed cake. This is my husband's favourite cake. Poppy-seed, he asked, to which she replied, Poppy-seed, yes: I have heard poppy-seed encourages patience and strengthens the memory. The visitor accepted the present without a word and did something she had not expected: he bade her farewell with a bow.

Waiting for the Guests

DIETER WELLERSHOFF

das Gefühl – the feeling

In Erwartung der Gäste

preperations

Sie war fertig mit ihren Vorbereitungen, über eine Stunde zu früh, *(for some)* und seit Minuten kämpfte sie gegen das Gefühl, sie müsse weg- *fight* *feeling* laufen. Es saß unter dem Brustbein und stieg in den Hals hoch. Ihr ganzer Leib wuchs zu einem starren Block zusammen. Was war das nun wieder? Was war los mit ihr? Sie blickte auf den gedeckten Tisch, die Damastdecke, das Berliner Porzellan,[1] den silbernen Ker- zenleuchter und dachte: Ich kann nicht! Ich muß weg! Weit weg von hier! Weg! Weg! Aber sie stand wie festgeleimt, und nur ihre Gedanken schnellten weg und schienen sich aufzulösen. Für Sekunden war ihr Kopf leer, und sie suchte herum nach dem verlorenen Fadenende: Ich habe mich doch gefreut.

Sie war heute früh voller Unternehmungslust aufgewacht und hatte den ganzen Tag mit ihren Vorbereitungen verbracht. Und noch vorhin, während sie den Tisch deckte, hatte sie das stärkende, bestätigende Gefühl gehabt, etwas Schönes herzustellen, mit dem sie übereinstimmte und worin sie sich zu erkennen gab. Es war der erste festlich gedeckte Tisch seit ihrer Scheidung, und obwohl sie das niemandem verraten wollte, bedeutete er für sie ihren sichtbar gemachten, neuen Anspruch auf Glück. Doch als sie zurückge- treten war, um das Arrangement noch einmal zu überblicken, war ihr der Tisch wie eine Täuschung erschienen: übertrieben feierlich und fremd. Und eine blinde Angst hatte sie überschwemmt.

Wenn sie doch schon da wären, dachte sie. Alles würde sofort ganz einfach sein. Die Sanders waren alte Kollegen und Wolfgang und Juliane ihre engsten Freunde. Es würde ein gelungener Abend werden. Man würde ihr Essen loben, und Juliane würde das Gespräch in Schwung bringen. Mit ihr wurde jede Gesellschaft ein Erfolg.

Sie rückte eine Gabel, einen Löffel zurecht und zog ihre Hand

Waiting for the Guests

She had finished her preparations over an hour too early, and for some minutes she had been fighting the feeling that she had to run away. It lay under her breastbone and was rising up in her throat. Her whole body was turning into a rigid block. What was it? What was the matter with her? She looked at the laid table, the damask tablecloth, the Berlin china, the silver candlestick and thought: I can't do it! I must get away! Far away from here! Away! Away! But she stood as if rooted to the spot, and only her thoughts sped away, seemed to dissolve into nothing. For a few moments her head was empty and she was searching around for the end of the lost thread: but I was happy.

She had woken up this morning filled with a spirit of enterprise and had spent all day on her preparations. And just before, while she was laying the table, she had had the invigorating, reassuring feeling of creating something beautiful with which she was in tune, through which she could express her identity. This was the first time since her divorce she had laid the table for a special occasion, and although she did not want anyone to know this, to her it signified a visible expression of her new claim to happiness. But when she had stepped back to look over the arrangements again, the table had seemed somehow false to her: excessively festive and alien. And a blind fear had swept over her.

If only they had arrived already, she thought. That would immediately make everything quite simple. The Sanders were old colleagues and Wolfgang and Juliane her closest friends. It would be a successful evening. They would praise the food and Juliane would get the conversation going. She turned every social gathering into a success.

She adjusted a fork, and then a spoon, then withdrew her

zurück. Allmählich wurde sie wieder ruhig. Juliane war eine zuverlässige Freundin, die immer alles verstanden hatte. Sie hatte sich immer mit allen Problemen zu ihr flüchten können. Das durfte sich nicht ändern, trotz allem, was sich verändert hatte. Sie wollten doch beide, daß es so blieb.

Wenn sie doch schon da wären! An diesem Tisch gab es nichts mehr herumzurücken. Die Gläser standen paarweise nebeneinander, das Besteck lag griffbereit geordnet neben den Tellern, die zarten Blumenmuster jedes Tellers waren dem Blick des Gastes zugedreht. In einer halben Stunde mußte sie das Filet Wellington[2] mit Eigelb überstreichen und in den Backofen schieben. Und sie konnte auch noch duschen und schnell bei Frau Klausmann anrufen und ein paar Worte mit David sprechen.

Nein, das war überflüssig. Er war ja gerne dort. Die beiden hatten sich aneinander angeschlossen. In den Monaten ihrer Ehekrise und auch in der schrecklichen Zeit nach ihrer Scheidung waren Frau Klausmanns kleine gemütliche Wohnung und ihr Garten für David ein zweites Zuhause geworden. Frau Klausmann hatte ein Recht auf ihn erworben. Sie wollte ihn für sich haben, wenn er bei ihr schlief. Wahrscheinlich las sie ihm gerade eine Geschichte vor, und dabei durfte sie nicht stören. Flüchtig sah sie die Szene: David, schon im Schlafanzug, saß im Sessel oder auf der Couch, und sein aufmerksames Gesicht, in dem der Mund ein wenig offen stand, schaute unverwandt zu Frau Klausmann hoch, die groß und mächtig in einem ihrer dunklen Kleider bei ihm saß und langsam, mit gleichmäßigem Nachdruck, aus einem Buch vorlas. Sie durfte sich da jetzt nicht einmischen, sie wurde nicht gebraucht. Vielleicht wäre es leichter gewesen, das Kind bei sich zu haben, morgen jedenfalls, beim Aufwachen, wenn Wolfgang wieder mit Juliane gegangen war. Dann wahrscheinlich würde sie Davids kleinen, zutraulichen Körper vermissen, der sie schon so oft getröstet hatte.

Sie ging in die Küche, um alles noch einmal zu überprüfen: das Filet, umhüllt von dem hellen Blätterteig, die Gläser mit den Krabbencocktails, den Obstsalat, den sie noch einmal abschmeckte und mit einem weiteren Spritzer Calvados übergoß. Die neuen

hand. Gradually she became calm again. Juliane was a reliable friend who had always understood everything. She had always been able to run to her with any problem. That must not be allowed to change, in spite of everything that had changed. For they both wanted things to stay the same.

If only they had arrived! There was nothing more to adjust on the table. The glasses were standing next to each other in pairs, the cutlery was lying next to the plates ready to use, the delicate floral patterns of each plate were turned towards the eyes of the visitor. In half an hour she had to baste the Beef Wellington with an egg yolk and then put it in the oven. And she had time to have a shower and quickly ring Mrs Klausmann and have a few words with David.

No, that was unnecessary. He was happy there. The two of them had became friends. During the months of her marital crisis and during the terrible time after her divorce Mrs Klausmann's small, cosy flat and her garden had become David's second home. Mrs Klausmann had earned a claim to him. She wanted him to herself when he slept at her house. Probably she was just reading him a story and she must not disturb that. Fleetingly she pictured the scene: David, already in his pyjamas, sitting in an armchair or on the sofa and his attentive face, with his mouth open a little, looking up intently at Mrs Klausmann, who was sitting beside him, tall and majestic in one of her dark dresses, reading slowly, in an even voice, from a book. She must not interfere now, she was not needed. Perhaps it would have been easier to have the child with her, tomorrow in any case when she woke up, when Wolfgang had left again with Juliane. Then she would probably miss David's small, trusting body which had consoled her so often.

She went into the kitchen to check everything once more: the fillet, wrapped in pale-coloured pastry, the glasses with the prawn cocktails, the fruit salad, which she tasted once more and over which she poured another dash of Calvados. The new

Sherrygläser für den Aperitif standen frisch gespült und blinkend
auf dem Tablett bereit. Die konnte sie eigentlich gleich nach
drüben tragen.

Obwohl es draußen noch hell war, hatte sie in Gedanken das
Licht angemacht. Sie brauchte immer viel Licht um sich herum.
Sie fühlte sich dann besser verbunden mit dem Raum. Doch da
war noch etwas anderes, eine Szene, die sie wegzuschieben versuchte, während sie das Tablett ins Wohnzimmer trug: Mitten im
hellen Licht lag sie mit Wolfgang zusammen. Sie liebten sich.
Etwas abseits stand Juliane und sah ihnen zu. Sie mußte das Tablett schnell auf die Anrichte stellen, weil ihr die Hände bebten. Sie
hatte nicht daran denken wollen, heute schon gar nicht. Das Bild
überfiel sie immer wieder, wenn Wolfgang sie zu lange alleine ließ.
Es war auch seine Schuld, wenn sie so hysterisch war.

Er hatte am Nachmittag nicht angerufen, obwohl er versprochen
hatte, es zu versuchen, und sie ihn so dringend darum gebeten
hatte. Sie hätte noch einen Augenblick der Vertrautheit gebraucht,
bevor er zusammen mit Juliane zur Wohnungstür hereinkam.
Doch sie hätte gleich davon ausgehen können, daß „versuchen"
bedeutete, er würde es nicht tun.

Nein, sie durfte nicht bitter sein. Heute war Sonnabend, und er
war nicht in seinem Büro. Er hätte unter einem Vorwand raus-
gehen oder heimlich von der Wohnung aus sprechen müssen, und
vielleicht war ihm das zu schwierig gewesen und nicht wichtig
genug. Ihr allerdings hätte es genügt, wenn er schnell einen einzigen Satz gesagt hätte: „Ich freue mich auf dich!" Oder: „Bis
heute abend, Liebling!" Ein einziger Satz von ihm hätte sie sicher
gemacht. Es enttäuschte sie, daß er so wenig darüber nachdachte,
wie er sie stützen und beruhigen konnte. Er wollte sich einfach
nicht vorstellen, wie schwierig alles für sie war, vor allem, wenn sie
auf ihn warten mußte, ohne zu wissen, wann oder ob er kommen
würde und wann er dann wieder ging. Es war ein dauerndes Sich-
anstemmen gegen die eigene Kraft, eine Fesselung von Armen und
Beinen, eine Augenbinde, die ihr alles Licht wegnahm.

Er hätte wirklich anrufen müssen.[3] Wie sollte sie Juliane

sherry glasses for the aperitifs were standing ready on the tray, freshly rinsed and sparkling. She might just as well take them next door straight away.

Although it was still light outside she had switched the light on absentmindedly. She always needed a lot of light around her. She then felt more in touch with the room. But there was something else, a scene she was trying to push aside as she was carrying the tray into the sitting room: in the middle of a pool of bright light she was lying with Wolfgang. They were making love. A little to one side Juliane was watching them. She had to put the tray down quickly on the sideboard, as her hands were shaking. She had not wanted to think of it, especially not today. The picture overcame her time and again if Wolfgang left her alone for too long. It was also his fault when she was so hysterical.

He had not called in the afternoon although he had promised to try and she had urgently asked him to. She could have done with another moment of intimacy before he came through the sitting-room door together with Juliane. She might just as well have worked on the assumption that 'try' meant he wouldn't.

No, she must not be bitter. It was Saturday today and he was not in his office. He would have had to go out under some pretext or other or call surreptitiously from the flat, and perhaps he would have thought it was too difficult and not important enough. For her it would have been enough if he had quickly said just one single sentence, 'I am looking forward to seeing you,' or, 'Until tonight, darling!' A single sentence from him would have made her feel secure. It disappointed her that he gave so little thought to how he could support her and calm her down. He just did not want to imagine how difficult everything was for her, especially when she had to wait for him without knowing when or whether he would come and when he would then go again. It felt as if she was constantly pushing against her own strength, like her arms and legs were bound, as if she wore a blindfold which excluded all the light.

He really ought to have rung. How could she face Juliane

entgegentreten, ohne dieses kleine heimliche Pfand? Es mußte doch ein paar unbewachte Sekunden geben, in denen er schnell ihre Nummer wählen und ein Wort zu ihr sagen konnte. Oder war er pausenlos mit Juliane zusammen? Auch im Badezimmer, und während sie sich umzogen? Sie konnte sich die beiden nicht vorstellen in solchen alltäglichen Situationen. Sprachen sie miteinander, berührten sie sich oder vermieden sie es? Sprachen sie vielleicht über diesen Abend und über sie? Und würde sich das Gespräch noch in ihren Gesichtern ausdrücken, wenn sie gleich hereinkamen? Mein Gott, was für ein Vorteil war es, zusammen in einer Wohnung zu leben! Wie viele Möglichkeiten der Verständigung hatten sie. Obwohl sie nach Wolfgangs Geständnissen[4] eigentlich keinen Grund zur Eifersucht hatte, fragte sie sich oft, was die beiden noch verband.

Fort damit! Nicht jetzt darüber nachdenken. Das machte sie nur unsicher. Sie neigte dazu, alles zu bezweifeln und dann wieder neue, überzeugendere Beweise seiner Liebe von Wolfgang zu verlangen. Sie überforderte ihn damit. Das war nicht klug. Gleich, wenn die beiden kamen, durfte sie nicht verkrampft wirken. Sie mußte gute Laune ausstrahlen. Sie wollte ihm gefallen und Julianes prüfendem Blick standhalten. Beide sollten sie sehen, daß sie glücklich war.

Alles stand bereit, auch die neuen Sherrygläser. Erst als sie auf dem Dachparkplatz des Kaufhauses ihren Wagen abschloß, war ihr eingefallen, daß sie vielleicht keine mehr besaß, und hatte für alle Fälle sechs neue gekauft. Seit sie sich von Ralf getrennt hatte, übersah sie ihren Haushalt nicht mehr. Denn zunächst hatte sie alles, was sie mitgenommen hatte, notdürftig in Schränke und Kommoden gestopft und dort vergessen, wie etwas, das sie nie wieder brauchen würde. Und erst, als sie begonnen hatte, Schritt für Schritt ins Leben zurückzukehren, stieß sie überall auf Lücken in ihrem Besitz. Neulich, als Wolfgang ihr die blühenden Zweige brachte, hatte sie die braunglasierte chinesische Vase gesucht, die ein Geschenk ihres Vaters war. Aber sie hatte sie nicht gefunden. In dem Schrank im Wohnzimmer, in dem oben rechts die Gläser,

without this small, secret token? There had to be a few
unguarded seconds in which he could have quickly dialled her
number and had a word with her. Or was he with Juliane all the
time, even in the bathroom and when they were changing? She
could not picture the two of them in such everyday situations.
Did they talk to each other, did they touch each other or did
they avoid touching? Were they perhaps talking about this
evening and about her? And would the conversation still be
reflected in their faces when they came in later? Goodness, what
an advantage it was to be living together in one place! How
many means of communication they had. Although after
Wolfgang's revelations she really did not have any reason to be
jealous, she often asked herself what the two still had in
common.

Banish the thought! No more thinking about it now. It only
made her insecure. She had the tendency to doubt everything
and then demand that Wolfgang offered new, more convincing
proof of his love. In doing so, she made excessive demands.
That was not wise. Later, when the two of them arrived, she
must not appear strained. She must radiate good humour. She
wanted to please him and withstand Juliane's critical gaze. They
should both see that she was happy.

Everything was ready including the new sherry glasses. It was
only when she was locking her car in the car park on the roof of
the department store that it had struck her that she might no
longer have any and so she had bought six new ones just in case.
Since her separation from Ralf she had not had any sense of control over her domestic affairs. For first of all she had stuffed all
the things she had taken with her temporarily into cupboards
and drawers and forgotten about them like things she would not
need any more. And only when she had started to return to life
step by step did she keep coming across gaps in her possessions.
Recently, when Wolfgang brought her a few sprigs of blossom,
she had looked for the Chinese vase with a brown glaze which
had been a present from her father. But she had not found it. In

links die Vasen, unten die Flaschen ihrer Hausbar und altes, nicht mehr benutztes Porzellan standen, war noch allerhand Krempel[5] zum Vorschein gekommen, Tabletts verschiedener Größe, eine angelaufene Silberschale, kunstgewerbliche Keramikaschenbecher, Weihnachtsbaumschmuck, ein Windlicht für den Garten, den sie nun nicht mehr hatte, nicht aber die Vase, deren etwas abgeflachte kugelige Form sie so sehr liebte.

War es möglich, daß Ralf sie beiseite geschafft hatte, als sie beschlossen, ihren gemeinsamen Hausstand aufzuteilen? Sie hatte jetzt manchmal Gedanken, deren sie sich früher geschämt hätte, die aber plötzlich eine einschneidende Wahrheit für sie enthielten. So konnte es gewesen sein: Ralf hatte die Vase an sich genommen und versteckt, nicht, weil er etwas von ihr behalten wollte, sondern um sie zu verletzen. Es war für ihn eine Genugtuung zu denken, daß ihr später etwas fehlen würde, woran sie hing.

Es konnte natürlich auch anders gewesen sein. Die Vase war vielleicht bei ihrem fluchtartigen Umzug zu Bruch gegangen, oder schon vorher, in dem letzten chaotischen Jahr ihrer Ehe, an das sie sich nur unzusammenhängend erinnerte. Sie hatte auffallende Erinnerungslücken, als sei ihr inneres Leben noch nicht wieder zusammengewachsen. Wenn sie sich jetzt danach umschaute, erblickte sie nur zwei Unglücksdarsteller, die in einem zermürbenden, sich dauernd wiederholenden Stück auftraten, zwei boshaft miteinander vertraute Menschen, von denen der eine, sie selbst, den anderen unerträglich reizte, indem sie immer wieder behauptete, daß ihre Liebe oder ihre Harmonie oder ihre Verbundenheit, oder wie immer sie es genannt hatte, noch unzerstört sei, und sie sich nur vorübergehend in einem fürchterlichen Wahn befänden. Gelegentlich hatte sie auch getrunken, wenn sie aus dem Dienst nach Hause kam und mit versiegenden Kräften versuchte, Ordnung in ihren Haushalt zu bringen, wenn sie schon keine Ordnung mehr in ihren Gedanken hatte, und vor allem nachts, wenn Ralf ohne Erklärung wegblieb und sie das Fernsehprogramm bis zu den letzten Nachrichten angestarrt hatte, oder wenn sie allein in dem großen Doppelbett lag und gegen ihren Willen auf sich nähernde und wieder

her cupboard in the sitting room in which the glasses were ranged top right, the vases on the left and at the bottom the bottles of her home bar and an old set of china she no longer used, all sorts of stuff had come to light: trays of different sizes, a tarnished silver bowl, art and craft ceramic cups, Christmas decorations, a light for the garden which she did not have any more, but not the vase, whose slightly flattened, spherical shape she loved so much.

Was it possible that Ralf had secreted it away when they had decided to divide up their joint household? Sometimes thoughts came to her now of which she would have been ashamed in the past, but which suddenly contained an incisive truth for her. That's how it might have happened: Ralf had taken the vase and hidden it, not because he wanted to keep something of hers, but to hurt her. It would have given him satisfaction to know that later she would be missing something to which she was attached.

It could, of course, have happened quite differently. Perhaps the vase had been broken in her hasty removal or even earlier, in the last chaotic year of their marriage, of which she only had disjointed memories. She had conspicuous gaps in her memory, as if her inner life had not grown together again. When she looked back on it now she could only see two unhappy actors, who were appearing in a gruelling, continually recurring play, two people who were spitefully familiar with each other, one of whom, she herself, would provoke the other beyond endurance by claiming over and over again that their love, their harmony, their bonds, or whatever she might have called it, were still unbroken, and that they were just temporarily caught up in a dreadful madness. Sometimes she took to drinking when she came home from work and with waning strength would try to bring some order to her household, when she no longer had any order in her thoughts, especially at night, if Ralf stayed out without an explanation and she had stared at the tele-vision until the final news bulletin, or when she was lying alone in the big double bed listening against her will to the sound of cars approaching then receding again in the peaceful nighttime

abflauende Motorgeräusche in der friedlichen Nachtstille ihres Wohnviertels lauschte, bis sie sich die Finger in die Ohren bohrte.

Das alles hatte sich geändert, seit sie mit Wolfgang zusammen war. In jedem Zimmer konnte sie nun neue Erinnerungen beschwören. Manchmal, wenn er gerade gegangen war, drückte sie ihr Gesicht in das Kissen, auf dem sein Kopf gelegen hatte, und stellte sich vor, sie könne so eine nachträgliche Nähe herstellen, die er vielleicht noch spürte.

Sie hatte auch jetzt mit den Fingern über die Decke gestrichen und erst Sekunden später begriffen, daß das eine Zärtlichkeit war. Hier würde Wolfgang sitzen, schräg gegenüber von ihr. Neben sich wollte sie Frau Sanders plazieren und Herrn Sanders zwischen sich und Juliane, die dann links von Wolfgang saß. Beide würden ihr schräg gegenüber sitzen, was vielleicht gut war, weil sie sich so gegenseitig weniger beobachten konnten. Aber sie konnte sie anschauen, beide. Für sich selbst hatte sie keinen Tischnachbarn eingeladen. Der Tisch war zwar groß genug, doch sie wollte allein sein. Sie wollte nicht verschleiern, daß sie allein war.

Sie überlegte, was sie anziehen sollte. Am besten ihr langes rotes afghanisches Gewand mit den vielen Stickereien, weil es ein Kontrast zu Julianes damenhafter Garderobe war. Kaum jemand trug noch so etwas, aber sie sah schön darin aus. Und heute abend hatte Wolfgang lange Zeit, sie anzusehen. Sie würde das Essen auftragen und hin und hergehen, o ja, und sie würde ihn bitten, die Weinflasche zu öffnen, so daß sie sich einbilden konnte, sie beide lebten zusammen und bedienten die Gäste.

Während sie sich auszog, um unter die Dusche zu gehen, spielte sie mit der Vorstellung, sie wären verheiratet und dies sei ihre gemeinsame Wohnung. Jetzt zum Beispiel war er im Wohnzimmer oder in der Küche. Sie konnte ihn rufen, und er würde kommen und sie abtrocknen und ihr vielleicht sagen, daß er sie so am schönsten fände. Und sie würde antworten, daß sie heute nichts unter dem Kleid anziehen wolle, damit er den ganzen Abend daran denken könne. Später, bei Tisch, inmitten ihrer Gäste,

stillness of her residential district, until she put her fingers in her ears.

That had all changed since she and Wolfgang had been together. She could conjure up new memories in every room now. Sometimes, just after he had gone, she would press her face into the cushion where his head had just rested and imagined that she could thereby achieve a closeness after the event, which he perhaps still felt.

Even now she had been brushing the cloth with her fingers and had only realized seconds later that it was a gesture of affection. Wolfgang would be sitting here, diagonally opposite her. Next to herself she wanted to place Mrs Sanders, and Mr Sanders between herself and Juliane, who would then be to the left of Wolfgang. Both would be sitting diagonally across from her, which would be good, because they would be able to watch each other less. But they could look at her, both of them. She had not invited a neighbour at table for herself. The table might be big enough, but she wanted to be on her own. She did not want to hide the fact that she was on her own.

She wondered what she should wear. Perhaps her long red Afghan robe with all its embroidery would be best, because it would contrast with Juliane's ladylike outfit. Hardly anyone wore this sort of thing any more, but she looked good in it. And tonight Wolfgang had plenty of time to look at her. She would serve the meal and walk to and fro, oh yes, she would ask Wolfgang to open the bottle of wine, so that she could imagine they were living together and serving the guests.

While she was getting undressed to go into the shower, she toyed with the idea that they were married and this was their flat. Now, for example, he was in the kitchen or in the sitting room. She could call him and he would come and dry her off and perhaps say to her that he found her at her most beautiful like this. And she would answer that she would wear nothing underneath the dress so that he could spend the whole evening thinking about it. Later at table amongst their guests she would

würde sie den Gedanken in seinen Augen aufblitzen sehen und ihm mit einem winzigen Zeichen, einem kaum merklichen Zucken ihrer Lippen vielleicht, darauf antworten.

Sie stieg aus der Dusche und frottierte sich, zog den Bademantel über und ging in die Küche. Das Filet mußte in den Backofen. Zehn Minuten nach Ankunft der Gäste konnten sie sich zu Tisch setzen. Sie wollte nackt sein unter dem Kleid. Wenn er noch anrief, würde sie es ihm sagen. Sie brauchten solche kleinen gemeinsamen Geheimnisse als Gegengewicht zu all dem Unausgesprochenen, das sie trennte. Sie wußte nicht, worüber er mit Juliane sprach. Er sagte nie etwas darüber, genauso wie sie ihm ihre verfänglichen Gespräche mit Juliane verschwiegen hatte.

Sie dachte ungern daran zurück. Es kam ihr jetzt wie eine Einmischung in ihr Leben vor, daß sie durch Julianes Erlaubnis und Regie mit Wolfgang verbunden war. Und doch war es so gewesen, zunächst einmal. Julianes verwirrende Reden waren der Anfang gewesen, und ihre eigenen Phantasien waren erst allmählich in diese Spur getreten.

Sie hatten über Sympathie gesprochen. Juliane hatte leichthin gesagt: „Wolfgang mag dich. Und ich mag euch beide. Ich würde ihn dir glatt ausleihen für eine Nacht. Das muß zwischen Freundinnen möglich sein." Darüber hatte sie gelacht, hatte es zur leeren Theorie erklärt. Doch war ihr damals wohl eine Hemmung genommen worden, obwohl sie noch nicht daran gedacht hatte, es zu versuchen.

Juliane hatte weiter diese lässige Toleranz gepflegt und Bemerkungen darüber gemacht, wie ähnlich Wolfgang und sie ihr erschienen – wie Geschwister, so unbewußt einstimmig, so im voraus verständigt. Es hatte ihr offenbar Vergnügen gemacht, lauter Ähnlichkeiten zu entdecken. Sie hatte dann „ihr beide" gesagt und sich auf diese Weise selbst abseits gestellt, oder nicht abseits, eher über sie. Oft, wenn es spät geworden war, hatte sie Wolfgang aufgefordert: „Fahr doch Claudia nach Hause." Sie selbst gab meistens vor, schon zu müde zu sein und ins Bett zu wollen. Einmal war sie auch übers Wochenende verreist, und das hatte sie ihr gegenüber angekündigt mit der Bemerkung: 'Du könntest dich ein bißchen um Wolfgang kümmern.'

see the thought flash through his mind and respond to him with a tiny little sign, a hardly discernible twitching of her lips perhaps.

She got out of the shower, dried herself, put on the bathrobe and went into the kitchen. The fillet had to be put into the oven. Ten minutes after the guests had arrived they could then sit down at table. She wanted to be naked under the dress. If he did call she would tell him. They had to have such small secrets between them as a balance to all the unspoken things which separated them. She did not know what he talked about to Juliane. He never said anything about it just as she had kept her tricky conversations with Juliane from him.

She did not like thinking back to them. It seemed to her like an interference in her life that through Juliane's permission and direction she was now linked to Wolfgang. And yet it had been like this first of all. Juliane's confusing speeches had been the beginning and her own fantasies had only gradually followed in this track.

She had talked about attraction. Juliane had said casually, 'Wolfgang likes you. And I like you both. I would lend him to you for a night just like that. Surely that's OK between friends.' She had laughed at this and dismissed it as an empty theory. But she had probably been freed from an inhibition then, although she had not yet actually thought of trying it.

Juliane had continued to cultivate this casual tolerance and had made remarks like how similar she and Wolfgang seemed – like brother and sister, so unconsciously on the same wavelength anticipating each other's thoughts. It had obviously given her pleasure simply to discover so many things in common. She had then said 'the two of you', thereby sidelining herself, or rather placing herself above them. Often, when it had got late, she had asked Wolfgang, 'Do take Claudia home.' She herself made out that she was too tired and wanted to go to bed. On one occasion she had gone away for the weekend and she had announced this to her with the comment 'You might look after Wolfgang a little.'

Der Schock war ihr in die Beine gefahren, als wäre sie entlarvt worden. Vor allem erschrak sie darüber, daß es sie so plötzlich packte. Steif und förmlich hatte sie zugesagt. Ja, sie würde ihn zum Essen einladen. Sobald Juliane gefahren war, hatte sie Wolfgang angerufen. Er war gekommen und über Nacht geblieben.

Wußte Juliane das alles nicht? Konnte sie es nicht ahnen? Sie mußte doch sehen, wie anders er jetzt aussah, wie sein Ausdruck, seine Haltung sich verändert hatten. Er konnte wieder lächeln, und es war ein Lächeln, das sein Gesicht öffnete, nicht die beflissene Maske höflicher Zustimmung, die er früher getragen hatte.

Er war in einer schlimmen Verfassung gewesen, gespannt, mit unsicheren Händen, unruhigen, ausweichenden Augen, so konventionell in allem, was er sagte und wie er sich benahm, so zurückgenommen auf unanfechtbare Korrektheiten, ein Mensch, der anderen kleinlaut beipflichtete und sich häufig räuspern mußte, um noch ein wenig Ton in der Stimme zu haben, ein halb ausgelöschter Mensch, der sich am Rand einer Depression bewegte und angestrengt, mit einer verzweifelten Tapferkeit aufrechthielt.

So hatte sie es gesehen, damals, als sie noch zusammen mit Ralf zu Julianes intellektuellen Abendgesellschaften kam, bei denen Wolfgang sich auf die Rolle eines fürsorglichen und unauffälligen Gastgebers beschränkte, während Juliane in der Runde das Wort führte, mit ihren weitgespannten, herrscherlichen Sätzen. Später, als sie nachmittags allein zu Juliane ging, um sich bei ihr auszusprechen, hatte sie Wolfgang meistens nur kurz gesehen. Er schaute herein, wenn er aus seinem Büro nach Hause kam, begrüßte sie und Juliane und zog sich nach ein paar Worten zurück. Seine ganze Haltung drückte aus, daß er sich nicht aufdrängen wolle. Er kam schon mit diesem Ausdruck herein: Hier bin ich, ich geh gleich wieder. Habt ihr alles, fehlt euch nichts? Und ihr, Claudia, ging es gut? Sie wußte nicht, ob Juliane ihm von ihren Problemen erzählt hatte und konnte nur abwehrend antworten – jaja, es ginge gut – womit sie ihm ungewollt das Wort abschnitt.

Damals, als sie zu Juliane ging, um mit ihr über die fortschreitende Auflösung ihrer eigenen Ehe zu sprechen, schienen ihr alle

The shock had gone to her legs, as if she had been unmasked. She was particularly shocked that it seized her so suddenly. Stiffly and formally she had agreed. Yes, she would invite him to dinner. As soon as Juliane had gone she had called Wolfgang. He had come and stayed the night.

Didn't Juliane know all this? Was it possible she didn't have an inkling? For she must see how differently he now looked, how his expression, his attitude had changed. He was able to smile again and it was the smile that opened up his face, not the studied mask of polite consent he had worn before.

He had been in a terrible state: tense, with nervous hands and restless, evasive eyes, so conventional in everything that he said and how he behaved, so restrained in an uncontroversial correctness, a person who timidly agreed with others and who had to clear his throat all the time in order to get a little tone into his voice, a half-obliterated man hovering on the edge of depression and straining with desperate courage to hold himself together.

That's how she had seen it when she had come to Juliane's intellectual soirées with Ralf, at which Wolfgang would restrict himself to the role of a caring and unobtrusive host, while Juliane held forth to the assembled company with her expansive, bossy remarks. Later, when she went to see Juliane in the afternoons on her own in order to unburden herself, she had usually only seen Wolfgang briefly. He looked in when he came home from his office, greeted her and Juliane, said a few words and then withdrew. His whole attitude suggested that he did not wish to intrude. When he came in he was already saying, here I am, but I'm not staying. Do you have everything, is there anything you want? And how was Claudia? She did not know whether Juliane had told him of her problems and could only answer defensively – yes, yes, she was fine which had the unintended effect of cutting him off.

At that time when she went to Juliane to discuss the progressive disintegration of her own marriage everyone around her

Menschen um sie herum weniger vom Unglück betroffen zu sein als sie selbst. Sie hatte Juliane so gesehen, wie sie sie brauchte und wie sie wohl auch gesehen werden wollte, mit diesem überlegenen Stil, den sie pflegte: Juliane, sportlich und teuer gekleidet, den Kragen der Bluse über den Kragen des Kostüms geklappt, im Halsausschnitt ein locker geschlungenes Chiffontuch, die kleine italienische Tasche an einem Tragriemen über die Schulter gehängt, so kam sie daher, umgeben von einem frischen Lemonenduft, Juliane, die Schicksallose, die Unangreifbare, deren Augen meistens von den getönten Gläsern einer großen, kühngeformten Brille verdeckt waren, wenn sie durch die Straßen ging, Juliane, die Praktische und Sachliche, die im Lehrerkollegium genauso dominierte wie zu Hause, und für sie, die Jüngere, die sich schwer hineinfand in den neuen Beruf, eine beschützende Mentorin war.

Hatte sie denn nie etwas anderes gesehen, bevor sie von Wolfgang erfuhr, daß es mit ihm und Juliane im Bett nicht klappte, daß sie beide ganz verzweifelt waren? War sie so blind gewesen, daß er sie erst darauf stoßen mußte?

Er hatte es ihr gestanden, als er zum erstenmal über Nacht bei ihr blieb und es zwischen ihnen klar war, daß sie miteinander schlafen würden. Er hatte ihr seine Hemmungen erklären wollen, die ihr, so befangen, wie sie sich selbst fühlte, viel weniger bewußt gewesen waren als ihm. Und vielleicht wollte er beängstigende Erwartungen abwehren, die er bei ihr vermutete. Jedenfalls sagte er: „Hab ein bißchen Geduld mit mir." Und als sie antwortete – „Geduld? Wieso denn? Das ist doch dumm. Ich brauche keine Geduld, wenn du bei mir bist" – als sie ihm das sagte, sich ihm ganz zuwendend, seinem gespannten, verletzbaren Gesicht, das sie mit kleinen, beruhigenden Küssen zu lösen versuchte, hatte er erklärend hinzugefügt: „Ich habe seit über einem Jahr nicht mehr mit Juliane geschlafen."

Wieso fühlte sie sich so erleichtert und glücklich, als er das sagte? Hatte er sie ins Recht gesetzt? Glaubte sie, nun alles zu verstehen? In diesem Augenblick empfand sie, daß er ganz ihr gehörte, und Juliane, die Bewunderte, Erwachsene, die ihnen beiden so

seemed to be less stricken with misfortune than she was. She had seen Juliane in the way she needed her to be, and probably also in the way she wanted to be seen, with that superior style which she cultivated: Juliane, with her sporty, expensive clothes, the collar of her blouse turned out over the collar of her suit, a loosely tied chiffon scarf round her neck, the small Italian hand-bag on a strap over her shoulder, that's how she came walking along, wafting fresh lemon scent, Juliane the fateless, the unassailable, whose eyes were usually obscured by the tinted len-ses of large boldly shaped glasses when she was walking along the road, Juliane, so practical and to the point, who dominated the teachers' common room just as much as at home, and who was for her, the younger of the two, who was finding it difficult settling into her new job, a protecting mentor.

So had she never seen anything else, before she learnt from Wolfgang that things were not working in bed for him and Juli-ane, that they were quite desperate? Had she been so blind that he had to make her notice it?

He had confessed it to her the first time he had stayed the night with her and it had become clear between them that they would sleep together. He had wanted to explain his inhibitions to her, of which she, self-conscious as she was, had been far less aware than he. And perhaps he had wanted to fend off alarming expectations, which he assumed she had. Anyway, he said, 'Be a little patient with me.' And she had replied, 'Patient? What for? That's just silly. I don't need patience when you are with me.' When she said this to him, turning fully towards him, to his tense, vulnerable face, which she tried to relax with light, soothing kisses, he had added as an explanation, 'I have not slept with Juliane for over a year.'

Why did she feel so relieved and happy when he said this? Had he made her feel she was in the right? Did she now think she understood everything? At that moment she felt that he was all hers, that Juliane the admired, the grown-up, who was so

überlegen war, keine Macht über sie hatte, Juliane wurde nicht
entthront, nur war sie nicht mehr anwesend, sie verschwand im
Hintergrund, und sie beide waren unerreichbar für alle, so eng
umschlungen, wie sie hier lagen auf dem aufgedeckten Bett, ge-
streift vom Lichtschein der Stehlampe, über die sie, das wußte sie
noch, irgend etwas hängen wollte, ein Tuch, ein Kleidungsstück,
um nicht geblendet zu werden. Statt dessen hatte sie die Lampe
nur ein Stück beiseite geräumt, so daß sie in einem weichen, ver-
schatteten Halblicht lagen. Es geschieht mit uns, hatte sie gedacht.
Sie hatte sich so wirklich gefühlt. Sie konnten sich jetzt heilen aneinander. Alles war richtig.

Als er ihr dieses unerwartete Geständnis gemacht hatte, war
der Druck von ihr genommen worden, das Gewicht einer verborgenen Niederlage, ihre Unterlegenheit. Sie hatte nicht mehr
an Juliane gedacht, sondern nur sich selbst gespürt. Sie war auf
einmal dieser pulsende, sich öffnende Körper, warm, fleischlich,
atmend, naß, gegen den es keinen Einspruch und kein verbrieftes
Recht gab. Das hatte er ihr ins Ohr geflüstert, als sie zusammen-
lagen und sich sanft bewegten. Dauernd sprach er zu ihr in beiden
Sprachen, mit diesem langsamen Gleiten in ihr und den geflüs-
terten Worten an ihrem Ohr, in ihrer Halsbeuge, während sie
stumm blieb und alles in sich einschloß, um es zu behalten.
Dann erst hörte sie, daß sie antwortete. Aber es waren nur Laute,
die sich aus ihr lösten, eine heller werdende Stimme, die wie
wachsendes Erstaunen klang und ihr nicht mehr wie ihre eigene
erschien. Für Augenblicke taute alles weg, und sie fanden sich
wieder, beieinander liegend, als hätten ihre Körper endlich ihren
Platz in der Welt gefunden und nichts brauchte mehr getan,
nichts mehr geändert zu werden. Das Lächeln auf ihren Gesichtern
hatte bedeutet: Wir sind da, wo wir immer schon sein mußten, du
und ich. Sie hatte das nie zuvor erlebt, und sie wußte, daß es ihm
auch so ging. Sie hatte gedacht, dies sei ein unverlierbares Pfand,
eine Gewißheit, die sie immer behalten würden. Sie hatte es
gedacht.

*

superior to them both, had no power over them. Juliane was not being dethroned, she was just no longer present, she disappeared into the background, and the two of them were beyond anybody's reach, so closely intertwined as they were lying here on the bed with the cover turned down, touched by the light of the standard lamp, over which, she still remembered this, she had wanted to put something, a scarf, an item of clothing, so as not to be blinded. Instead, she had just put the lamp a little to one side, so that they were lying in a soft, shaded half-light. It is happening between us, she had thought. She had felt so real. They could now heal each other. Everything was right.

When he had made this unexpected confession to her, the pressure had been taken off her, the weight of a hidden defeat, her inferiority. She had no longer been thinking of Juliane, but she had only felt her own self. She was suddenly this pulsating, opening body, warm, fleshy, breathing, wet, against which there was no objection, no vested right. That is what he had whispered into her ear as they were lying there, moving gently. He spoke to her constantly in both languages, through this slow sliding inside her and the words whispered into her ear, into her neck, while she remained silent, enclosing everything inside her in order to keep it. Only then did she hear that she was answering. But they were only sounds which were loosening up inside her, a voice that was growing lighter, which sounded like growing astonishment and no longer appeared to her like her own. For moments everything melted away and they found themselves lying next to each other again as if their bodies had finally found their place in the world, and nothing needed to be done any more, nothing needed to be changed. The smiles on their faces had meant: we are here, where we always should have been, you and I. She had never experienced this before and she knew that he had not either. She had thought that this was a token that could not be lost, a certainty they would always keep. This is what she had thought.

*

Er war dann neben ihr eingeschlafen, und sie hatte sich wachgehalten, um ihn zu betrachten. Ein wenig hatte sie sich wie ein Kind gefühlt, dem ein wunderbares Geschenk gemacht worden ist und das nun, in einer Glückslähmung versunken, davor sitzt, um es ununterbrochen anzuschauen. Sein Gesicht schien jünger geworden zu sein. Es war entspannt und glatt und warm durchblutet. An der Halsader hatte sie seinen ruhigen Pulsschlag beobachtet, und vorsichtig, um ihn nicht zu wecken, hatte sie sich neben ihn gelegt und die Decke an sich hochgezogen. Sie lag ausgestreckt auf dem Rücken und wollte noch einmal den Kopf drehen, um ihn von der Seite zu betrachten, da kam ihr Juliane vor Augen, wie sie sie gesehen hatte, einige Tage zuvor im Lehrerzimmer in einem kurzen, unbewachten Moment.

Sie war dort in einer Freistunde allein gewesen und hatte in der Ecke bei den Lexika gesessen, um ein paar historische Daten nachzuschlagen. Plötzlich war Juliane hereingekommen, hatte ihre Mappe auf den Tisch gelegt und sich gesetzt, den Kopf in beide Hände vergrabend. Sie hatte einen Augenblick reglos dagesessen, dann hatte sie den Kopf ein wenig gehoben und mit den Fingerspitzen vorsichtig die Schläfen massiert. Gleich danach war die Bewegung wieder erstarrt, und sie hatte aufgestöhnt.

„Mein Gott, was ist, Juliane?" hatte sie gefragt und in ein aufgerissenes, aufgewühltes Gesicht geblickt.

„Sag doch, daß du hier bist", hatte Juliane sie angefahren.

„Ich habe gedacht, du hast mich gesehen", hatte sie sich verteidigt, und Juliane hatte gleich eingelenkt und gesagt, sie habe Kopfschmerzen. Das hatte sie sofort geglaubt.

Doch nun, während sie dort lag, noch gesättigt und berauscht von der Liebe mit Julianes Mann, war ihr die Szene anders erschienen. Sie waren auf einmal zu dritt in einem einzigen Raum, und Julianes schönes, aufgewühltes Gesicht blickte direkt zu ihnen herüber. Trotzdem hatte sie keine Angst empfunden, nur eine aufwallende Zärtlichkeit für ihre Freundin. Sie hätte sie umarmen mögen, um ihr zu sagen: Siehst du, so ist das nun mal. Das ist nicht mehr zu ändern. Leide bitte nicht so fürchterlich.

*

He had then fallen asleep next to her and she had kept herself awake in order to look at him. She had felt a little like a child who had been given a wonderful present and who now, immersed in a paralysis of happiness, was sitting in front of it in order to look at it all the time. His face seemed to have grown younger. He was relaxed and smooth and pulsating with warm blood. She had watched the even pulse in his jugular vein and quietly, so as not to wake him, she had lain down beside him and pulled up the cover. She was lying stretched out on her back, and was about to turn her head once more to look at him from the side when Juliane came to her mind as she had seen her a few days ago in the staff room in a brief, unguarded moment.

She had been there on her own in a free period and had been sitting in a corner near the encyclopedias in order to look up a few historical facts. Suddenly Juliane had come in, put her brief-case on the table and sat down and buried her head in both hands. She had sat motionless for a moment, then she had lifted her head and carefully massaged her temples with her fingertips. Soon afterwards she had stopped moving again and had groaned.

'My God, what's the matter, Juliane?' she had asked, looking into a terrified, ravaged face.

'Don't announce yourself,' Juliane had snapped at her.

'I thought you had seen me,' she had defended herself and Juliane had immediately come round and said that she had a headache. She had believed it at once.

But now, as she lay there, still fulfilled and intoxicated from having made love to Juliane's husband, the scene had taken on a different light. The three of them were suddenly in the same room and Juliane's ravaged, beautiful face was looking directly at them. Nevertheless she had not felt any fear, just a budding tenderness towards her friend. She could have put her arms around her to tell her: look, that's just the way it is. It cannot be changed any more. Please don't suffer so terribly.

*

Aber konnte Juliane überhaupt leiden? Ließ sie es zu? Waren es nicht doch nur Kopfschmerzen und beruflicher Ärger gewesen, die sie momentweise so verwandelt hatten? Sie war sofort bereit gewesen, es so zu sehen, weil es ihren Wünschen entsprach. Ja, Juliane erfüllte ihre Wünsche, indem sie sich so wunderbar hielt. Stimmte vielleicht auch die Umkehrung, daß Juliane immer Schwächere brauchte, von denen sie sich unterscheiden konnte und von deren Bewunderung sie lebte?

In ihrer Vorstellung war sie es gewesen, die Julianes Freundschaft suchte. Sie hatte in ihr alles gesehen, was ihr fehlte, diese anscheinend anstrengungslose Überlegenheit, mit der Juliane alles in der Hand hatte, ihren Beruf, ihren Haushalt und vor allem auch sich selbst. Während sie Angst hatte, eine in ihr bereitliegende Angst, zu versagen und sich zu verlieren, die sie immer wieder heimsuchte. Sie konnte sie manchmal hören, etwas entfernt, eine falsche Musik, eine zittrige Geigenstimme, die immer weiter spielte und sich immer aussichtsloser in einen Irrtum verlor, ohne daß sie etwas dagegen tun konnte, obwohl sie selbst es war, die spielte, vor einem entsetzten Publikum und außerhalb ihres eigenen Verstandes, der sich verzweifelt bemühte, sich ins Gedächtnis zu rufen, wie das Stück weiterging.

So war es gewesen, damals. Der Dirigent hatte abgeklopft, es war ein Augenblick brausender Leere um sie herum gewesen, und das fragende Gesicht des Dirigenten war vor ihr erschienen. Sie hatte genickt, aber sie wußte, daß das nur die Einwilligung in die Katastrophe war. Denn als das Orchester erneut einsetzte, hatte sie nach wenigen Takten wieder die Melodie verloren und war hinausgerannt.

Sie hatte geglaubt, daß ihr Leben zu Ende sei, und sich in eine schwer faßbare Krankheit fallen lassen, einen Nervenzusammenbruch mit jähen Schweißausbrüchen und wiederkehrenden Wellen hohen Fiebers. In der trockenen Hitze brannte die Angst weiter, aber es gab auch tranceartige Halbträume, in denen ihr eine vergessene Glücksgestalt erschien, der Schneemann, den ihr Vater – auch damals war sie krank gewesen – auf dem Balkon ihres Zimmers für sie gebaut hatte und ihr eines Morgens zeigte. Die

But was Juliane capable of suffering? Did she admit it? Had it not been merely a headache and the aggravations of work which had transformed her in that moment? She was immediately willing to see it like that, because it corresponded to her wishes. Yes, Juliane fulfilled her wishes by bearing up so wonderfully. Was the reverse also true perhaps, that Juliane needed weaker people from whom she could set herself apart and on whose admiration she lived?

In her mind it had been she who had sought out Juliane's friendship. She had seen everything in her that she was lacking, this seemingly effortless superiority with which Juliane controlled everything, her job, her household and above all herself. Whereas she had a fear, always lurking within her, that she might fail, that she might lose herself, a fear which overcame her time and again. She could sometimes hear it a short distance away, music that was out of tune, the shaky sound of a violin which went on playing and which went ever more hopelessly astray without her being able to do anything about it, although it was she herself who was playing in front of a horrified audience and outside her own mind, which was desperately trying to recall how the piece went on.

That's how it had been, then. The conductor had stopped the orchestra, there had been a moment of resounding emptiness around her, and the inquiring face of the conductor had appeared before her. She had nodded, but she knew that she was consenting to a disaster. For when the orchestra had started up again she had lost the melody again after a few bars and had run out.

She had thought that her life was at an end, and had let herself slide into an illness that was hard to diagnose, a nervous breakdown with sudden outbreaks of perspiration and recurrent bouts of high temperature. In the dry heat the fear smouldered on, but there were also trance-like semi-dreams in which a forgotten image of happiness appeared to her, the snowman that her father had built – she had also been ill then – on the balcony of her room and shown her one morning. The small white

kleine, weiße Gestalt bewachte die Grenze, über die sie nicht
hinaus durfte. Eine Zeitlang blieb sie dort, in der Nähe des kleinen,
weißen Idols mit den schwarzen Augenpunkten, dann hatte sie sich
der Welt vorsichtig wieder zugewandt.

Neben ihrem Bett standen die Blumensträuße von Ralf, der zu
dieser Zeit noch ein fürsorglicher Freund war. Sie hatte ihn geheira-
tet, weil er da war, als sie ihn brauchte. Sie liebte ihn als eine
beruhigende Notwendigkeit und mit einem Verlangen nach Über-
einstimmung, das ihn wahrscheinlich überfordert hatte. Zur Musik-
hochschule war sie nicht mehr zurückgekehrt. Statt dessen ging sie
zur Universität, um Lehrerin zu werden. Alles hatte sie getan, um
wegzukommen von der Angst.

Doch eines Tages war die Angst wieder da. Vielleicht weil sie
schwanger war und ahnte, noch nicht begriff, daß ihre Ehe sich
aufzulösen begann. Plötzlich war sie wieder laut geworden, die
falsche Geigenstimme, die sich entfernte und sie zurückließ mit leer-
geräumtem, rasendem Verstand, der nichts mehr zu fassen bekam.
Unfähig zu sprechen, stand sie in einem Klassenzimmer vor einer
Wand von starrenden Gesichtern, die ihr keinen Ausweg ließen.
Sie stand da, ohnmächtig, und verlor ihr Ich, fühlte körperlich ihr
immer rascheres Auseinanderrinnen, ihre Verflüchtigung. Auf einmal war Juliane da gewesen, der Lemonenduft, ihre ruhige
Stimme. Juliane hatte sie untergehakt und war mit ihr nach
draußen gegangen. In einem kleinen Café in der Nähe der Schule,
wo sie sich in einer Ecke gegenübersaßen, war sie allmählich aus
ihrer Erstarrung herausgekommen und hatte vor sich das schöne,
kluge Gesicht ihrer neuen Freundin gesehen. Dieses Gesicht, das
sie anlächelte, hatte sie Mut fassen lassen. Aber ihr Mut war ab-
hängig von diesem Gesicht geblieben.

Mut war das wichtigste, was man im Leben brauchte. Sie hatte ihr
Kind David genannt, weil der Name Mut versprach. Monatelang
schien, das Kind ihrer Ehe einen neuen Sinn zu geben. Doch
allmählich hatte sie begreifen müssen, daß das eine Täuschung
war.

Zuerst war sie noch zusammen mit Ralf zu Julianes abendlichen

figure guarded the border over which she must not step. For
a time she remained there, next to the small white idol with
black dots for eyes, then she cautiously turned back to the
world.

Next to her bed there were bouquets of flowers from Ralf,
who was still a caring friend to her at this time. She had married
him because he was there when she needed him. She loved him
as a comforting necessity and out of her desire for harmony,
which had probably overtaxed him. She did not return to the
music academy. Instead she went to university in order to
become a teacher. She had done everything to get away from
this fear.

But one day the fear had returned. Perhaps because she was
pregnant or because she sensed without understanding yet that
her marriage was beginning to disintegrate. Suddenly it could
be heard again, the out-of-tune sound of a violin, which receded
and left her behind with an emptied, racing mind which was
unable to grasp anything. Incapable of speaking, she was standing in a classroom in front of a wall of staring faces which did
not leave her any escape. She was standing there, powerless, losing her own self, physically feeling her accelerating disintegration, her dissolution. Suddenly Juliane had been there, the
scent of lemon, her quiet voice. Juliane had taken her by the
arm and had gone outside with her. In a small coffee-house near
the school, where they sat opposite each other in a corner, she
had gradually emerged from her numbness and had looked into
the beautiful, intelligent face of her new friend. This face, which
was smiling at her, had enabled her to pluck up her courage.
But her courage had remained dependent on this face.

Courage was the most important thing you needed in life. She
had called her child David because the name promised courage.
For months the child seemed to give her marriage a new
meaning. But gradually she had had to accept that it was a
delusion.

First she had gone with Ralf to Juliane's discussion evenings.

Gesprächsrunden gegangen. Er hatte dort fremd gewirkt, so ausfallend und zynisch verstockt, daß sie sich seinetwegen vor Juliane schämte. Immer häufiger wurde Juliane zum Anlaß ihrer Streitereien. Er nannte sie die „Dame Perfekta" und bedauerte wortreich den „armen Wolfgang", der an „diese kalte Prestigefrau, diese Dompteuse" geraten sei. Sie hörte aus diesen Schmähungen eine wütende Bewunderung für Juliane heraus. Vielleicht hatte er nicht ertragen können, daß Juliane ihm keine Beachtung schenkte. Vielleicht flößte sie Menschen wie ihm ein Gefühl von Minderwertigkeit ein. Jedenfalls verzerrte er sich mehr und mehr.

In dieser Krisenzeit war sie immer häufiger zu Juliane gegangen und hatte sich von ihr neue Kräfte geliehen. Juliane war ihr besseres Ich, an dem sie sich aufrichtete. Schon wenn Juliane ihr die Tür öffnete und den Arm um ihre Schulter legte und, mit der lässigen Bestimmtheit ihrer Gastfreundschaft, ihr Tee machte oder einen Schnaps anbot, und auch schon, wenn sie bloß daran dachte, wie Juliane sich ausdrückte und bewegte, wenn sie in der Erinnerung den Klang ihrer Stimme hörte, hatte sie sich gestärkt gefühlt.

Seltsam sich vorzustellen, daß sie nicht allein die Bedürftige gewesen war. Während sie fürchtete, an der Großmut ihrer Freundin zu schmarotzen, hatte Juliane sie immer enger an sich herangezogen und sich durch Ratschläge und freundschaftliche Umarmungen unentbehrlich gemacht. Verständnisvoll und geduldig hatte Juliane ihr zugehört, wenn sie von ihrem Unglück erzählte, denn das hatte ihr geholfen, ihr eigenes Unglück zu ertragen oder es jedenfalls vor allen zu verbergen, bis es in einem unbewachten Augenblick so unverhüllt in ihrem Gesicht erschien, daß sie, die ungewollte Zeugin, erschrocken zurückgewichen war und es gleich wieder aus ihrem Bewußtsein getilgt hatte. Es war ein aufgerissenes, ein schreiendes Gesicht gewesen, entstellt von einer Qual, für die es keinen Ausweg gab, außer dem einen, heimlichen, in verborgenen Momenten zum Vorschein zu kommen und Julianes in die Hände vergrabenes Gesicht zu verwüsten, bis sie es schnell, mit einer Anspannung ihres Willens, wieder unter Kontrolle brachte.

Alles das hatte sie erst später verstanden, nach Wolfgangs

He had seemed out of place there, so aggressive, so cynically stubborn that she felt ashamed of him in front of Juliane. More and more frequently Juliane became the cause of their quarrels. He called her 'Lady Perfect' and effusively pitied Wolfgang, who had fallen into the clutches of 'this cold status-conscious woman, this animal tamer'. She could detect a furious admiration for Juliane in these insults. Perhaps he had not been able to bear the fact that Juliane took no notice of him. Perhaps she induced a feeling of inferiority in people like him. In any case he became more and more twisted.

During this period of crisis she had gone to Juliane more and more often, in order to seek new strength from her. Juliane was her better self from whom she could take courage. As soon as Juliane opened the door to her and put her arm round her shoulder and, with the relaxed assurance of her hospitality, made some tea for her or offered her a glass of Schnapps, or even when she just imagined how Juliane expressed herself and moved, when she heard the sound of her voice in her mind, she felt invigorated.

Strange to think that she had not been the only one in need. While she had been afraid of exploiting her friend's magnanimity, Juliane had drawn her closer to herself and made herself indispensable through advice and friendly embraces. Juliane had listened to her full of understanding and patience when she had told her of her misfortune, because it had helped her to bear her own misfortune or at least to hide it from everybody, until in an unguarded moment it so plainly appeared in her face that she, the unintentional witness, had been taken aback and shied away and obliterated it from her consciousness straight away. It had been a ravaged, screaming face, disfigured by a torture from which there was no relief, except to manifest itself secretly in a secluded moment and to devastate Juliane's face, which she buried in her hands, until she brought it under control again with an assertion of her will-power.

She had understood all this only later, after Wolfgang's

unerwartetem Geständnis, daß er und Juliane schon lange nicht
mehr miteinander schliefen und nichts mehr zu tun wußten, als
darüber hinwegzuleben. Sie liebte Juliane nur noch mehr, wenn
sie sich vorstellte, wie sie litt und ihren ununterbrochenen
Kampf um ihre Haltung ausfocht. Juliane war so tapfer in ihrer
Einsamkeit, in die sie sich selbst verbannte durch irgendein selbst
auferlegtes Gebot, nie eine Schwäche oder einen Schmerz zu
zeigen. Was zwang sie dazu? Weshalb mußte sie sich vor allen
Menschen verschließen? Konnte sie nicht glauben, man würde sie
verstehen? Sie hätte sie gerne umarmt, um sie fühlen zu lassen,
daß sie nicht allein war. Doch als sie es begriff, als ihr Julianes ver-
störtes Gesicht wieder vor Augen kam, lag sie an Wolfgangs
Körper geschmiegt in ihrem Bett, und nun war sie es selbst, die
Juliane verletzte, Wolfgang und sie, die auf ihre Kosten glücklich
waren.

Wußte es Juliane? War es möglich, daß sie nichts wußte, weil irgendein Schutzmechanismus sie davor bewahrte wahrzunehmen,
was um sie herum geschah? Wie sollte sie Julianes unverminderte
Freundlichkeit deuten, ihre häufigen Anrufe, die Kunstpostkarte
mit dem erotischen Motiv, die sie ihr aus einer Ausstellung
schickte: ein nacktes, sich küssendes Paar, das leidenschaftlich
umschlungen am Fenster eines düsteren Zimmers stand? Juliane
hatte nichts zu dem Bild geschrieben, nur daß sie mit Wolfgang in
dieser Ausstellung gewesen sei, die ihnen bloß teilweise gefallen
habe. Ihre Schrift war energisch und klar wie immer. Sie sah nicht
nach Lüge und Verstellung aus. Und doch waren gerade Julianes
Klarheit und gleichbleibende Freundlichkeit eine undurchdring-
liche Mauer, vor der sie stand. Es war die Mauer, hinter der auch
Wolfgang immer wieder verschwand, wenn er bei ihr gewesen war
und sie sich heftig und fast verzweifelt geliebt hatten, wie dieses
Paar auf der Kunstpostkarte, die sie oft betrachtete, als könne sie
davon eine Antwort bekommen auf Fragen, die sie ihm nicht zu
stellen wagte und die er immer verwischte und die danach, wenn
er gegangen war, wieder in ihr auftauchten, wie Sand unter
abfließendem Wasser, bedeckt mit sterbenden oder sich

unexpected confession that he and Juliane had not been sleeping together for some time and did not know what to do about it except try and live as if nothing had changed. She loved Juliane all the more when she imagined how she was suffering and fighting the continual battle to keep her composure. Juliane was so brave in her loneliness, into which she exiled herself through some self-imposed edict never to betray a weakness or pain. What forced her to do this? Why did she have to barricade herself against everyone? Could she not believe that they might understand her? She would have liked to have put her arms round her, to let her feel that she was not alone. But when she understood this, when she remembered Juliane's ravaged face, she was lying in bed nestling against Wolfgang's body, and now it was she herself who was hurting Juliane, she and Wolfgang, who were being happy at her expense.

Did Juliane know? Was it possible that she knew nothing because some protective mechanism saved her from noticing what was happening around her? How should she interpret Juliane's undiminished friendliness, her frequent telephone calls, the postcard of an erotic motif which she had sent her from an exhibition: a naked, kissing couple, who were standing at the window of a dark room embracing passionately? Juliane had said nothing about the picture, just that she and Wolfgang had been at this exhibition, which they had liked only in part. Her handwriting was forceful and clear as always. It did not look like lies and deception. And yet it was precisely Juliane's openness and friendliness that erected this impenetrable wall which she was now facing. It was a wall behind which Wolfgang also disappeared again every time he had been with her and they had made violent, almost desperate love, like this couple on the postcard, at which she looked often, as if she might be able to get from it answers to the questions which she did not dare to ask him and which he always blotted out and which, when he had gone again, reappeared in her mind like sand under receding water, covered in dying sea creatures or those which were

verkriechenden Meerestieren, vielfältig gezeichnete Fläche voller
Spuren einer heimlichen Angst.

Was war es? Was verschwieg er ihr?

Sie hatte sich mit ihm über Juliane zu verständigen versucht,
doch kleine Zeichen von Abwehr oder Unwillen, die sie bei ihm
bemerkte, hatten sie verstummen lassen. Zunächst hatte sie sogar
gedacht, sie seien sich einig, Juliane für Stunden völlig zu
vergessen. Aber Juliane blieb nur unantastbar und wartete im
Hintergrund. Das machte sie schon einsam, wenn er noch bei ihr
war. Sie spürte schon im voraus, wann er gehen würde. Seine
Hand, die auf ihr lag, verlor ihr Interesse, wurde schlaff und reglos,
zog sich zurück. Sein Körper streckte sich und grenzte sich von ihr
ab. Bald danach würde er seufzend auf seine Uhr blicken und sie
verlassen.

Sie blieb dann liegen und sah ihn weggehen mit einem Lächeln
und einer kurzen kraulenden Bewegung seiner Fingerspitzen in der
Luft, ein Zeichen von Zärtlichkeit, das sie erwiderte, obwohl es für
sie ein Ausdruck von Traurigkeit war. Sobald er sich abwandte
und aus der Zimmertür verschwand, hielt sie die Luft an. Denn
gleich mußte das leise Geräusch folgen, mit dem die Wohnungstür
ins Schloß fiel, ein kurzes Knacken oder Schnappen, mit dem er sie
nicht nur verließ, sondern auch für ihre Gedanken vollkommen
unsichtbar wurde. Er verschwand hinter der Mauer, wo Juliane auf
ihn wartete.

Manchmal allerdings hatte sie sich aufgebäumt gegen dieses
Verschwinden, das immer selbstverständlicher zu werden drohte,
als sei es zwischen ihnen ausgemacht, daß sie immer nur warten
müsse, wann er kam und ging. Sie hatte auf einmal begriffen, daß
dies schon ein Vertrag war, der ihr unterschoben wurde, damit sie
ohne nachzudenken unterschrieb, ein Vertrag nicht nur mit ihm,
sondern eben auch mit Juliane, der stillen Partnerin dieser Kom-
promisse. Juliane beanspruchte Wolfgang weiterhin für sich, zu
einem Teil, den sie nicht überschauen und bewerten konnte, so
daß sie auch unsicher wurde, was denn ihr Teil sei, was diese
stundenweisen Zärtlichkeiten, diese Seufzer und Beteuerungen

seeking cover again, an expanse of complex markings, full of the traces of a secret fear.

What was it? What was he keeping from her?

She had tried to communicate with him about Juliane, but the little signs of resistance or annoyance which she picked up from him had made her fall silent. At first she had even thought that they had an understanding to forget about Juliane completely for some hours. But Juliane remained untouchable, waiting in the background. This was already making her feel lonely when he was still with her. She sensed in advance when he would go. His hand, which was lying on her, lost interest, became limp and motionless and withdrew. His body stretched and separated itself from her. Soon afterwards he would sigh and look at his watch and leave her.

She then remained lying there and watched him leave with a smile and a short, tickling wave of his fingertips in the air, a sign of tenderness to which she responded, although for her it was an expression of sadness. As soon as he turned away and disappeared through the door, she held her breath, for soon would follow the quiet sound of the door of the flat closing, a brief clicking or snapping sound, with which he was not only leaving her, but which made him also completely invisible in her mind. He disappeared behind the wall where Juliane was waiting for him.

Sometimes, however, she had struggled against this disappearance, which more and more was in danger of being taken for granted, as if it had been agreed between them that she just had to wait on his comings and goings. She had suddenly realized that this already amounted to a contract, which was being foisted on to her so that she would sign it unthinkingly, a contract not just with her, but also with Juliane, the silent partner of these compromises. Juliane was still claiming Wolfgang for herself to an extent that she could not have a clear view of or assess, so that she also became uncertain what her role was, what these caresses, these sighs and these assertions for hours at a time,

überhaupt bedeuteten, die immer abgebrochen und gelöscht
wurden mit dem Schnappgeräusch der Wohnungstür.

Als Wolfgang sich wieder einmal lächelnd mit dem kleinen
Handzeichen zum Gehen wandte, hatte sie dieses kurze, knack-
ende Geräusch schon im voraus gehört. Da war sie aufgesprungen
und hatte ihn in der Tür festgehalten. Wie einen Verirrten, fast
schon Verlorenen hatte sie ihn an sich gerissen und mit wilden,
ziellosen Küssen überschüttet, um ihm einzureden, daß er ihr
gehöre, daß sie ihn nicht mehr loslasse, nie mehr, niemals! Und
während sie ins Zimmer und zu ihrem Bett zurückgingen, hatte sie
sich vorgestellt, Juliane sei anwesend und müsse alles mit ansehen,
was sie und Wolfgang miteinander machten. Das hatte sie sofort in
eine kalte, hysterische Raserei getrieben, in ein verzweifeltes Klam-
mern und Bäumen, in dem sie ihn und auch sich selbst immer
mehr verloren hatte. Je fordernder sie den anderen Körper an sich
riß, um so mehr fühlte sie, daß Julianes Blick ungerührt blieb, als
verfüge sie über ein geheimes Wissen, gegen das nichts auszu-
richten war. Und auf einmal war ihre Umarmung zu einem wüsten
Gerüttel geworden, mit dem sie sich gegenseitig abschüttelten,
um weit voneinander entfernt zu sein, jeder ein einsamer Über-
lebender, ausgelöscht, sprachlos und vielleicht, dank der barmher-
zigen Verdunklung ihrer Sinne, auch ohne Gedanken.

Allein konnte sie sich nicht auflehnen. Auch ihre Phantasien münd-
eten in Demütigungen und Niederlagen. Und Wolfgang war dabei
nicht auf ihrer Seite. Sie hatte ihm nie von ihren Phantasien erzählt, weil sie fürchtete, daß sie ihm fremd seien, und er sich nicht
mit ihr verbünden würde bei diesen heimlichen Anschlägen auf
Julianes Übermacht. In letzter Zeit hatte sie oft Angst, seine
Erwartungen nicht zu erfüllen, weil sie sich nicht auf ihn einstellen
konnte, wenn er unangekündigt kam. Wie in der vergangenen
Woche, als er am späten Abend bei ihr klingelte und, ohne ihr Zeit
zu lassen, mit ihr schlafen wollte. Sie hatte ihn erst am nächsten
Abend erwartet. Aber da konnte er nicht, weil Juliane etwas vor-
hatte. So war er einen Tag früher gekommen, nur für eine Stunde,

which were always broken off and obliterated by the noise of the door of the flat as it snapped shut, really meant.

When Wolfgang turned to go again, smiling with a little wave of the hand, she had heard this short, clicking sound in advance. So she had leapt up and had held on to him in the doorway. Like someone who has gone astray and is almost lost she had seized him, covering him with wild, aimless kisses in order to persuade him that he belonged to her, that she would not let him go again, never again, never! And as they went back into the room and to her bed, she had imagined Juliane was there and had to witness all this, what she and Wolfgang were doing together. That had thrown her immediately into a cold, hysterical frenzy, into a desperate clinging, convulsive state in which she had lost him and also herself more and more. The more demandingly she was clutching the other body to her own, the more she felt that Juliane's gaze remained unmoved, as if she had some secret knowledge at her disposal, against which there was no match. And suddenly her embrace had turned into a wild shaking, with which they were both trying to push each other away in order to put distance between them, each a lonely survivor, obliterated, speechless and, perhaps thanks to the merciful clouding of her senses, without any thoughts.

On her own she could muster no opposition. Her fantasies also ended in humiliation and defeat. And Wolfgang was not on her side in this. She had never told him of her fantasies because she was afraid that they were alien to him and that he would not become her ally in these secret assaults on Juliane's superior power. Recently she had often been afraid of not fulfilling his expectations because she could not adjust to him if he came unannounced. Like last week, when he rang her doorbell late one evening and wanted to sleep with her without giving her enough time. She had been expecting him to come the following evening. But he could not make it then because Juliane had something planned. So he had come a day earlier, just for an

und wollte ungeduldig seine Ration Liebe von ihr einfordern, ohne die er sich in seinem Gleichgewicht gefährdet fühlte.

Während sie noch getrennt in zwei Sesseln saßen, weil sie lieber erst mit ihm reden wollte, wußte sie schon, er würde gleich aufstehen, um sie zu umarmen und unter Küssen nach ihren Brüsten und Beinen zu tasten. Und indem sie das dachte, hatte der Film auch schon begonnen. Er war bei ihr, noch heftiger und fordernder als sonst, und sie hatte, in sich zusammenschrumpfend und erstarrend, seinem Drängen nachgegeben. Sie war in eine Grube gefallen, war wie ein Stein gewesen, der im Wasser versank und auf dem Grund eine modrige Wolke aufwühlte. Dort, in ihrem inneren Dunkel, hatte sie verborgen gelegen, unterhalb des Tumults ihrer gespielten Leidenschaft, mit der sie ihn angestrengt zu täuschen versuchte. Doch das schien er gespürt zu haben. Denn als er bald danach ging, kam er ihr ernüchtert vor und schien nun selbst bemüht zu sein, das mit den üblichen Zärtlichkeiten vor ihr zu verbergen.

In zehn Minuten kamen die Gäste, und sie fühlte sich unfähig, ihnen entgegenzutreten. Wie sollte sie die wohlgelaunten Scherze von Kurt Sanders ertragen und die Geschwätzigkeit seiner Frau? Und Julianes Freundinnenlächeln, das sie nicht mehr verstand, und daneben Wolfgang, zweideutig und ein wenig hölzern, ein wenig auf der Hut, weil er sich von ihr bedroht fühlte?

Warum hatte er nicht angerufen, um ihr zu helfen? Konnte es überhaupt einen Grund geben, sie so im Stich zu lassen? Ruhig, dachte sie. Sie mußte die Ruhe in sich selber finden. Dies hier war ihre Wohnung, hier mußte sie sich behaupten. Konnte sie noch irgend etwas tun? Sie ging zum Fenster und schaute hinaus. Die Straße war menschenleer, und es standen weniger Autos als sonst in den Parktaschen. Viele Leute waren übers Wochenende weggefahren. Das hätten sie und Wolfgang auch tun sollen: wegfahren, weg aus dieser Stadt, aus der Nähe von Juliane, weg von all den Zwängen und Rücksichten, in denen sie hier lebten. Dann vielleicht hätten sie einen Entschluß fassen können, eine mutige, alle Zweideutigkeiten beendende Entscheidung. Aber Wolfgang hatte

hour, and impatiently wanted to claim his ration of love from her, without which he felt his equilibrium was threatened.

While they were still sitting apart in two armchairs because she wanted to talk first, she already knew that he would get up in a minute to embrace her and, showering her with kisses, grope for her breasts and legs. And while she was thinking this the film had already started. He was even more pressing and demanding with her than usual and, shrivelling up inside and becoming rigid, she had succumbed to his urging. She had fallen into a pit, had been like a stone sinking into the water and stirring up a murky cloud on the bottom. There, in her inner darkness, she had been lying hidden, below the commotion of her feigned passion with which she was straining to deceive him. But he seemed to have sensed this. Because when he went soon after, he appeared sobered to her, and now seemed himself to be at pains to hide this under the usual caresses.

Her guests were due to arrive in ten minutes and she felt incapable of facing them. How was she to bear Kurt Sanders's good-humoured jokes and the talkativeness of his wife? And Juliane's friend's smile, which she could no longer understand, and next to her Wolfgang, ambivalent and a little wooden, a little on his guard, because he felt threatened by her?

Why had he not called in order to help her? Could there really be any reason to leave her in the lurch like this? Calm down, she thought. She must find the calm in herself. This was her flat, here she had to stand up for herself. Was there anything else she could do? She went to the window and looked out. The street was deserted, and there were fewer cars than usual in the parking bays. Many people had gone away for the weekend. She and Wolfgang ought to have done the same: gone away, out of this town, out of Juliane's presence, away from all the constraints and considerations of their life here. Then perhaps they might have been able to make a decision, a bold decision which would put an end to all ambiguity. But Wolfgang had

nie einen solchen Vorschlag gemacht, und sie hatte nicht daran zu denken gewagt.

Beinahe heftig drehte sie sich um: die Blumen, die übermäßig vielen Blumen! Sollte sie zwei Sträuße in Davids Zimmer schaffen und den Kerzenleuchter wegnehmen? Nein, das wäre nur eine neue Täuschung, um die erste zu verleugnen. Es brachte sie nicht näher an die Wahrheit heran. Sie mußte hinsehen. Sie mußte die Spur finden. Da war etwas, das sich schon den ganzen Tag zeigen wollte. Es verbarg sich in ihrer Unruhe. Es kam und ging. Immer wieder entglitt es ihr.

Heute morgen auf dem Dachparkplatz des Kaufhauses hatte es begonnen, als sie aus dem Auto stieg. Schon während sie die Tür abschloß, hatte sie bemerkt, daß sie hier oben zwischen den Reihen geparkter Autos ganz allein war. Da war ein großer dunkelblauer Ford die Rampe hochgekommen und hatte hinter ihr gehalten. Zwei dunkelhaarige Männer mit Schnauzbärten, wohl Ausländer, hatten zu ihr herübergeblickt. Wahrscheinlich warteten sie darauf, daß die Parktasche frei wurde. Denn als sie den Kopf schüttelte, fuhren sie weiter. Sie hatte sich unbehaglich gefühlt und statt des Treppenhauses die Rolltreppe im Inneren des Kaufhauses benutzt. Doch die Beklemmung hatte nicht nachgelassen, sondern sich nur verändert. Die langsame Sinkbewegung durch die weiten, lichterfüllten Stockwerke voller Menschen und Warenangebote hatte ihr eine Empfindung von Unwirklichkeit und künstlicher Ruhe gegeben. Es war wie ein Luftanhalten, ein langes Untertauchen. Und dann kam es: Eine Gruppe von Schaufensterpuppen, Männer und Frauen in Ferienkleidung, die sich lachend, mit ausgreifenden Gebärden zu begrüßen schienen, stieg gleichmäßig neben ihr hoch, während sie tiefer sank. Das ist es, hatte sie gedacht. Genauso! Genauso! Aber sie konnte nicht sagen, was sie meinte. Es blieb eine leere Offenbarung, als mache ihr jemand einen Trick vor, der ganz einfach zu sein schien und den sie doch nicht verstand. Unwillkürlich hatte sie nach dem rollenden Handlauf gegriffen, unter dem sie ein Rumpeln spürte, kleine Unebenheiten, über die er hinwegglitt. Alles verflüchtigte sich

never made such a suggestion and she had not dared to
think of it.

She turned round with an almost violent movement: the
flowers, the excessive number of flowers! Should she put two
bunches in David's room and take the candlestick away? No,
that would only be a new deception to deny the initial one. It
did not bring her any closer to the truth. She had to concen-
trate. She must find the trail. There was something that had
been trying to show itself all day. It was hiding within her dis-
quiet. It came and went. Time and again it slipped away from
her.

It had started this morning on the roof car park of the department store, when she got out of the car. When she was locking
the car door she had noticed that up here between the rows of
parked cars she was quite alone. Then a large dark-blue Ford
had come up the ramp and stopped behind her. Two dark-
haired men with moustaches, foreigners perhaps, had looked
over to her. Perhaps they were waiting for the parking bay to
become vacant. For when she shook her head they drove on.
She had felt uncomfortable and instead of using the staircase
she had used the escalator inside the store. But the anxiety had
not stopped, it had just changed. The slow descent through the
vast, brightly lit floors full of people and displays of goods had
given her a feeling of unreality and artificial calm. It was like
holding one's breath or being submerged for a long time. And
then it appeared: a group of dummies, men and women in holiday outfits who seemed to greet her, laughing and making
exuberant gestures, rose steadily up alongside her as she sank
deeper. This is it, she had thought. Exactly! Exactly! But she
could not say what she meant. It remained an empty vision, as
if someone were showing her a trick which seemed to be quite
simple but which she nevertheless did not understand. She had
involuntarily gripped the rolling handrail, beneath which she
felt a rumble, some small bumps over which it was gliding.
Everything was slipping away again. Then she reached the

schon wieder. Dann kam das Ende des Treppenlaufs, und sie hatte
ihre Gedanken wieder ihren Einkäufen zugewandt.

Noch einmal hatte sie sich geweigert zu erkennen, was sie längst
wußte: Alles war Verstellung und Täuschung. Doch zugleich lag
alles auf der Hand. Sie mußte nur den Mut haben hinzublicken,
um den Zusammenhang der Szenen zu verstehen, in denen sie alle
spielten: Juliane und Wolfgang waren sich einig. Sie hatten alles
miteinander abgesprochen, um ihre kaputte Ehe zu retten. Alles
war nach Julianes Regie gelaufen. Julianes angebliche Reise und
Wolfgangs erster abendlicher Besuch bei ihr waren der Anfang
einer Ehekur, die Juliane ihm und sich verordnet hatte und deren
Verlauf sie im Hintergrund verfolgte. Denn natürlich erzählte
Wolfgang ihr von seinen kurzen Liebesstunden, und über dieses
Erzählen waren sie wohl allmählich selbst wieder hinübergeglitten
in eigene Zärtlichkeiten, eigene Umarmungen, in denen sich alles
wiederholte, was sie und Wolfgang miteinander machten. Alles
geschah jetzt doppelt, die Worte, die Seufzer, die Berührungen.
Und vielleicht wußte inzwischen niemand mehr, was die ursprüng-
liche Wirklichkeit und was ihr Spiegelbild war, oder vielleicht war
alles Wirkliche längst verflogen, und es handelte sich nur noch um
Spiegelungen von Spiegelbildern, und jedes Paar sah dem anderen
zu. So wie sie es von Juliane träumte, mochte die es auch von ihr
träumen. Vielleicht kamen Wolfgang und Juliane heute abend
hierher, um sich in ihrer Wohnung besonders verbunden zu
fühlen und verstohlene Zeichen auszutauschen, wie sie es selbst
phantasiert hatte, und um dann, nach Stunden freundschaft-
licher Plauderei, in erregter Einigkeit wegzugehen. War es so?
Wer war der Betrogene? Gleich, wenn sie kamen, würde sie es
sehen können. Sie mußte nur standhalten, dann würde sie es
sehen!
    Nein, sie würde nichts sehen. Julianes Lächeln würde alles ver-
bergen. Ihr ruhiges, klares Gesicht war das Zentrum der Verwor-
renheit. Denn vielleicht war alles anders. Wirklich war vielleicht
nur die Fratze des verborgenen Leidens, die sie einen Augenblick
lang gesehen hatte. Juliane konnte nicht mehr lieben. Vielleicht

foot of the escalator and she focused her thoughts on her shopping again.

Once again she had refused to acknowledge what she had known for some time: everything was pretence and deception. And yet everything was obvious. She only had to have the courage to look in order to understand the context of the scenes in which they were all acting: Juliane and Wolfgang were in agreement. They had agreed everything between them in order to save their broken marriage. Everything had followed Juliane's directions. Juliane's supposed trip and Wolfgang's first visit to her had been the beginning of a marriage therapy which Juliane had prescribed for herself and him and whose progress she was monitoring in the background. For Wolfgang would be telling her, of course, about his brief hours of love-making and through this reporting they themselves had gradually slipped into intimacies and embraces of their own again, in which all she and Wolfgang did together was repeated. Everything was happening twice now, the words, the sighs, the physical contact. And perhaps nobody knew any more by now what was the original reality and what was its mirror image, or perhaps all reality had long vanished, it was only a matter of reflections and mirror images, and each couple was watching the other. Whatever she was dreaming about Juliane was probably being dreamt of about her. Perhaps Wolfgang and Juliane were coming here this evening in order to feel particularly close in her flat and exchange surreptitious signs, as she herself had pictured in her fantasies, and in order to then leave, after hours of friendly chat, in excited harmony. Was it like this? Was she the cheated party? In a minute, when they arrived, she would be able to see the truth. She only had to hold her ground, then she would see it.

No, she would not see anything. Juliane's smile would hide everything. Her calm, clear face was the focus of the confusion. Perhaps it was all different. Perhaps it was only the grimace of hidden suffering which she had seen for a moment. Juliane was incapable of loving any more. Perhaps she just did not want to,

wollte sie es auch nicht, konnte es nicht hoffen, wollte so bleiben, wie sie war. Doch sie hatte Wolfgang für sich behalten wollen und für ihn eine Ersatzfrau gesucht, eine passende, willfährige Stundengeliebte, bei der er sich holen konnte, was sie ihm nicht geben wollte, und die sie beeinflussen und kontrollieren konnte, weil sie ihre Freundin war. Das war die beste Lösung auf die Dauer. Sie entsprach ihrem kühlen Verstand. Sie wollte alles in der Hand behalten. Wollte dabeisein und darüberstehen. Sie hatte alles eingefädelt wie eine Kupplerin. Alles, was geschah, sollte noch von ihr kommen. Wolfgangs Umarmungen waren von ihr gewährte Zärtlichkeiten. Sie ließ alles zu, sie konnte es zurücknehmen. Nein, das würde sie nicht tun. Alles war gedacht als eine dauerhafte Einrichtung, eine Routine, die ihre Ehe stützte. Juliane hatte sie als das Flickstück eines Bündnisses benutzt, von dem sie offenbar nichts verstand.

Was war es? Was hielt die beiden zusammen und war stärker als das, was sie und Wolfgang miteinander erlebt hatten, so stark, daß alles andere daran zunichte wurde?

Denn das hatte doch schon angefangen, sein unauffälliger aber stetiger Rückzug aus dem gemeinsamen Traum auf Gewohnheiten, die sie immer mehr eingrenzten und die allmählich die Leidenschaft herabzogen auf die reizvolle Abwechslung einer erotischen Extratour, einer gelegentlichen Fickstunde. Sie waren vielleicht schon dort angekommen. Alles war nur noch eine Spielerei, die nichts bedeutete, weil sie ein Arrangement unter aufgeklärten Freunden war, die sich danach ohne Schwierigkeiten zu einem gemeinsamen Essen trafen. Man wußte alles, und es störte nicht. Man konnte darüber hinweglächeln. Es war das, was alle machten, um sich zu erfrischen und in Balance zu halten. Vielleicht war Juliane, als sie Wolfgang zu ihr schickte, zu einem anderen Mann gefahren, um sich dort zu holen, was sie brauchte, und ihm zu geben, was er vermißte. Nicht alles, nicht das Ganze, sondern immer nur eine Abschlagszahlung, gerade so viel, um nicht hineinzugeraten. Denn darunter, im Dunkeln, gab es das Leiden, dem gegenüber man hilflos und ratlos war. Man mußte vorsichtig sein. Man kam nur kurz aus seinen Festungen heraus, um sich zu

could not hope for it, wanted to stay as she was. But she had wanted to keep Wolfgang for herself and had found a replacement woman for him, a suitable, willing lover, for a few hours at a time, from whom he could get what she no longer wanted to give him, and whom she could influence and control because she was her friend. That was the best solution in the long term. It suited her cool intellect. She wanted to keep everything under control, wanted to be part of it and above it. She had engineered everything like a matchmaker. Everything that happened was to be initiated by her. Wolfgang's embraces were the intimacies she had granted. She permitted everything and she could take it back. No, she would not do that. Everything was intended to be a permanent arrangement, a routine that supported her marriage. Juliane had used her to patch up a pact which she did not understand.

What was it? What was keeping the two of them together and was stronger than anything she and Wolfgang had experienced together, so strong that everything else had to be wrecked by it?

For that had already started, his unobtrusive, but steady retreat from their common dream into habit, which they were limiting more and more, and which diminished their passion to the charming diversion of an erotic excursion, the occasional hour of fucking. Perhaps they had already reached this point. Everything had just turned into a little game which no longer meant anything because it was an arrangement among enlightened friends who subsequently met for a meal without any problem. Everyone knew everything, and wasn't bothered. One could brush it aside with a smile. It was something everybody was doing to recharge their batteries and keep themselves in balance. Perhaps when Juliane had sent Wolfgang to her, she herself had gone to another man to get what she needed, and to give him what he was missing. Not everything, not all at once, but just one instalment, just enough not to get sucked in. For underneath, in the dark, there was only suffering, in the face of which you felt helpless and at a loss. You had to be on your guard. You only left your fortress briefly to touch like blind

berühren wie Blinde mit ausgestreckten Händen. Da war der
andere, das andere Leben, erschreckend fühlbar und deutlich.
Man zog sich klug davon zurück.

War es so? Sah sie es richtig? Sie konnte alles so oder so sehen,
als sei das Ganze ein Suchbild, das sich ständig veränderte und
in dem auch sie sich verzerrte und ihren Umriß verlor. Wie sollte
sie ihre Gäste empfangen? Wer war sie? Was wußte sie? Heute
morgen war sie mit einem Gefühl von Gewißheit erwacht. Sie
war glücklich gewesen und stark. Das würde sie nun nicht mehr
wiederfinden. Es war ihr genommen worden, oder sie selbst
hatte es zerstört. Sie hatte es nicht festhalten können und
wieder ihre Stimme verloren, wie damals auf dem Podium,
als die Lähmung sie ergriff. Wieder spürte sie den ersten
Schatten dieser Dunkelheit, die von innen kam, und konnte es
schon hören: Es klang krank und falsch und zog sie von sich
fort. Gleich, wenn die Gäste kamen, würde sie verwandelt sein.
Starr und unkenntlich würde sie in der Tür stehen, unfähig zu
sprechen. Kommt, kommt schnell, dachte sie, helft mir! Nein,
kommt nicht!
     Sie hörte das Klingeln. Doch sie konnte nicht mehr öffnen. Sie
klingelten anhaltend, als wäre es ein Alarm. Wer waren sie? Was
wollten sie von ihr? Sie konnte nicht mehr öffnen. Sie mußte
unsichtbar werden, sich in einen Winkel verkriechen. Aber die dort
draußen würden hereinkommen, früher oder später, und man
würde sie finden.
     Also gut, sie stand hier. Das waren ihre Gäste, die kommen und
wieder gehen würden. Mehr würde es nicht sein.
     Sie hatte auf den Türöffner gedrückt. Im Treppenhaus ging das
Licht an, und unten waren jetzt ihre munteren Stimmen. Sie
kamen schnell die Treppe hoch, mit Blumen und kleinen Ge-
schenken, zuerst die beiden Sanders, dann Juliane, ihr Lemonenduft und leichte Küsse auf beide Wangen, und Wolfgang gleich
danach, der heimlich ihre Hand drückte.
     Alle lächeln sie in diesem Augenblick. Und man wird so leicht,
man könnte davonfliegen. Vielleicht sollte sie sich festhalten, sollte

people with outstretched hands. There was the other person, the other life, terrifyingly tangible and clear. You wisely withdrew from it.

Was it like this? Did she see it correctly? She could see everything in different ways, as if the whole thing were a picture puzzle which was changing constantly and in which she herself was also being distorted and losing her outline. How should she receive her guests? Who was she? What did she know? This morning she had woken up with a feeling of certainty. She had been happy and strong. She would now not find that again. It had been taken from her, or she had destroyed it herself. She had not been able to keep hold of it and had lost her voice again, like the time on the stage when paralysis had seized her. Again she was feeling the first shadow of this darkness which came from within and she could already hear it: it sounded sickly and false and pulled her away from herself. In a minute, when her guests arrived, she would be transformed. Rigid and unrecognizable, she would stand in her door, unable to speak. Come, come quickly, she thought, help me! No, don't come!

She heard the doorbell ring. But she could not open the door any more. They were ringing continuously, as if it were an alarm. Who were they? What did they want from her? She could no longer open. She had to become invisible, hide away in a corner. But those people outside would come in, sooner or later, and she would be discovered.

So be it, she was standing here. These were her guests; they would come then go again. There would be no more to it than that.

She had pressed the door opener. The light went on on the stairs and downstairs cheerful voices could now be heard. They were coming up the stairs quickly with flowers and little presents, first the Sanders, then Juliane, her lemon scent and light kisses on both cheeks, and Wolfgang immediately afterwards, who pressed her hand surreptitiously.

They are all smiling at this moment. And you feel so light you could fly away. Perhaps she should hold on to something, should

sich an Wolfgangs und Julianes Arme hängen, um etwas zu spüren, sich selbst, die anderen, ihre Körper, die auch nur Lügen und Täuschungen waren, die man aber anfassen, die man berühren konnte, ohne daß sie einfach verschwanden.

Kommt herein! Kommt herein!

take Wolfgang's and Juliane's arm, in order to feel something, herself, the others, their bodies, which were also just lies and deceit, but which you could take hold of, which you could touch without them simply disappearing.

Come in! Come in!

Eating Mussels (*Excerpt*)

BIRGIT VANDERBEKE

Das Muschelessen (*Exzerpt*)

Die Muscheln haben ganz still in der Schüssel gelegen und waren
tot, und da hat meine Mutter plötzlich Angst bekommen, daß wir
zu aufsässig[1] wären, und hat gejammert, daß sie sich solche Mühe
gegeben hätte mit unsrer Erziehung, aber wir haben schon gewußt,
daß sie sich bloß nicht getraut hat, gegen den Vater etwas zu
sagen, der jetzt bestimmt schon befördert wäre; sie hat einen
Heidenrespekt[2] vor dem Vater gehabt, weil er Naturwissenschaftler
gewesen ist, was mehr wert als Schöngeist[3] war, es hat damals noch
als abgemacht gegolten, daß ich auch zur Naturwissenschaft
neigen würde, weil die Musik und die Literatur, überhaupt die
gesamte Kultur, nur ein Feierabendgeschäft wären und die Welt
sich nicht weiterentwickeln könnte, wenn nicht Naturwissenschaftler und Techniker sie ergründen und tat- und entscheidungs-
kräftig beeinflussen würden, wogegen das Musische, hat mein
Vater gesagt, reiner Überfluß wäre und keinen Motor zum Laufen
bringt, das hat er deshalb gesagt, weil meine Mutter seit der Flucht
ihre Geige im Schlafzimmerschrank stehen hatte, und nur manchmal hat sie, wenn sie traurig gewesen ist, am Klavier gesessen und
Schubertlieder gespielt und gesungen, die ganze Winterreise[4] vor
und zurück, dabei hat sie geweint, und es hat wirklich schaurig
geklungen, obwohl meine Mutter einmal eine schöne Stimme
gehabt haben muß, und Geige haben wir sie nur einmal spielen
hören, da hat sie auch sehr geweint, und wir haben uns auf die
Lippen gebissen, um nicht zu lachen, weil es gräßlich geklungen
hat und nach Katzenmusik,[5] sie hat geschluchzt dabei und gesagt,
daß die Geige so kratzt, ist kein Wunder, im kalten Schlafzimmerschrank, da gehört sie ja auch nicht hin, und wenn man jahrelang nicht gespielt hat; und da hat sie uns dann doch leid getan.
Später ist die Geige auf einmal zerbrochen gewesen, als sie sie aus

Eating Mussels (*Excerpt*)

The mussels had been lying quite still in the bowl and were dead, and then my mother suddenly became anxious that we were too rebellious and started whining that she had taken such care over our education; but we knew already that she simply did not have the courage to say anything against father, who was bound to have received his promotion by now. She had immense respect for my father because he was a scientist, which was worth more than any man of letters. It was then still taken for granted that I also inclined toward science, because music and literature, indeed all cultural matters, were things you did in your spare time, and the world could make no progress if scientists and technicians did not investigate it and influence it with their decisions and actions, while fine arts, my father said, were simply superfluous and would never get an engine to work. He said this because my mother had left her violin lying in the wardrobe since the escape, and only occasionally, when she was sad, did she sit at the piano and play Schubert lieder and sing the whole of the *Winterreise*, over and over again, while she was crying, and it really sounded quite awful, although my mother must have had a beautiful voice once. We heard her play the violin only once, then she also cried a lot, and we had to bite our lips not to laugh, because it sounded ghastly, like caterwauling. And she was sobbing at the same time, saying that it was no wonder that the violin was scraping so much, because it did not belong in the cold bedroom wardrobe, and it hadn't been played for years. And then we felt sorry for her after all. Later the violin suddenly got broken when she wanted to take it out of the bedroom wardrobe, for she sometimes did

dem Schlafzimmerschrank holen wollte, das hat sie nämlich manchmal heimlich gemacht, daß sie sie aus dem Schlafzimmerschrank
geholt hat, und dann hat sie sich im eisigen Schlafzimmer aufs Bett
gesetzt und die Geige betrachtet, dabei hat sie immer geweint, und
dann hat sie sie ins grüne Futteral zurückgegeben, das ist immer
eine richtige Beerdigung gewesen,[6] sie hat den Geigenkasten im
Schlafzimmerschrank beerdigt und ist ganz verweint aus dem
Schlafzimmer rausgekommen.

this secretly, and then she sat down on the bed in the ice-cold bedroom, always crying while she looked at the violin. And then she put it back into the green lined case, that was always like a proper funeral, she buried the violin case in the bedroom wardrobe and emerged from the bedroom tear-stained.

The Good Old Days

GABRIELE WOHMANN

Bessere Zeiten

Gegen zwei Uhr verlangte es die Gernsteins[1] nach ihrer gewohnten
Mittagspause. Überhaupt: Gewohnheiten! Wichtig, sich daran zu
halten. Es war ein warmer und sonniger Tag am Wochenende.
Samstag. Appetit hatten die Gernsteins und durstig waren sie auch,
Bedürfnisse, die sie befriedigen konnten; nur dem Wunsch, sich
etwas frische Luft zu verschaffen, stand, kaum hatten sie vier Fenster geöffnet, der Verkehrslärm entgegen.

Mach bitte wieder zu, bat Frau Gernstein ihren Mann, während
sie selber schon zwei Fenster schloß.

Es wird von Jahr zu Jahr schlimmer mit dem Verkehr, sagte
Frau Gernstein. Wie schön wäre es, wenn man jetzt ein paar
Schritte gehen könnte. Einfach ein bißchen den Waldweg entlang.

Wir könnten ein Stück mit dem Auto fahren, schlug Herr
Gernstein vor.

Frau Gernstein rührte er in diesem Moment, denn seine Stimme
hatte mutlos geklungen. Seinen Vorschlag in die Tat umzusetzen,
hatte der Gute überhaupt keine Lust. Er machte einen überan-
strengten Eindruck, und ein Mittagsschläfchen wäre das Beste für
ihn.

Nur nicht, doch jetzt nicht, rief Frau Gernstein.

Was denn: jetzt nicht, nur nicht?

Autofahren, bis zu irgendeinem Waldweg oder so. Jetzt ist
Pause. Ausruhen. Du brauchst das.

Eine Zeitlang schwiegen sie, sie beobachteten den Verkehr,
denn wenn man ihn schon hören und riechen mußte, empfahl es
sich, ihn auch zu sehen. Besser, man bekam deutlich mit, worunter
man zu leiden hatte.

Hast du den da gesehen? Herr Gernstein klang aufgeregt.

Wen? Welchen?

The Good Old Days

At about 2 o'clock the Gernsteins felt a desire for their customary lunch break. Well, habits are habits! Important to stick to
them. It was a warm, sunny day at a weekend. Saturday. The
Gernsteins were hungry, and thirsty as well, needs which they
could satisfy; only the noise of the traffic – they had barely
opened four windows – stood in the way of their desire to get
some fresh air.

Please close them again, Mrs Gernstein asked her husband, as
she herself closed two windows.

The traffic is getting worse every year, Mrs Gernstein said.
How nice it would be if one could go for a little walk now. Just a
little way down a path in the woods.

We could go somewhere in the car, Mr Gernstein suggested.

At this Mrs Gernstein felt somewhat moved, because his
voice had sounded despondent. The dear man had no desire
to put this plan into action at all. He gave the impression
that he was under strain; a little nap would be the best thing
for him.

Please, let's not, not now, Mrs Gernstein called out.

Let's not what now?

Go for a drive to some path in the woods or whatever. It's
time we had a break. Time for a rest. You need it.

For a time they were silent, they were watching the traffic,
for if they had to hear and smell it, they might as well see
it too. Better to have a clear grasp of what you had to
suffer.

Did you see that one? Mr Gernstein sounded excited.

Who? Which one?

Den weinroten Mercedes oder was es war. Slalomfahrer. Von der rechten Fahrspur über die mittlere auf die linke, hat mindestens drei andere Fahrzeuge in Bedrängnis gebracht.

Mercedes gibt es kaum in Weinrot, oder? Frau Gernstein war stolz darauf, sich in Automarken sehr gut auszukennen. Darunter, daß sie selber nicht imstande war, ein Auto als Fahrerin zu benutzen, litt sie wie unter Analphabetentum. Sie hatte Freundinnen, die sie dieser Befähigungslücke wegen immer wieder einmal verspotteten. Eine von denen kam ihr jetzt in den Sinn, während noch ihr Mann vor sich hinschimpfte:

Wie sie wieder rasen, wie riskant sie überholen, phantasielose Idioten, hirnlose. Nimm dem deutschen Autofahrer sein Recht, so schnell zu fahren, wie er will, und er ist sicher, du hast ihm seine Freiheit genommen. Schöne Freiheit, armselige.

Und der Wald, und die Tiere, die Umwelt, sagte Frau Gernstein, fand es aber schwach, ihr fiel nichts Vehementes ein, weil sie nach wie vor an ihre kritische und in jeder Lebensbeziehung selbständige Freundin Andrea denken mußte. Andrea hatte ihr eine Weile damit zugesetzt, sie müsse autofahren lernen, und sich erboten, ihr Prinzipielles beizubringen, vor jedem offiziellen Fahrunterricht. Du mußt dich doch völlig amputiert fühlen! Du brauchst plötzlich das Auto, du willst plötzlich weg, also beides gibt es, den Nutzwert und den Lustwert, ja, und dann mußt du erst umständlich deinen lieben Mann bitten, ob er wohl die Güte habe und so weiter. Und selbst wenn er dann die Güte haben sollte, es wäre nicht dasselbe. Das einzig Wahre ist: du kannst selbst über dich bestimmen. Und was dir nicht sonst noch alles entgeht: Fahrtrausch, du hörst Musik, du fängst zu schweben an, du bist unabhängig . . . Frau Gernstein war daran gewöhnt, daß Herr Gernstein derlei Bekundungen mit *QUATSCH* und *UNFUG* kommentierte, und dadurch fühlte sie sich ein wenig getröstet.

Gerade mußte ich daran denken, daß wir vor zwanzig Jahren noch bei Autofahrten sogar auf der Autobahn einfach da, wo es

The ruby-coloured Mercedes or whatever it was. Slalom driver – from the right-hand lane across the middle to the left, endangering at least four other vehicles.

You don't usually get ruby-coloured Mercedes, do you? Mrs Gernstein prided herself that she knew about different types of cars. That she was unable to use a car as a driver was something she suffered as if it were illiteracy. She had girlfriends who from time to time made fun of her because of this gap in her competence. One of them sprang to her mind while her husband was still grumbling away:

Look at them tearing along, look how dangerously they are overtaking, unimaginative idiots, mindless fools. Deprive the German motorist of the right to drive as fast as he likes and he will be convinced that you have taken away his liberty. Wonderful liberty, but how pitiful.

And the forest, and the animals, the environment, Mrs Gernstein said, but she found it a little lame, she could not think of anything forceful because her mind went back again to her friend Andrea, her critical attitude and her independence in every aspect of her life. Andrea had pressed her for some time to learn to drive, had offered to teach her some of the basics before she started official driving lessons. You must feel like a complete amputee. You need the car straight away, you suddenly want to get away, so there are both aspects, the utility value and the pleasure value, yes, and then you have to go to the trouble of asking your dear husband if he might be so kind as to, etcetera. And even if he were to be so kind as to, it would not be the same. The only certainty is: you can determine your own destiny. And all the other things you are missing: the buzz of driving, you are listening to music, you start floating, you are independent . . . Mrs Gernstein was used to Mr Gernstein describing such statements as *NONSENSE* and *RUBBISH*, and that consoled her a little.

I was just thinking that when we went out in the car twenty years ago, even on the motorway, we were able to pull off to

schön war, rechts raus in ein Waldstück fahren konnten, um ein Picknick zu machen, sagte sie.

Und zwar ein Picknick mit allem Drum und Dran, fügte Herr Gernstein hinzu. Deine Mutter hat auf dem Spirituskocher Fleischwurst in mitgebrachtem Wasser heißgemacht, dein Vater, ich sehe ihn noch, wie er ein deprimiertes Gesicht gezogen hat, wenn kein Senf da war.

Die Gernsteins lachten, glücklich in der Erinnerungswehmut.

Oder ist es mehr als zwanzig Jahre her?

Egal, es waren bessere Zeiten.

Für uns, bessere Zeiten. Sind wir elitär, was meinst du?

Von mir aus.

Auch für die Natur waren das bessere Zeiten, egoistisch sind wir nicht.

Bessere Zeiten! Die jetzigen Autobesitzer denken anders darüber.

Jetzt fährt einfach jeder.

Und jede. Denk an all die Zweitwagen.

Gut, sind wir eben elitär.

Ja, was bleibt uns übrig?

In dem Punkt gab es zwischen den Gernsteins keinen Streit. Neuzeit und Fortschritt hatten sich längst als folgenschwere Phantome erwiesen, die Menschen saßen in der Sackgasse, bedroht von Überfüllung, Erstickung, Bruchlandung der Erde, Ende der Atemluft. In wie vielen Jahren auch immer, ihr Wohlbefinden als Bewohner ihres Viertels, als Fußgänger da und dort, und auch wenn sie auf einstmalige Autofahrten zurückblickten, es hatte starke Einbußen erlitten.

Gegen drei Uhr fühlte Herr Gernstein, auf Befragen seiner Frau hin, sich wieder fit.

Ungewöhnlich lang pausiert, heute, sagte er. Wundere dich also nicht, wenn es von nun an etwas flotter geht.

Du bist der beste Fahrer, den ich überhaupt kenne, sagte Frau Gernstein aus Liebe, denn sie wußte, dieses Kompliment gehörte unter den Favoriten an Komplimenten für ihren Mann auf den ersten Platz.

Sie richteten sich in ihren Sitzen auf, legten die Gurte an.

the right into a little stretch of woodland to have a picnic,
she said.

And a picnic with all the trimmings, Mr Gernstein added.
Your mother warmed up Frankfurters on the camping stove
in water she had brought with her, your father, I can see
him now, how depressed he looked if there wasn't any mus-
tard.

The Gernsteins were laughing, happy in the wistfulness of
their memories.

Or is it more than twenty years ago?

No matter, they were better times.

For us, better times. Are we elitist, do you think?

I don't care if we are.

And they were better times for nature too, we are not being
selfish.

Better times! Today's motorists are of a different opinion.

Now every man jack drives.

And every woman. Just think of all the second cars.

Well, we are just elitist.

Yes, what other choice do we have?

On this point there was no disagreement between the Gernsteins. The new age and progress had long proved to be phan-
toms of great consequence; human beings were in a cul-de-sac,
threatened by overcrowding, suffocation, the crash-landing of
the earth, no more air left to breathe. However many years you
might want to take into account, their well-being as residents of
their area, as pedestrians anywhere, had taken quite a knock,
even if you looked back over former car journeys.

At about three o'clock, when his wife inquired, Mr Gernstein
felt fit again.

Had an unusually long break today, he said. So don't be surprised if things move at a bit more of a pace, now.

You are the best driver I know, Mrs Gernstein said lovingly,
because she knew that, among her husband's favourite compli-
ments, this one took first place.

They sat up in their seats, put on their seat belts and

Verließen ihre Parklücke im Autobahnrastplatz, vorbei an der Rast-
stätte.

Schon wenige Minuten später, eingefädelt in den dichten Verkehr in Richtung Grenze, kamen die Gernsteins gut vorwärts mit
zahlreichen Geschwindigkeitsüberschreitungen, gemütlich aufge-
pflanzt hinter der Frontscheibe ihres Autos, das ihnen so sympa-
thisch war wie ein Haustier.

drove out of their parking space in the layby past the restaurant.

Only a few minutes later the Gernsteins had filed into the
heavy traffic heading for the border. They were making good
progress, often breaking the speed limit, comfortably in place
behind the front windscreen of their car, of which they were as
fond as if it were a pet.

Lascia

JUDITH HERMANN

Lascia[1]

Vor ein paar Jahren reiste ich mit meinem Freund David durch
Sizilien. Unsere Reise ging zu Ende, unsere Beziehung auch, in
Catania[2] brach das Auto zusammen und war vor Ablauf von
drei oder vier Tagen nicht wieder fahrbar. Wir fügten uns, weil
uns nichts anderes übrig blieb, mieteten ein Zimmer in einer
Absteige[3] und liefen, verfeindet bis zur Sprach- und Blicklosig-
keit, Straßen aus schwarzem Lavastein ziellos hinauf und
hinunter. Es war unglaublich heiß und wir waren zu Tode erschöpft, aber im Gehen ertrugen wir uns gerade noch. In
diesem Zustand wurden wir die Opfer Francescos, der uns auf
dem Domplatz ansprach und dann, weil wir ihn nicht energisch
genug abwehrten, durch alle Straßen hindurch unerbittlich verfolgte. Er würde uns für ein Trinkgeld, für ein Garnichts, nach
Taormina fahren. Oder irgendwohin. Auf den Ätna. Er schrie
es – „Vulkano!", nie wäre uns die Idee gekommen, auf den
Ätna zu fahren, aber jetzt erschien uns diese Möglichkeit wie
ein Zeichen, ein Schicksal, vielleicht eine Rettung. Wir einigten
uns auf ein Honorar von 200.000 Lire, zahlten 50.000 für
Benzin an, gingen zu seinem Auto zurück, das er in der Nähe
des Domes geparkt hatte. Francesco war Rumäne, ein kleiner,
dicker, weißhaariger Mann, er sprach von allen Sprachen die
nötigsten Sätze, er schien verschlagen,[4] nicht wirklich gefährlich
zu sein. Er lief vor uns her und wir folgten ihm, David griff beinahe nach meiner Hand. Er setzte sich in Francescos marodem
Fiat[5] auf den Beifahrersitz, weil ihm sonst schlecht geworden
wäre, Francesco bemerkte das, verstand es aber falsch und warf
mir einen bedeutungsvollen Blick zu, ich sah weg und stieg
hinten ein. Der Beifahrersitz hatte ein riesiges Loch, das mit Zeit-
ungen und Plunder ausgefüllt war, Francesco startete, gab Gas

Lascia

A few years ago I was travelling through Sicily with my boyfriend David. Our trip was coming to an end, as was our relationship; in Catania our car broke down and was not going to be in a drivable state again for three or four days. We put up with it because we had no other choice, rented a room in some cheap guest house and roamed aimlessly up and down the streets with their black lava stone paving – daggers drawn to the point where all communication had ceased, we did not exchange so much as a glance. It was incredibly hot and we were utterly exhausted, but we could just about tolerate each other only when we were walking. In this state we fell prey to Francesco, who spoke to us on the cathedral square and who then proceeded to pursue us relentlessly through the streets because we did not fend him off firmly enough. For a tip, for almost next to nothing, he would drive us to Taormina. Or anywhere. Up Mount Etna. He shouted it: 'Volcano!'. It would never have occurred to us to go up Mount Etna but now this opportunity appeared to us like a sign, a stroke of fate, possibly salvation. We agreed a fee of 200,000 lire, paid a deposit of 50,000 lire for petrol and went back to his car, which he had parked near the cathedral. Francesco was a Romanian, a small, fat, white-haired man; he knew the essential phrases in every language. He seemed cunning but not really dangerous. He charged ahead and we followed him; David almost reached for my hand. He got into the passenger seat in Francesco's decrepit Fiat, because he would have felt sick otherwise; Francesco noticed this, but misunderstood it and gave me a meaningful look; I looked away and got into the back. The passenger seat had a huge hole in it which had been packed with newspapers and other stuff. Francesco started the car, put his foot down on the

und fuhr los, und David sackte zunehmend ein und wurde kleiner und kleiner, bis er von hinten wie ein Kind aussah. Francesco bestand darauf, dass wir seine rumänischen Zigaretten rauchten, er hielt eine offene Zigarettenschachtel vor Davids Gesicht. „No, grazie", sagte David und schüttelte den Kopf, Francesco sagte sehr bestimmt: „Smoke. Romania. Zigaretten gut." Und also rauchten wir, eine nach der anderen, bis wir eingehüllt waren in dicken, gelblichen Qualm. Wenn David sein linkes Bein nach rechts zog, um ihm Platz fürs Schalten zu lassen, bog Francesco es sanft wieder zurück, er sagte „bequeme, bequeme" und dann „lascia", worüber er aus unerfindlichen Gründen in lang anhaltendes Gelächter ausbrach. David versuchte von Zeit zu Zeit, sich hochzuziehen und gerade zu sitzen, gab es dann auf. Wir blieben im Stau stecken, und Francesco ließ uns ein Album betrachten, in dem fünfzig Fotos von Frauen klebten, die allesamt aussahen wie Prostituierte oder Transsexuelle, ich war ratlos, David höflich, er nahm sich für jedes Foto Zeit, nie Zeit genug für Francesco, der immer wieder die Seiten zurückblätterte, zeigte und mit den Fingern darauf schlug, seinen Oberkörper hin und her wiegte. Es war erstickend im Auto und wir hatten nichts zu trinken dabei. David sagte, er würde gerne an einer Tankstelle halten um Wasser zu kaufen, und Francesco schüttelte abwehrend den Kopf und kramte eine angebrochene Wasserflasche unter seinem Sitz hervor, aus der wir alle tranken, er selber als Erster. Er gähnte oft und lange und hatte eine groteske Art, den Mund dabei weit aufzusperren. Ich konnte mich nicht zurückhalten, zu sagen: „Schlafen Sie schlecht?" Er sagte, er könne eigentlich gut schlafen, aber er habe Angst zu schlafen. Er kannte das deutsche Wort *Angst*. Er sagte, er würde fürchterlich träumen, wenn er schlafe, und dabei drehte er sich um und sah mir ins Gesicht, und für den Bruchteil einer Sekunde war mir so, als würde *ich* fürchterlich träumen, jetzt gerade, immerzu, machtlos und hingegeben, und dann drehte er sich wieder weg. Als wir, schon fast aus der Stadt heraus, schneller fuhren, wollte David sich anschnallen, Francesco sagte „Lascia", diesmal entschieden drohend, nahm den Gurtstecker und bog ihn hinter den Sitz. David versuchte es später noch einmal, dann nicht mehr, auch nicht, als Francesco unglaublich riskant zu überholen

accelerator and drove off, and David gradually sank deeper into
the hole, becoming smaller and smaller until he looked like a
child from the back. Francesco insisted on us smoking his
Romanian cigarettes, he held an open cigarette packet under
David's nose. 'No, grazie,' said David shaking his head. Francesco replied very firmly, 'Smoke. Romania. Cigarettes good.'
And so we smoked one after the other until we were shrouded in
thick, yellowish smoke. When David moved his left leg to the
right in order to leave him enough room to change gear he
gently moved it back again, he said 'easy, easy,' and added 'lascia', which sent him into prolonged laughter for some impenetrable reason. David tried from time to time to pull himself up
and sit up straight, but then gave up. We got stuck in a traffic
jam and Francesco let us look at an album which contained fifty
photos of women who all looked like prostitutes and trans-
sexuals; I was at a loss; David politely took time over each photograph, but never enough time for Francesco, who kept turning
the pages back again, pointing and tapping with his fingers
while he rocked his torso back and forth. It was stifling in the
car and we had nothing to drink with us. David said that he
would like to stop at a petrol station to get some water and Francesco shook his head and fished out an opened water bottle
from under his seat from which we all drank, he first. He often
gave lengthy yawns, opening his mouth wide in a grotesque
manner. I could not refrain from saying, 'Do you have trouble
sleeping?' He said he actually could sleep well, but that he was
afraid of sleeping. He knew the German word *Angst*. He said if
he slept he would have terrible dreams and with that he turned
round and looked me in the face, and for a split second I felt as
if *I* was in a terrible dream, that very moment, for ever helpless
and in a state of surrender: and then he turned round again.
When we had almost left the town and had started to go faster,
David wanted to put his seat belt on. Francesco said 'Lascia',
this time with decided menace, took the safety belt clasp and
bent it behind the seat. David tried again a little later but then
gave up, even when Francesco started to overtake in the most

war begann. Wenn er nichts sagte, sagten wir auch nichts. Ich
kämpfte gegen eine ungeheure Müdigkeit. Wie es David ging,
konnte ich nicht sehen, er schien in dem Loch völlig versackt zu sein.
Einmal redete Francesco längere Zeit, ich hörte nicht genau zu, ich
verstand vielleicht, dass er sagte, es gebe so etwas wie eine
elementare, tiefe Befriedigung, Glück, das keine Rücksicht auf ein
Nachher nimmt. Er redete sich in Rage – „Capisci?[6] Capisci?" –,
unterbrach sich dann wieder und fuchtelte mit der Hand vor David
herum. David sagte „Si, si, si. Capito,[7] ja", er klang schwach und ich
ahnte, dass er in Bedrängnis war, dennoch war ich froh, überhaupt
seine Stimme zu hören. „Non capisci", schrie Francesco, „non capisci", er seufzte und schwieg und fing dann wieder von vorne an, das
Glück, die Rücksicht, das Nachher, du weißt. Wenn ich mich nicht
täusche, lag irgendwann für Sekunden seine Hand auf Davids Bein.
David drehte sich zu mir um und versuchte, mich anzuschauen. Er
sah seltsam aus und ich berührte kurz seine Schulter. Irgendwo auf
einem der Ätnahänge hielten wir, nach Stunden so schien es,
„Andiamo",[8] sagte Francesco und stieg aus. Als wir nicht sofort
folgten, schlug er hart mit der Faust gegen die Autofensterscheibe.
Wir stiegen aus, ich war wie gelähmt, obwohl ein kühler, erfrisch-
ender Wind ging. Francesco zeigte in eine Richtung, in die David
dann auch einfach losging, schleppend und wie benommen,
Francesco folgte ihm. David und ich suchten keine Nähe mehr,
obwohl ich mich ihm nah fühlte oder vielleicht genau deshalb.
Francesco häufte uns schwarze Steine in die Hände, die wir trugen
wie Kinder. In einer Höhe von etwa 2000 Metern endete die Straße
an einer Touristenstation und dem Anfang einer Seilbahn, die außer
Betrieb war. Der Wind war jetzt heftig, und was Francesco unaufhörlich sagte, war nicht mehr zu verstehen. Er kaufte uns an einem
Kiosk einen 27-Bild-Fotoapparat und zeigte David, was er foto-
grafieren sollte. David fotografierte, Francesco hatte mit dem
Kioskverkäufer Blicke gewechselt, die mich aufs Äußerste beun-
ruhigten. Wir stiegen auf die kleinen, erloschenen Nebenkrater aus
winzigen, braunen Steinen, die unter uns wegrutschten. Francesco,
zwischen uns, umklammerte mit der linken Hand mein, mit der
rechten Davids Handgelenk, sein Griff war hart. Der Kraterrand

reckless manner. If he did not speak we did not speak either. I
was fighting enormous fatigue. I could not see how David was,
he seemed to have shrunk into the hole completely. At one time
Francesco was talking for quite a while; I was not listening properly; I understood perhaps that he was saying that there was
something like an elementary, deep satisfaction, a happiness
which had no regard for what comes after. He talked himself
into a frenzy – 'Capisci? Capisci?' he interrupted himself again,
gesticulating with his hands in front of David. David said, 'Si, si,
si. Capito. Yes.' He sounded weak and I sensed that he was in
difficulty and yet I was glad just to hear his voice at all. 'Non
capisci,' shouted Francesco, 'Non capisci.' He sighed, fell silent
and then started all over again, happiness, regard, what comes
after, you know. If I am not mistaken his hand was resting on
David's leg for a few seconds. David turned round to me and
tried to look at me. He looked strange and I touched his shoulder briefly. Somewhere on the slopes of Mount Etna we
stopped, after some hours it seemed. 'Andiamo,' said Francesco
and got out. When we did not follow immediately he hit the
windscreen hard with his fist. We got out, I felt as if I was para-
lysed, although there was a cool, refreshing wind blowing. Francesco was pointing in a particular direction, in which David
then simply set off, shuffling, as if in a daze; Francesco followed
him. David and I no longer sought proximity, but I was feeling
close to him, perhaps for that very reason. Francesco heaped
black stones into our hands which we carried like children. At a
height of about 2000 metres the road ended at a tourists' stop
and the beginning of a cable railway, which was out of service.
The wind was now strong and we could no longer understand
Francesco's incessant chatter. At a kiosk he bought us a 27-
picture camera and told David what he should take photos of.
David took photos; Francesco had exchanged glances with the
kiosk salesman which I found extremely unsettling. We climbed
on to the small, extinct side craters made up of tiny brown
stones, which slipped from under us. Francesco, walking
between us, grasped my wrist with his left hand and David's

kaum breiter als ein Fußpfad, mir war schwindelig, der Wind
nahm mir den Atem und ich fühlte mich fiebrig. Beim Abstieg löste
Francesco seinen Griff und nahm uns stattdessen an der Hand, ich
starrte auf meine Füße, unter denen die Asche abwärts glitt. Es war
früher Nachmittag, als wir über einen anderen Weg wieder zurück-
fuhren. In einem völlig ausgestorbenen, verlassenen Dorf hielt Francesco an, kletterte über Zäune, brach einen ganzen Arm voll
Blumen und stopfte sie nach hinten zu mir auf die Rückbank, aus
den Blättern krochen Insekten heraus. David schlief. Die
Landstraße wurde breiter, ging in eine Schnellstraße über, die Aus-
schilderungen zeigten alles Mögliche an, Catania war nicht
darunter. Ich richtete mich auf, mit letzten Kräften wie mir schien,
um Francesco nach dem Weg zu fragen. Er antwortete nicht und
schob stattdessen eine von den vielen Kassetten, die zwischen
seinen Füßen herumlagen, in den Autorekorder, rumänische
Musik, absolut unerträglich, er drehte die Lautstärke so weit auf,
dass er mich nicht verstanden hätte, hätte ich weiter gefragt, aber
ich fragte nicht mehr. Wir hielten an einer Tankstelle, David
wachte auf und rieb sich die Schläfen. Wir hätten aussteigen
können, weglaufen, wir stiegen nicht aus, wir blieben sitzen, reglos,
bis Francesco zurückkam, einstieg, weiterfuhr. Wir verließen die
Schnellstraße, ich hatte den Eindruck, dass wir uns von einer anderen Seite her wieder dem Ätna näherten. In einer Mondland-
schaft hielten wir, Francesco stieg aus dem Auto und kümmerte
sich nicht mehr um uns, er lief über die Aschehügel und rauchte
pausenlos, ich sah selbst aus der Entfernung, dass ihm die Hände
zitterten. Die rumänische Musik brach ab. Ich konnte den Wind
hören und das schmirgelnde, sandige Geräusch, mit dem die Asche
verwehte, ich schloss die Augen. Als ich irgendwann wieder auf-
wachte oder zu mir kam, befanden wir uns in den Straßen
Catanias.

Es ist nichts geschehen. Wir zahlten Francesco das vereinbarte
Geld, das Geld für den Fotoapparat, für das Benzin, für ich weiß
nicht was. Wir wollten ihn jetzt loswerden, wir waren hochmütig
genug. Wir waren in der Stadt, zurück, in Sicherheit, wir zahlten
einen absurden Betrag, eine Art Lösegeld, wie David es später

with his right; his grip was hard. The edge of the crater was
hardly wider than a footpath, I felt dizzy, the wind took my
breath away and I felt feverish. As we climbed down Francesco
loosened his grip and took us by the hand instead; I stared at my
feet, beneath which the ash was sliding downhill. It was early
afternoon when we headed back by a different route. In a
completely uninhabited, deserted village Francesco stopped,
climbed over some fences and plucked a whole armful of flowers
which he stuffed in next to me on to the back seat; insects came
crawling out of the leaves. David was asleep. The country road
became wider, changing into a fast road, the signs were showing all sorts of places, Catania was not one of them. I hoisted
myself up, rallying the few ounces of strength left within me in
order to ask Francesco the way. He did not answer but instead
pushed one of the many cassettes lying around between his feet
into the cassette player, Romanian music, absolutely unbear-
able, he turned the volume up so high that he would not have
understood me had I gone on asking, but I did not ask again
any more. We stopped at a petrol station, David woke up and
rubbed his temples. We could have got out, run away; we did
not get out, we remained seated, motionless until Francesco
came back, got in and drove off. We left the fast road and I had
the impression that we were approaching Mount Etna again
from a different side. We stopped in a kind of lunar landscape,
Francesco got out of the car and no longer bothered with us; he
ran across heaps of ash smoking incessantly; even at a distance I
could see that his hands were shaking. The Romanian music
broke off. I could hear the wind and the grating, sandy noise
of the ash blowing away; I closed my eyes. When I woke
again or came round at some point we were in the streets of
Catania.

Nothing happened. We paid Francesco the agreed sum, the
money for the camera, for petrol and goodness knows what else.
We now wanted to get rid of him; we were arrogant enough.
We were back in town, safe, we paid an absurd sum, a kind of
ransom money, as David later called it, Francesco disappeared,

nannte, Francesco verschwand, es ist nichts geschehen. In der Nacht in der Pension Holland International wachte ich auf. David neben mir lag reglos, am Fenster bewegten sich die Gardinen im Zugwind. Aus den Nachbarzimmern war nichts mehr zu hören, aber aus der Tiefe des Hofes kam ein Geräusch wie das Plätschern von Wasser. Ich ging zum Fenster und lehnte mich hinaus. Zuerst sah ich die Katzen auf den Dächern der Autos, dann das Wasser, das schon fast den ganzen Hof überschwemmt hatte, es wirkte schwarz unter einem diffusen gelben Nebel aus Licht. Im Parterre gegenüber wusste ich ein Universitätsinstitut für Kommunikationswissenschaften. Am frühen Morgen hatten hier Studenten gesessen, sich leise unterhalten, Kaffee getrunken, gelesen. Die Luft schien sehr rein und klar gewesen zu sein, daran erinnerte ich mich. Ich konnte nicht sehen, woher das Wasser kam.

nothing had happened. During the night in the Holland International guest house I woke up. David was lying next to me, motionless, at the window the curtains were moving in the draught. There was no more sound coming from the neighbouring rooms, but from far below in the yard came a noise like the splattering of water. I went to the window and leant out. First I saw the cats on the roofs of the cars and then the water which had nearly flooded the whole of the yard; it seemed black under the diffuse yellow fog of light. I knew there was a University Institute of Communication Studies opposite on the ground floor. Early in the morning students had been sitting there, talking quietly, drinking coffee and reading. The air seemed to be clean and clear, that much I remembered. I could not see where the water was coming from.

Chicago/Shanty Town

GEORG KLEIN

Chicago/Baracken

Mich hat die Kunst meiner Frau nach Chicago gebracht, und ihr Wagemut zog mich unter die schwarzen Balken der Baracken. Falls Sie Urlaubsgelüste oder die Launen Ihrer Geschäfte an die großen Seen Nordamerikas führen, liegt es in Ihrem Ermessen, ob Sie Ihren kostbaren Kopf durch denselben Türstock ins Finstere stecken. Ich rate Ihnen zu nichts – weise Sie nur darauf hin, dass der Sears-Tower, eines der höchsten Gebäude der Welt, ein Aussichtsdeck besitzt. Die 20 Dollar, die Sie für die Auffahrt bezahlen werden, sind ein fairer Preis.

Und wenn Sie dann oben an der Seeseite vergeblich nach einem soliden Horizont Ausschau gehalten haben, wenn Ihnen das glitzernde Süßwasser und der Himmel über den unsichtbaren kanadischen Ufern im angestrengten Starren zu einem Blaugrau verschwimmen, dann ist es Zeit, im Kreislauf der Touristen zur landeinwärts gewandten Seite der Panoramaetage hinüberzugehen. Lassen Sie dort – die Stirn am Glas – den Blick auf den Loop, auf das durch eine alte Hochbahnlinie klar umrissene Zentrum Chicagos hinunterstürzen. Die Baracken, die ich meine, sind als ein kleiner, aber dennoch deutlicher schwarzer Fleck hinter den Geleisen zu erkennen.

Es hat seinen eigenen Reiz, es bringt in aparte Verlegenheiten, als bloßer Gatte einer bekannten Musikerin durch die USA zu reisen.[1] Die Kulturstiftung der Deutschen Bank, die die Auftritte meiner Frau organisierte, hatte ihr einen Tourneeleiter zur Seite gestellt. Von frühmorgens bis spät in die Nacht stand der junge Mann, gebürtiger Nürnberger und Doktor der Amerikanistik, mit Sightseeing-Angeboten und Sicherheitshinweisen in Bereitschaft.[2] Aber vom ersten Tag an torpedierte meine Frau seine Vorschläge und seine Einwände mit zwei kargen Sätzen, entweder mit „Mein

Chicago/Shanty Town

It was my wife's art that brought me to Chicago and it was her daring that led me to these black-beamed slums. If you ever find yourself, whether on holiday or due to the vagaries of your business, in the American Great Lakes it's up to you whether you poke your precious head into the dark behind this particular door. I am not suggesting that you should. All I am saying is that the Sears tower, one of the highest buildings in the world, has a viewing platform. The twenty dollars which you pay to go up there is a fair price.

And if at the top you have failed to discern a definite horizon on the lakeside and if the glistening water and the sky above the invisible Canadian shoreline are beginning to merge into a bluey grey in your fixed gaze, then it is time to follow the stream of circulating tourists to the side of the viewing platform which faces inland. There, with your forehead pressed against the glass, let your gaze drop down to the loop, the centre of Chicago, which is clearly encircled by an elevated railway. The slums I am referring to are a small but nevertheless clearly discernible black dot behind the railway lines.

Travelling through the States merely as the husband of a famous musician has its own attraction, its own exquisite embarrassment. The culture fund of the Deutsche Bank, which organized my wife's concerts, had given her a tour manager. From early in the morning until late at night the young man, who was born in Nuremberg and had a doctorate in American Studies, was on hand to offer sightseeing tours or security advice. But from day one my wife torpedoed his suggestions and objections with two crisp sentences, saying either 'My husband has already

Mann hat schon eine andere Idee" oder mit „Mein lieber Mann
passt schon auf mich auf!" Dass beides gelogen war, konnte der
wackere Exil-Franke[3] nicht wissen. Und als ihm meine Frau an
unserem zweiten Chicago-Tag bei Kaffee und Cream Cake erzählte, wo wir gewesen seien und was uns dort zugestoßen sei,
stand ihm der Mund so lange offen, dass man sich um die Feuchte
seines Gaumens sorgen musste.

Meine Frau ist Schlagzeugerin, fachgenau gesagt Solo-
Perkussionistin. Das Stück, mit dem sie in den USA auftrat, hatte
ihr eine bekannte Leipziger Neu-Tönerin quasi auf Hände und
Füße geschrieben. Falls Sie sich in eine Aufführung verirren und
wie ich nur schwer Zugang zur modernen Musik finden sollten,
käme Ihnen die zweistündige Suite wahrscheinlich nur wie ein
infernalisches, von kurzen Ruhepausen gegliedertes Lärmen[4] vor.
Aber aus der bloßen Anschauung würden Sie zumindest begreifen,
welche Kondition solche Solostücke verlangen. Und es müsste
Ihnen einleuchten,[5] dass es einer dermaßen trainierten Vortrags-
künstlerin nahe liegt, ihren Mann auf exzessiven Fußmärschen
kreuz und quer durch die Großstädte der Alten und Neuen Welt
zu schleppen.

In Chicago hatte uns die Deutsche Bank in einem Apartment im
Sheffield Historical District untergebracht. Nach Jahrzehnten des
Niedergangs vibriert dieses einstige Arbeiterviertel seit kurzem in
einem heftigen Aufschwung. Fast gleichzeitig mit den jungen
Künstlern ist das Geld dorthin gekommen. Galerien, eine Vielfalt
kleiner Restaurants, Boutiquen und Accessoirlädchen säumen die
größeren Straßen. Als wir am späten Nachmittag des Ankunfts-
tages zu unserem Gang Richtung Zentrum aufbrachen, sah ich,
wie auf der anderen Straßenseite ein Mann im Plastikoverall eine
Atemmaske über sein Gesicht zog. Dann warf er einen Kom-
pressor an und richtete den Lauf einer Farbpistole auf die Fassade
eines Backsteinhäuschens, um es bis unter die Dachrinne kanarien-
gelb zu spritzen. Eine knappe halbe Stunde später sind wir, nur
noch drei Straßenzüge vom Loop entfernt, den Negern in die
Hände gefallen.

Glauben Sie mir, ich habe versucht, wenn die Rede auf unser

thought of something different,' or 'My dear husband will look after me.' That both statements were lies was something the Franconian in exile could not know. And when on our second day in Chicago my wife told him over coffee and cream cakes where we had been and what had happened to us, his mouth hung open in amazement for so long that we feared his palate might dry out.

My wife is a drummer or, to use the accurate term, a solo percussionist. The piece which she was performing in the United States had almost literally been custom-made for her by a well-known contemporary female composer from Leipzig. Should you wander into a performance and, like me, find modern music fairly inaccessible, the two-hour suite will strike you as little more than some infernal row punctuated only by brief respites. But by just watching her play you would understand what physical stamina such solo pieces require. Then it would be obvious to you why the idea of dragging her husband on excessively long hikes all over the cities of the Old and the New World should suggest itself to such a fit performer.

In Chicago the Deutsche Bank had put us up in an apartment in the Sheffield Historical District. After decades of decline the former working-class area had recently experienced a vibrant boom. The money had arrived almost simultaneously with the young artists. The main streets are lined with galleries, a variety of small restaurants, boutiques and shops selling accessories. When in the late afternoon on the day of our arrival we set out towards the town centre, I noticed a man in plastic overalls on the other side of the road pulling a breathing mask over his face. Then he started up a compressor and pointed the shaft of a painting gun at the façade of a small brick house in order to paint it canary yellow up to the guttering. About half an hour later, only three roads from the loop, we fell into the hands of the negroes.

Believe me, I have tried, whenever our adventure has come

Abenteuer kam, von Schwarzen, von Farbigen, von Amerikanern afrikanischer Herkunft zu sprechen. Aber stets waren diese Bezeichnungen der Erzählung abträglich. Und als meine Frau einmal hörte, wie ich mich mit drei herkulischen amerikanischen Bürgern afrikanischer Abstammung abmühte, unterbrach sie mich mit dem Zwischenruf: „Aber es waren doch Neger!" Auf jeden Fall waren es drei, und ich habe ihre Attacke nicht kommen sehen, als wir aus der Steuben Street in die Lincoln Avenue einbogen und das grandiose, als architektonisches Weltwunder gerühmte Hochbaupanorama des Loop bereits vor Augen hatten.

Später hat man uns erklärt, dass die Häuser, die wir auf der Lincoln Avenue passierten, Überbleibsel eines ehrgeizigen städtischen Wohnprojekts der späten sechziger Jahre sind. Vor kurzem, zur Jahrtausendwende, war ein Drittel der zehnstöckigen Gebäude gesprengt worden, die meisten anderen hatte man geräumt, ihre Türen und ihre unteren Fenster waren zugemauert oder zumindest mit Brettern vernagelt. Nur eine Hand voll Blöcke längs der Straße wurde noch von schwarzen Familien bewohnt. Vielleicht machte mich die Musik, die aus fast jedem Fenster drang, arglos, vielleicht dachte ich unter dem Einfluss eines deutschen Sprichworts, dass einer, der gerade so laut Musik höre, nicht gleichzeitig daran denken könne, Passanten auszurauben. Aber dann sah ich, wie drei junge Männer aus dem Fenster einer Erdgeschosswohnung sprangen, und wunderbar locker und eindeutig zielstrebig zu uns auf die andere Straßenseite trabten.

Nur an mir liegt es, dass man uns sofort als Touristen identifiziert. Meine Frau vermag, egal wie, allein durch ihr forsches, federndes Ausschreiten[6] fast überall wie eine Ortskundige zu wirken. „Schlurf nicht so!", sagt sie oft in aufmunterndem Ton zu mir oder „nicht glotzen, nur gucken!" Glauben Sie mir, drei große, breitschultrige Neger sind in der Lage, einen hilflos glotzenden Touristen so lückenlos zu umringen, dass es mit jedem Weiterschlurfen vorbei ist.

Einer hatte eine zerknitterte Zeitschrift aus dem Halsausschnitt seines Sweatshirts gezogen und hielt sie mir mehr auf als vor das Gesicht, alle drei redeten auf mich ein, zupften an meiner

up in conversation, to call them blacks, coloureds or Americans
of African origin. But these terms always detracted from the
story. And when my wife overheard me once droning on
about three Herculean American citizens of African origin, she
just interrupted me by calling out, 'But they were negroes.' In
any case there were three of them and I did not foresee their
attack when we turned from Steuben Street into Lincoln
Avenue and could already see the high-rise panorama of the
loop, which is praised as one of the architectural wonders of the
world.

Later it was explained to us that the houses we went past in
Lincoln Avenue were the remainder of an ambitious urban housing project of the late 1960s. A short while ago, at the millen-
nium, one-third of the ten-storey block had been blown up,
most of the others had been vacated and the doors and lower
windows had been bricked up or at least boarded over. Only a
handful of blocks along the road were still inhabited by black
families. Perhaps it was the music ringing out from almost every
window which put me off my guard or perhaps, under the influence of some German proverb, I was thinking that someone
who was listening to such loud music could not possibly be thinking of robbing passers-by at the same time. But then I saw three
young men jump out of the window of a ground-floor flat, and
with a wonderfully relaxed but purposeful stride, head towards
us on the other side of the road.

It is entirely my fault that we are immediately identified as
tourists. My wife manages, no matter how, to appear like
someone who knows the vicinity, simply because of her bold,
brisk pace. 'Don't drag your feet,' she will say to me encouragingly, or 'Don't stare, just look.' Believe me, three broad-
shouldered black men are able to surround a helplessly staring
tourist so completely that dragging of feet is no longer an
option.

One of them had pulled a crumpled magazine out of the neck-
line of his sweatshirt and held it more into than in front of my
face; all three were keeping on at me, pulling at my clothes,

Kleidung und schubsten mich nicht allzu fest, aber in unheimlicher Abstimmung hin und her. Ich verstand, dass es sich bei dem Druckprodukt, das ich zu riechen bekam, um eine Art Arbeitslosen- oder Obdachlosenzeitschrift handelte, dass die drei Hünen dieses Heft verkauften und milde Gaben für ein Wohn- oder Beschäftigungsprogramm sammelten und dass alle Spender, vor allem die großzügigen, von Gott gesegnet seien.

Seit sie bekannt ist und regelmäßig ins Ausland eingeladen wird, weigert sich meine Frau, Englisch zu sprechen. Sie sagt, als deutsche Kulturschaffende, vor allem als Musikerin, sei verpflichtet, die deutsche Sprache zum Erklingen zu bringen. Dem amerikanischen Kulturattaché in Peking, Mister Simon Hardstone, den wir auf der Frühlingsparty des dortigen Goethe-Instituts kennen lernten, hat sie mit einem herzlichen „Guten Tag, wie geht's, Herr Hartstein!"[7] die Hand geschüttelt.

Sogar die drei Neger, die uns umstellt hielten, ging sie auf Deutsch an, fragte sie unter anderem, ob das Projekt, für das sie sich engagierten, religiös ausgerichtet sei oder ob sie das mit dem Segen Gottes mehr metaphorisch gemeint hatten. Ich bin der Letzte, der meine Frau für naiv hielte. Aber auf der Lincoln Avenue, in einem Anfall moralischer Schwäche,[8] zweifelte ich doch an ihrem tausendfach erwiesenen Wirklichkeitssinn. Ich wollte es alleine richten, ich zückte mein Portemonnaie, mit ein paar Dollar gedachte ich uns freizukaufen und vergaß, dass ich unser gesamtes Bargeld bei mir trug, dass meine Börse mit großen Banknoten gespickt war.

Meine Frau und ich, wir haben uns vor ihrer Haustür kennen gelernt. Ich klingelte an dem kleinen Reihenhäuschen, das sie damals in Mannheim zusammen mit zwei befreundeten Musikerinnen gemietet hatte, um ihr ein Paket zuzustellen. Ich weiß nicht, ob Ihnen der United Parcel Service ein Begriff ist, diese US-Firma die der ganzen Welt, auch unserer Deutschen Post, das Päckchenverteilen vormachen will. Ich war seinerzeit gerade eine Woche dabei und fühlte mich äußerst unwohl am Steuer des ungetümen amerikanischen Lieferwagens.

Warum konnten wir unser Frachtgut nicht mit Transportern

pushing me about, not very hard but in an ominously coordinated fashion. I understood that the printed matter I was forced to smell was some magazine published for the unemployed or the homeless, that the three hulks were selling this magazine and collecting kind donations for a housing or employment project and that all donors, especially generous ones, would be blessed by God.

Since she has become well known and been invited abroad regularly, my wife refuses to speak English. She says that as a creative representative of German culture, especially as a musician, it is her duty to let the German language ring out. When we met the American cultural attaché in Peking, Mr Simon Hardstone, at the spring party at the local Goethe Institute, she shook his hand with a hearty 'Guten Tag, wie geht's, Herr Hartstein!'

Even the three negroes who had surrounded us she addressed in German asking, among other things, whether the project they were promoting was for a religious organization or whether they had used the term 'God's blessing' more metaphorically. I would be the last person in the world to call my wife naive. But on Lincoln Avenue, in a fit of moral weakness, I did begin to doubt her grasp of reality, which she had demonstrated over and over again. I wanted to deal with it singlehandedly; I pulled out my wallet, intending to buy our freedom with a few dollars, and forgot that I was carrying all our cash, that my wallet was packed with large notes.

My wife and I met for the first time at her front door. I rang the doorbell of a small terraced house in Mannheim, which she had rented with two musician friends, in order to deliver a parcel. I don't know whether you're familiar with United Parcel Service, that US firm that wants to teach the whole world, including our Deutsche Post, how to deliver parcels. At the time I had only been with them for a week and I felt ill at ease at the wheel of this huge American van.

Why could we not deliver our freight in vans made by

von Daimler, Volkswagen, Fiat oder zumindest mit in Europa gebauten Fords zustellen? Wieso wurden diese gewaltigen, mit tausend Nieten protzenden Blechungetüme über den Atlantik geschafft, und wieso war alles bei UPS, auch das affig kurze Uniformjäckchen, in dem ich steckte, braun? Meine Frau meinte später, wäre ich postgelb oder gar in einem meiner karierten Freizeithemden bei ihr erschienen, hätte sie mich bestimmt nicht auf einen Kaffee hereingebeten. Braun stehe mir unheimlich gut,[9] dagegen solle ich – UPS hin, UPS her – nie anzukämpfen versuchen.

So habe ich mein United-Parcel-Service-Jäckchen über meine Kündigung hinweg behalten, und in unserem Gepäck war es schließlich zurück in sein Herstellungsland geflogen. Ich trug es, als ich 100 Dollar für ein obskures Wohlfahrtsprojekt spendete und mich einer der Sammler bei Entgegennahme des Geldes plötzlich fragte, ob wir aus „Doitschländ" seien. Ich sehe die Lippen, die Zähne, die Zunge und den Schlund noch vor mir, die dieses Doitschländ phonetisch nicht ganz korrekt und doch rätselhaft richtig hervorbrachten. „Netherlands!" wollte ich lügen, „Switzerland!" oder zumindest „Austria!", aber es war zu spät, meine Frau hatte schon geantwortet und außer Deutschland auch noch Berlin als unseren augenblicklichen Wohnsitz preisgegeben.

Am nächsten Tag zeigte uns unser Tourneeleiter mit zitterndem Zeigefinger auf einer Chicago-Karte, wo wir genau in die Falle gegangen waren. Die verkommenen Sozialbauten füllten drei große Karrees, zwischen den abbruchreifen Blöcken habe sich keinerlei Gewerbe, nicht die mieseste Kneipe gehalten. Als letzte Bastion abendländischer Kultur sei vor einem halben Jahr ein Männerwohnheim der Heilsarmee niedergebrannt worden. Westlich schließe sich ein ehemaliges Bahngelände an, auf dem noch einige Altmetallhändler und Autoreparaturwerkstätten ein befristetes Dasein führten. Auch hier seien die Schuppen und Hallen bereits zum Abriss bestimmt. Und dass die alten Holzhäuser, die so genannten Black Barracks, davon ausgenommen seien, halte er für unwahrscheinlich. Einen Denkmalschutz in unserem skrupulösen Sinne gebe es in den USA natürlich nicht.

Daimler, VW, Fiat or at least Ford Europe? Why were these enormous metal rivet-bedecked monsters being shipped across the Atlantic, and why was everything at UPS, even the silly short uniform jacket which I was wearing, brown? My wife said later that, had I appeared on her doorstep wearing postman's yellow or, indeed, one of my check leisure shirts, she would never have asked me in for coffee. Brown suited me terribly well, UPS or no UPS, and I should never try to deny it.

So I kept my United Parcel Service jacket even after I had handed in my notice, and it had eventually flown back to the country of its origin in our luggage. I was wearing it when I donated 100 dollars to an obscure welfare project and when one of those collecting suddenly asked me, when he took the money, whether we were from 'Doitschländ'. I can still picture the lips, the teeth, the tongue and even the throat which articulated Doitschländ in a manner not quite phonetically correct but mysteriously accurate. 'The Netherlands', I wanted to lie, 'Switzerland' or at least 'Austria', but it was too late; my wife had already replied and had not only specified Germany but also Berlin as our present place of residence.

The next day our tour manager, with a trembling forefinger, pointed out on a map of Chicago the exact spot where we had fallen into the trap. The run-down social housing filled three large squares between the blocks awaiting demolition; no business, not even the lowest dive of a pub, had managed to keep going there. As the last bastion of Western culture a Salvation Army hostel for young men had been burnt down there six months previously. At the western edge there was a former railway yard, on which a few scrap metal dealers and car-repair workshops were eking out an existence. Here the workshops and hangars were also marked out for demolition. And he thought it improbable that the old wooden houses, the so-called Black Barracks, were exempted from this. There was no such thing as a preservation order in our scrupulous understanding of the term in the United States.

Als wir, halb geführt, halb abgeführt, die Holzbauten erreicht hatten, als ich, meiner Frau folgend, die Stufen zu einer verglasten Souterraintür hinunterstieg, war meine Panik bereits in einen verstörten Fatalismus übergegangen. Wenn unsere Neger jetzt in bestem Goethe-Sprachkurs-Deutsch „April April! Hereingelegt!"[10] gerufen hätten, hätte ich dies mit dem gleichen idiotischen Seufzer quittiert, der mir vermutlich auch entfahren wäre, hätte mich jener Hieb auf den Hinterkopf getroffen, den ich mir als einen alles auslöschenden Gong auf dem Weg zu den Baracken so schrecklich gut hatte vorstellen können. Aber man berührte uns nicht mehr, man schob uns einmal hinein. Eine der schwarzen Hände, vor denen ich mich umsonst gefürchtet hatte, zog die Tür hinter mir zu, und wir standen mutterseelen allein zu zweit in ARNO'S ATLANTIC HARDWARE.

Ich weiß nicht, ob ich Ihnen wünschen soll, Arno kennen zu lernen. Als er aus dem Hinterraum seines Eisen- und Haushaltswarengeschäfts auf uns zukam, spürte ich jenen Ganzkörperschauer, mit dem mich bis dahin nur hohes Fieber oder die wenigen wirklich guten Horrorszenen der Filmgeschichte beglückt hatten. Auch in freier Wildbahn, selbst unter den Negern, die uns zu ihm geführt haben, muss der alte Mann riesig wirken. Hier, unter der niedrigen Decke des Ladens, zog sein gewaltiger Schädel wie ein käsiger Mond durch einen Schwarm blitzender Meteoriten – durch Himmelskörper, die in kosmischer Gewitztheit die Form von Pfannen, Töpfen, Schöpflöffeln, Gießkannen und Bügelsägen angenommen hatten.

„Kaffee oder Tee?", fragte er. Und als meine Frau „Bitte Tee! Aber nicht zu dünn, Herr Arno!" antwortete, griff er in eine Tasche seines grauen Kittels, und eine schwarz gerahmte Brille fand auf seiner Nase Platz. Zuvor, ohne die dicken Gläser seiner Sehhilfe, musste sich Arno allein mit der Kraft der Erinnerung durch den mit Hindernissen verstellten Verkaufsraum bewegt haben. Wohlgefällig, für meinen Geschmack mit etwas zu viel Wohlgefallen, studierte er das Gesicht und die Gestalt meiner Frau, sah dann kurz auf mich und verschwand mit einem „Ach, das will also Ihr Mann sein!" im Hinterzimmer seines Ladens.

When, half guided, half frog-marched, we had reached the
wooden buildings, and when, following my wife, I walked down
some stairs to a glass basement door, my panic had already
changed to a bewildered fatalism. If our negroes had now called
out in their best Goethe language-course German 'April! April!
Hereingelegt!' I would have dismissed this with the same idiotic
sigh that I would have uttered if I had actually been hit by that
blow on the back of my head which I had been able to picture
so terribly clearly on my way to the barracks as a gong which
blotted out everything. But we were not touched again, we were
simply pushed in. One of the black hands of which I had been
unnecessarily afraid pulled the door shut behind me and we
were standing all alone, the two of us, in ARNO'S ATLAN-
TIC HARDWARE.

I don't know whether I should wish it upon you that you
should meet Arno. When he came out of the back room of his
hardware and household goods shop I felt the same shiver run
all over my body that I had only previously felt when running a
fever or watching a particularly good scene in a horror film.
Even out in the open, even alongside the negroes who had led
us to him, this old man would strike you as enormous. But here,
underneath the low ceiling of the shop, his enormous skull
circled like a pale moon through a galaxy of sparkling meteor-
ites, through celestial bodies which the wit of the universe had
allowed to take the shape of frying-pans, pots, ladles, jugs and
hacksaws.

'Coffee or tea?' he asked. And when my dear wife replied,
'Tea, please Mr Arno. But not too weak, Mr Arno!', he put his
hand into the pocket of his grey overalls and a pair of black-
rimmed spectacles found its place on his nose. Before that, without the help of these thick lenses, Arno must have found his way
through this obstacle-bestrewn sales room purely by memory.
Appreciatively, to my mind a little too appreciatively, he examined my wife's face and figure, then glancing briefly at me, he
disappeared into the back room of his shop, saying, 'So he fan-
cies himself as your husband!'

Vielleicht habe ich mich deshalb auf die Trittleiter gesetzt. Sie wird Ihnen, wenn Sie Arnos Atlantic Hardware betreten, links vor der Verkaufstheke auffallen. Es handelt sich um keine vollwertige Leiter, sondern nur um eine so genannte „Hausfrauenhilfe". Aus einem stabilen, etwa hüfthohen Hocker lassen sich drei Stufen herausklappen. So hat man beim Fensterputzen, Vorhang-aufhängen und Regaleinräumen sicheren Stand. Als Arno zurück-kam und ein Tablett auf die Theke stellte, ging meine Frau hinten im Laden auf und ab und sah sich die Waren an. Arno beugte sich über mich und drückte mir eine Teetasse auf den Schoß.

„Du siehst blass aus, Landsmann." Und in ein Flüstern fallend, fragte er, ob mich seine Nachbarn, die Bimbos, so erschreckt hätten.

„Sind Sie Rassist, Herr Arno?" Meine Frau, gegen die man jeden Luchs schwerhörig nennen muss,[11] schlängelte sich aus einem Winkel voll mit Gasflaschen und allerlei Schweißgerät.

„Quasi im Gegenteil! Fräulein!", rief ihr Arno entgegen. Eher noch glaube er an den Unwert der gesamten menschlichen Spezies als an eine Höherwertigkeit der pigmentarmen Völker. Und mich fragte er, ob ich nicht etwas Milch zum Tee nehmen wollte, es sei Rohmilch, direkt von der Kuh, handgemolken von einem deutsch-stämmigen Farmer in Wisconsin. Leider brauche man hier, bei den bigotten Amis, nur für solche Vollfettprodukte und für gottes-lästerliche Bücher einen Waffenschein. Er hatte also bemerkt, wo mein ihm ausweichender Blick gelandet war. Ein Teil der Verkaufs-theke war verglast und ließ in eine Schublade blicken, in der Revolver und Pistolen in einem wüsten Durcheinander ihre Läufe kreuzten.

„Kannst Du schießen, Kleiner?" Was hätte ich Arno antworten können: Ich habe noch vor dem Abitur den Kriegsdienst ver-weigert und meinen Zivildienst in einer Seniorenwohnstätte am Ammersee abgeleistet.[12] Das Pflegeheim war voll mit alten Krieg-ern, die, während ich sie rasierte, ihnen die Katheder wechselte oder sie in Windeln legte, damit prahlten, wie sie mit ihren Stukas oder Panzerabwehrkanonen einen russischen Tank nach dem an-deren geknackt hätten.

Perhaps that is why I sat down on the stepladder. If you go into Arno's Atlantic Hardware, you will notice it on the left-hand side in front of the counter. We are not talking about a full-size ladder here, but one of those so-called 'housewife's aids'. Three steps fold down from a solid waist-high stool. So if you are cleaning windows or hanging curtains or clearing shelves you can stand quite safely on them. When Arno came back and put a tray on to the counter, my wife was pacing up and down in the back of the shop looking at the goods. Arno bent over me and pressed a cup of tea into my lap.

'You look pale, compatriot.' And dropping his voice to a whisper, he asked whether his neighbours, the bimbos, had frightened me so much.

'Are you a racist, Mr Arno?' My wife, compared to whom even a lynx would be hard of hearing, was wiggling her way out of a corner full of glass bottles and welding equipment.

'Almost the opposite, Miss!' Arno called out in her direction. He would rather believe in the worthlessness of the whole human race than in the superior value of a race which lacked a certain amount of pigment in their skin. And he asked me whether I would like some milk in my tea, unpasteurized milk straight from a cow which had been milked by hand by a native German farmer in Wisconsin. Unfortunately, here among these bigoted Americans only full fat products and blasphemous publications require a licence. So he had noticed what my wandering eyes had fallen upon. Part of the counter was made of glass, allowing you to look into a drawer in which lay a confused jumble of revolvers and pistols, their barrels all crisscrossed.

'Do you know how to shoot, boy?' What could I have said to Arno? Even before my Abitur I had become a conscientious objector and had done my spell of civic duty in an old people's home at the Ammersee. The home had been full of war veterans who were boasting how they had taken out one Russian tank after another with their Stukas and anti-tank guns, while I was shaving them, changing their catheters or putting them into nappies.

„Pe Null Acht! Neun Millimeter Luger, deutsche Dienstpistole zweier Weltkriege!"[13] Arnos langer, gelber Zeigefingernagel klopfte über einer zierlichen Pistole aufs Glas. Dies sei seine einzelhändlerische Wunderwaffe. Da leuchteten den Yankees die Augen. Die gepflegten Exemplare, aus Beständen der DDR-Volkspolizei, seien bei ihm als „The Original Adolf's & Eve's Home Gun" erhältlich.

„Heißt das, Herr Arno, Sie haben sich auf Nazi-Devotionalien spezialisiert?"[14]

„Reiner Broterwerb, Fräulein!" Arno reichte meiner Frau mit einem knackenden Bückling ihre Tasse und ließ ein wenig der schwerflüssigen Milch in den Tee tropfen. Das Service war wunderschön, und ich hob die Zuckerdose, um nach der Prägung der Manufaktur zu sehen. Obschon wir vorgewarnt waren, überraschte mich der rote Adler, der ein goldenes Hakenkreuz krallte. So viel Geschmack, so viel in funktionaler Form gemäßigten Willen zur Schönheit hatte ich den Mächten des Bösen nicht zugetraut.

„Entwurf Albert Speer!",[15] klärte mich Arno auf. Das Service komme bei ihm nur selten auf den Tisch. Zuletzt habe er vor zehn Jahren mit seinem Lieblingsgegner aus Anlass der deutschen Wiedervereinigung alten kubanischen Rum daraus geschlürft. Er goss meiner Frau, die ohne Absetzen leer getrunken hatte, nach und hielt mir mit der anderen Hand ein Zigarettenetui unter die Nase. Ich hatte mir das Rauchen im Frühjahr nach zahllosen Fehlversuchen endlich abgewöhnt, aber ich weiß, dass ich, solange meine Lungen atmen, vom Rückfall bedroht bin. Mit umgeleiteter Gier, mit ehelicher Demut sah ich meine Frau einen der sehr schlanken filterlosen, offensichtlich selbst gedrehten Glimmstängel[16] rauchen, während Arnos Finger – seine Pranken hätten einem Schmied zur Ehre gereicht – lange behutsam über die im Etui verbliebenen Zigaretten strichen, bis er sich eine herauszupfte und sich von meiner Frau Feuer geben ließ.

„Rauchen haben die Männer früher spätestens im Krieg gelernt!" Das war in meine Richtung gesprochen, aber ich schwieg, denn vom Krieg verstehe ich, Gott sei Dank oder leider Gottes, nur wenig. Mehr als ich hat mein Vater, der im ersten Kriegsjahr

'P zero eight! Nine millimetre Luger – German service pistol
in two world wars!' Arno's yellowed index finger was tapping on
the glass above a dainty pistol. This was the retailer's wonder
weapon. This made Yankee eyes light up. These well-preserved
samples from the stocks of the East German Police Force could
be bought from him as 'The Original Adolf's & Eve's Home
Gun'.

'Does this mean, Mr Arno, that you specialize in Nazi
memorabilia?'

'Purely to earn my keep, Miss!' Bowing smartly, Arno passed
my wife her cup and let a few drops of the thick milk trickle
into the tea. The tea-set was very beautiful and I lifted up the
sugar basin in order to look at the manufacturer's stamp.
Although we were forewarned, the red eagle clutching a golden
swastika surprised me. I would not have credited the powers of
evil with such determination to achieve beauty in a functional
shape.

'Designed by Albert Speer,' Arno enlightened me. The
set was only seldom brought out in his house. The last time,
ten years ago, he and his favourite opponent had been sip-
ping old Cuban rum out of it on the occasion of German
reunification. He poured another cup for my wife, who
had emptied hers in one go, and with his other hand he
waved a cigarette case under my nose. I had finally given
up smoking in the spring after countless failed attempts but
I know that as long as my lungs are breathing I am in danger
of relapsing into the habit. With suppressed greed and con-
jugal meekness I watched my wife smoking one of these slim,
filterless fags, while Arno's fingers – a blacksmith would have
been proud of his paws – gently stroked the cigarettes remaining
in the case until he finally plucked one out and asked my wife
for a light.

'Men learnt to smoke during the war, if not sooner!' This had
been directed at me, but I said nothing, because thank goodness, or unfortunately, I only know very little about war. My
father, who was born in the first year of the war and who

geboren wurde und als fünfjährige Halbwaise in den Frieden
ging, unter diesem Erfahrungsmangel gelitten. Mit inquisi-
torischem Furor konnte er jeden ungefähr 20 Jahre älteren
Mann, ohne dass der zu Wort kam, ohne dass der überhaupt
anwesend sein musste, als potenziellen Massenmörder entlarven.
Als mein Vater letztes Jahr starb, hat meine Mutter im
Hobbykeller, raffiniert in der Trennwand zur Sauna-Kabine
verborgen, zusammen mit ein paar zerfledderten „Playboys",
die sie nicht überraschten eine erstaunlich große Sammlung
Landserhefte und zahlreiche Weltkrieg-II-Fotobände
gefunden.

„Erzählen Sie uns, was Sie nach Chicago verschlagen hat?"
Damit stellte meine Frau, die geschwätzige Männer hasst, dem Alten
einen erstaunlichen Freibrief aus. Und der große Arno nahm sich die
Zeit, um von etwas zu berichten, was ich, nicht ohne Neid, als einen
heroischen Lebensplan gelten lassen muss. Herr Arno ist Amateur-
philologe und Amateurübersetzer. Ich verrate kein Geheimnis. Wer
will, kann sein Projekt sogar auf einer Internet-Seite besuchen. Amateur komme, so hat er es uns etymologisch erklärt, von indogerman-
isch „amut", der Zuchthengst. Im Sanskrit sei das Wort „amuta" als
ein heiliger, außerhalb kultischer Zusammenhänge verbotener Ausdruck für die eheliche Vereinigung belegt. Seit über einem halben
Jahrhundert, seit man ihn als jungen Kerl aus britischer Kriegsge-
fangenschaft entlassen habe, sei er mit der Übersetzung eines einzigen deutschen Buches ins Englische beschäftigt.

Arno griff hinter sich in ein Regal und warf ohne Rücksicht auf
das dünnwandige Nazi-Porzellan einen gewaltigen Folianten auf
die Ladentheke. Als er ihn irgendwo in der Mitte aufgeschlagen
hatte, sahen wir links oben eine vergilbte Buchseite eingeklebt.
Darüber und darunter und in drei rechts davon gezogenen
Spalten war mit winziger Schrift – es sah wie Stenografie aus –
in verschiedenfarbigen Tinten jeder Freiraum voll gekrit-
zelt.

„Textkritik, seelenhistorische, sprachvegetative Textkritik!" Ein
Fausthieb Arnos zwang dem Wälzer ein pneumatisches Ächzen ab
und ließ die Löffelchen im Service des großdeutschen Baumeisters

entered peacetime as a five-year-old half-orphan, suffered rather more from this lack of experience. With inquisitorial frenzy he could expose any man who was about twenty years older as a potential mass murderer; the latter didn't have to say a word, he didn't even have to be present. When my father died last year my mother discovered carefully hidden in the partition wall between his work room in the basement and the sauna, along with some tatty copies of *Playboy*, which did not come as a surprise to her, an astonishingly large collection of soldiers' magazines and numerous photograph albums of the Second World War.

'Tell us, what brought you to Chicago?' In asking this, my wife, who hates talkative men, surprisingly gave him carte blanche. And big Arno took his time relating what I can only describe, not without envy, as a heroic plan for life. Mr Arno is an amateur philologist and translator. I am not betraying any secrets. Anyone who cares to can even visit his project on a website. Amateur, he said, explaining the etymology to us, derives from the Indo-Germanic 'amut', a pedigree stallion. In Sanscrit the word 'amuta' could be shown to be a sacred expression, forbidden outside the context of cults, for marital intercourse. For half a century now since he had been released from captivity as a British prisoner of war he had been engaged in translating a single German text into English.

Arno reached for something on the shelf behind him and threw a folio-volume down on the counter without any regard for the delicate Nazi china. He opened it somewhere in the middle, and we saw a yellowed page from a book which had been stuck into the top left-hand corner. Above and below, and in three columns which had been drawn to the right of it, tiny writing was scribbled in every inch of space in different-coloured inks – it looked like shorthand.

'Textual criticism, tracing the history of the spirit, the vegetative growth of language itself!' A blow from Arno's fist forced a pneumatic moan out of the massive tome and made

klingeln. Gewissenhafte Textkritik als Grundlage jeder gründlichen Übersetzung sei das irdische Fegfeuer, sei Höllenarbeit zu Lebzeiten. Bis ins späte 18. Jahrhundert, bevor die besten deutschen Säfte von nationaler Kleingeisterei aufgesogen worden seien, habe man in der Heimat noch zu arbeiten gewusst. Aber dann seien die armen Schufter, die Rackerer, die Wühler, die Kärrner, der Humus der höheren Arbeit nach Amerika ausgewandert. Hier in Wisconsin und Illinois hatten sie sich niedergelassen. Und deshalb sei es kein Zufall, dass man in Chicago bereits 1938 die erste vollständige Übersetzung von „Mein Kampf" in Druck gegeben habe.

„Ist sie gut?" Meine Frau traf damit, wie so oft, auf ihre Weise ins Schwarze. „Gottverdammich! Nein!" Arno riss sich die Brille von der Nase, als hätte er das Machwerk vor Augen und könnte dessen Anblick nicht ertragen. Ausgerechnet ein Christenhund, ein aus der Lüneburger Heide ausgewanderter Sektierer,[17] habe die Worte des Führers ins Amerikanische gebracht. Verharmlosend und verschlimmbessernd sei die Übertragung vom ersten bis zum letzten Satz. Wie solle man den Faschismus vernünftig bekämpfen, solange keine vernünftige Übersetzung seines theoretischen Hauptwerks ins Amerikanische – in die Weltsprache! – vorliege.

Ich wagte nicht, Herrn Arno, ein Beruhigen-Sie-sich-doch! zuzurufen. Und zum Glück schien er selbst bemerkt zu haben, dass er sich unbekömmlich echauffiert hatte.[18] Seine Brille, die seine Rechte eben noch wie eine Waffe durch die Luft geführt hatte, fand zurück in sein Gesicht. Aus den hinteren Seiten seines Arbeitswälzers zog er ein Heftchen. Er murmelte ein „Entschuldigen Sie mich für eine Minute, Fräulein . . ." und begann mit einem klobigen Kugelschreiber, rasend schnell, waagerecht und senkrecht und waagerecht in das Heft zu krakeln. Schließlich riss der das beschriebene Blatt heraus, griff sich einen Gummierstift – ich las den Markennamen GUTENBERG[19] – und klebte das Blatt vor meine Knien auf die Front der Verkaufsbarriere.

Erst viel später, als Arno längst mit meiner Frau über ausgewählten Beispielen für die Übertragung deutscher Prosarhythmen brütete, lehnte ich mich zurück, um mit Muße einen Blick auf die

the teaspoons tingle in the great German masterbuilder's tea-service. Conscientious textual criticism as the basis of any translation was like purgatory, like labouring in hell in your lifetime. Right up until the late eighteenth century, before the best German life juices had been sapped away by national petty-mindedness, people in the fatherland had known how to work. But then all those poor things who had been drudging, slaving and toiling away, who were the soil from which higher pursuits sprang, had emigrated to America. Here in Wisconsin and in Illinois they had settled. And therefore it was no coincidence that already in 1938 the first complete edition of *Mein Kampf* had gone to press here.

'Is it good?' As so often my wife hit the bull's eye. 'Goddamn! No.' Arno tore the glasses from his nose as if he had the shoddy piece of work in front of him and could not bear the sight of it. Of all people a wretch of a Christian, a sectarian from the Lüneburg Heath, had rendered the words of the Führer into American English. The translation toned down and dis-improved the original from beginning to end. How could fascism be fought effectively if there was no decent translation of its main theoretical work into American English, the world language!

I did not dare to call out 'Calm yourself' to Mr Arno. And fortunately he himself seemed to have noticed that he had worked himself up unduly. His glasses, which he had been brandishing in the air like a weapon with his right hand, found their way back on to his nose. Out of the back pages of his folio he pulled out a little notebook. He mumbled an 'Excuse me a minute, Miss . . .' and at a rate of knots he started to scrawl diagonally and vertically into his notebook with a bulky biro. Finally, he tore out the page on which he had been writing, took out a glue stick – I read the brand name GUTENBERG – and fixed it to the sales counter.

Only much later, when Arno had been pondering over select examples for the rendition of German prose rhythms with my wife, did I lean back in order to cast a leisurely glance over the

Zettel zu werfen, die dort, kreuz und quer übereinander gepappt, Arnos Ladentheke panzerten. Es waren, soweit ich sah, immer Blätter aus alten deutschen Kreuzworträtselheften. Keinem Kästchen war sein Buchstabe vorenthalten worden, auch wenn er oft nur einem runenartigen Haken oder einem flüchtigen Kringel glich: Niederschlesische Kreisstadt am Queis, sechs Buchstaben. So verging uns die Zeit. Und irgendwann hatte sich der Chicagoer Mond, ein scharf umrissener, fleckenlos weißer Diskus, in eines der Fenster der schwarzen Baracke geschoben.

Jene drei schwarzen Amerikaner, denen ich in der Hoffnung, dass sie uns dann unbeschadet ziehen lassen würden, 100 Dollar gespendet hatte, meinten, während sie sich das Geld umständlich teilten, wenn wir schon aus Deutschland bis zu ihnen nach Chicago gekommen seien, dann müssten wir auch ihren Deutschen besuchen. In einer Art Comic-Pathos, mit weit aufgerissenen Augen und erhobenen Fäusten nannten sie ihn Arno The Great Cold Warrior. Und als ich ihr Auseinandertreten mit einem „Thank you, good bye!" zu einem hastigen Weitergehen, zur Flucht nutzen wollte, rief meine Frau: „Halt, wo rennst Du denn hin? Vielleicht hat dieser Arno schon jahrelang mit niemandem mehr Deutsch gesprochen!"

So kam es, dass ich eine amerikanische Nacht auf der Hausfrauen-leiter in Arnos Atlantic Hardware verbrachte. Im Sitzen döste ich schließlich ein und hörte im Halbschlaf, wie Arno aus dem Originaltext und aus seiner Übersetzung zitierte, wie meine Frau mit den Finger-knöcheln, mit den Fäusten, und mit den Ellenbogen ihre rhythmischen Korrekturen und Verbesserungsvorschläge trommelte.

Zuletzt, gegen Morgen, schrak ich nicht einmal mehr hoch, wenn ihr Fuß, wenn ihr Knie gegen die Ladentheke donnerte, um einen wichtigen Akzent zu setzen. Fast träumte ich, zumindest kam ich im Halbschlaf pendelnd, einer Art Traum nahe. Ich fantasierte, meine Frau, die Avantgardistin, trommle Arno auf seiner Hartware, auf seinen Geräten und Werkzeugen, ein Liedchen aus der Heimat vor. Sie, die man mit bestimmten Harmonien zur Weißglut reizen kann, hatte sich auf dem Blech die nötigen

pieces of paper which had been stuck all over Arno's counter.
As far as I could see they were all pages out of old German
crossword magazines. There wasn't a single box which
didn't have a letter written in it, even if it only resembled a
rune-like tick or a casual little circle: Lower Silesian town
on the river Queis, six letters. So we whiled the time away.
And at some point the Chicago moon, a sharply outlined,
spotless, white disc, had filled one of the windows of the black
shack.

Those three black Americans to whom I had donated 100
dollars in the hope that they would then let us go unharmed,
felt, while they were clumsily sharing out the money, that if
we had come all this way from Germany to Chicago then we
really ought to meet their German. With a kind of comic
pathos, they referred to him as Arno The Great Cold
Warrior, their eyes wide open, their fists raised. And when I
wanted to take advantage of the fact that they were
stepping aside to escape with a quick 'Thank you, goodbye',
my wife called out: 'Stop! Where do you think you are
going? Arno may not have spoken to anyone in German for
years.'

So it came about that I spent a night in America on Arno's
housewife's stepladder. Sitting upright, I eventually dozed off
and half asleep I heard Arno reading from the original and from
his translation, while my wife drummed her rhythmic correc-
tions and suggestions for improvement with her knuckles, fists
and elbows.

Eventually towards morning I was not even startled when
her foot or her knee came thundering down against the
counter to mark an important point of emphasis. I was
almost dreaming, at least I was drifting into a sort of semi-
sleep. I was imagining that my wife, the avant-garde artist, was
drumming a little song from home to Arno on his hardware, his
pieces of equipment and his tools. She who can almost be driven
into a frenzy by certain harmonies had been able to produce the

Dreiklänge zusammengesucht. Es war etwas Kleines, es war etwas Eingängiges, was sie da spielte, und Arno brummte und schluchzte den einfältigen Text dazu.

„Für uns", sagte meine Frau, als wir Arno verließen und uns durch die Sozialruinen auf den Weg zu unserem Apartment machten, „für uns und vielleicht auch für unsere Kinder ist das Reich noch weit genug. Noch kann es uns alles – einen salzigen und einen süßen Ozean![20] – mit seinen deutschen Ländern umfangen halten."

required triads on the metal objects. What she was playing was small, accessible, while Arno was mumbling or sobbing the simple lyrics that went with it.

When we left Arno to make our way to our apartment through the dilapidated social housing, my wife said, 'For us and perhaps for our children the German empire is still large enough. With its German lands it can still encompass everything for us – a salty and a sweet ocean!'

Grandfather and the Decision-makers

CHRISTOPH HEIN

Grossvater Und Die Bestimmer

Als Mutter mich weckte und sagte, dass wir gleich aussteigen müssten, hatte ich Mühe, mich zurechtzufinden. Ich wusste nicht, wo ich war und wieso ich aufstehen sollte. Ich saß auf der Holzbank eines Eisenbahnabteils. Draußen war es stockdunkel, nirgends war ein Licht zu sehen. Ich lehnte mich in die Ecke zurück und sah Mutter zu, wie sie die Arme meiner Schwester in die Jacke fädelte. Das Baby lag in der Reisetasche und schlief. Mutter reichte mir meine Strickjacke und nahm, während ich sie gähnend anzog, unsere Tasche und den Koffer aus dem Gepäcknetz, um sie vor die Abteiltür zu stellen. Die Lokomotive pfiff durchdringend, bevor sie ihre Fahrt verlangsamte. Als der Zug in der Station einlief und abbremste, prallten die Stoßdämpfer aufeinander und ein metallener Stoß lief knirschend durch die Eisenbahnwaggons.

Auf dem Bahnsteig brannte eine einzige Lampe, das Gebäude war nicht zu erkennen. Mutter rief mich, sie stand mit Dorle und dem Baby bereits im Abteilgang. Ich hängte mir rasch den Rucksack um, nahm den Koffer auf, den Mutter mir vor die Füße gestellt hatte, und lief ihnen hinterher.

Großvater erwartete uns. Er hob mich aus der offenen Tür, drückte mich an sein stoppeliges Gesicht und stellte mich auf den Boden. Dann sprach er mit Mutter, die das Baby aus der Tasche genommen hatte und im Arm hielt. Mir war kalt, und ich war müde. Ich legte meinen Kopf an Großvaters Arm und schloss die Augen.

Hinter dem Bretterverschlag, der das Bahnhofsgebäude absperrte, stand der Kutschwagen mit zwei Pferden. Rechts und links neben dem Kutschbock brannten Petroleumlampen, zwei würfelförmige Kandelaber mit geschliffenen Gläsern an den

Grandfather and the Decision-makers

When mother woke me and told me that we had to get off soon, I found it difficult to get my bearings. I did not know where I was and why I had to get up. I was sitting on a wooden bench in a railway compartment. Outside it was pitch black; there wasn't a light anywhere to be seen. I leant back in the corner and watched my mother threading my sister's arms into her jacket. The baby was lying in the carry-cot asleep. My mother passed me my cardigan and while I put it on yawning, she lifted our bag and the suitcase down from the luggage rack in order to put them in front of the compartment door. The engine let out a penetrating whistle before it started to slow down. When the train entered the station and braked, the shock absorbers clamped shut and a grinding metallic jolt ran through the railway carriages.

On the platform a single lantern was burning, it was hard to make out the building. Mother called me; she was already standing in the corridor with Dorle and the baby. I quickly slipped on my rucksack, picked up the case which my mother had put down in front of my feet and ran after them.

Grandfather was waiting for us. He lifted me out of the open door, pressed me against his stubbly face and put me down on the ground. Then he spoke to mother, who had taken the baby out of the cot and was holding it in her arm. I felt cold and I was tired. I put my head against grandfather's arm and closed my eyes.

Behind the wooden partition which fenced off the station building stood the carriage and pair. To the right and left of the coach box paraffin lamps were burning, two cube-shaped candelabra with polished plates in the sides, which protected the

Seiten, die die Flammen vor Wind und Regen schützten, Großvater blieb vor der Kutsche stehen und sah uns erwartungsvoll an.
Da Dorle und ich nichts sagten, fragte er, ob wir uns nicht freuten,
mit den Pferden aufs Gut kutschiert zu werden. Doch ich war so
müde, dass ich nur wortlos nickte. Mutter und Großvater setzten
uns in den Wagen. Mutter gab mir das Baby auf den Schoß und
verstaute mit Großvater das Gepäck in der Holztruhe, die hinten
an der Kutsche mit Ledergurten angeschnallt war. Mutter stieg zu
uns in den Kutschkasten und Großvater kletterte auf den Bock, ich
konnte seinen Rücken durch das kleine vordere Fenster des
Coupés sehen. Ich bemühte mich, richtig wach zu werden, denn
ich wollte die Fahrt genießen und nichts verpassen, aber die Kutsche wackelte so gleichmäßig über die Landstraße, dass ich fest
einschlief.

In den Sommerferien fuhren wir jedes Jahr zu den Großeltern.
Großvater war nach dem Krieg Gutsverwalter[1] geworden. Er hatte
schon vor dem Krieg ein Landgut[2] geleitet, sogar während der
Kriegsjahre, da er von der Wehrmacht freigestellt worden war.
Doch das in Schlesien sei damals ein richtiges Rittergut gewesen,
hatte mir Mutter erzählt, viel größer und schöner als das in
Holzwedel. Großvater habe als Verwalter alles allein bestimmen
und entscheiden können, da der Baron ein alter Mann gewesen sei,
der sich nicht um seine Landwirtschaft kümmerte, sondern das
gute Geld, das Großvater für ihn erarbeitete, für Projekte mit
einem Heißluftballon verpulverte. Er lebte in Breslau und erschien
nie auf seinem Gut, weil er Großvater grenzenlos vertraute. Gegen
Ende des Krieges waren die Großeltern mit der ganzen Familie auf
dem Treck[3] vor der anrückenden Front bis nach Sachsen-Anhalt
gezogen, wo man dem erfahrenen Inspektor angeboten hatte, ein
Staatsgut zu übernehmen.

Mutter und Großmutter erzählten uns viel über diese Zeit und
den Flüchtlingszug mit Pferdefuhrwerken durch halb Deutschland.
Die Familie war nach der langwierigen Flucht bei dem Bruder der
Großmutter untergekommen. Sie wohnten dort in einer provisor-
isch ausgebauten Dachwohnung, durch rasch zusammengenagelte
Bretterwände waren drei dürftige kleine Räume entstanden,

flames against wind and rain. Grandfather stood still in front of the carriage looking at us expectantly. As Dorle and I were not saying anything he asked us whether we were looking forward to being driven to the estate by the horses. But I was so tired that I only nodded without saying a word. Mother and grandfather put us into the carriage. Mother put the baby on my lap and with grandfather stowed away the luggage in a wooden box which was strapped on to the back of the carriage with leather belts. Mother got into the carriage with us and grandfather climbed on to the box; I could see his back through the little window in the coupé. I made an effort to wake up properly, because I wanted to enjoy the trip and not miss anything. But the carriage swayed so evenly along the country road that I fell fast asleep.

In the summer holidays we went to my grandparents every year. Grandfather had become an estate manager after the war. He had already run an estate before the war, and even during the war, as he had been discharged by the army. But the one in Silesia had been a proper manor, much bigger and more beautiful than the one in Holzwedel. As the manager grandfather had been able to make all the decisions himself, as the baron had been an old gentleman who did not take an interest in his country estate, but used up the good income grandfather was creating for him by pursuing hot-air balloon projects. He lived in Breslau and never showed his face on the estate, as he had total confidence in grandfather. Towards the end of the war my grandparents had moved with the whole family, trekking ahead of the advancing front, as far as Sachsen-Anhalt, where the experienced inspector had been offered the management of a state-owned estate.

Mother and grandmother told us a lot about those times and the trek of refugees with horse-drawn carriages halfway across Germany. After the protracted escape the family had found a home with grandmother's brother. There they lived in a make-shift flat in the loft; three rather basic small rooms had been created by hastily nailing some wooden boards together, and

und Großvater hatte sich an einen Cousin in Bayern gewandt, weil er hoffte, dort Arbeit und Wohnung zu finden. Als er das Angebot erhielt, das Staatsgut Holzwedel zu übernehmen, stand bereits der Tag der Übersiedlung in ein niederbayrisches Dorf fest, trotzdem entschloss er sich, das Gut zumindest in Augenschein zu nehmen. Nach der Rückkehr erkundigten sich Großmutter und sein Schwager, ob ihm das Gut zusage und er sich den Umzug nach Bayern überlegen wolle. Großvater erwiderte nichts, schüttelte nur zweifelnd seinen Schädel hin und her und strich sich über die Glatze.

„Und was nun, Wilhelm", fragte Großmutter ihn im Bett, nachdem sie den ganzen Abend darauf gewartet hatte, dass er etwas sagte.

„Etwas Besseres wird uns wohl nirgends angeboten."

„Also Holzwedel und nicht Bayern?"

„Ich denke, ich sollte das Gut nehmen, Klara. Der Boden ist gute Börde, die Stallungen machen einen vernünftigen Eindruck, das Haus kann man reparieren, und die Leute, na, die Leute, die bieg ich mir hin."

Als Großmutter mir das erzählte, sah sie mich an und sagte: „So ist er, dein Großvater, so ist er immer gewesen. Ich habe nur zu ihm gesagt: ‚Das dachte ich mir schon. Dann können wir ja endlich schlafen.' "

Holzwedel bestand aus einem großen, mit einer Steinmauer umgebenen Gutshof. In der Mitte stand das stattliche Gutshaus, in dem der Verwalter wohnte und wo sich die Büroräume sowie die lange, gefliese Gutsküche befanden. Die Vorderfront des Hofes wurde von einer hohen Mauer begrenzt mit einem gewaltigen Tor, dessen Einfassung mit steinernen Kugeln verziert war, auf der Mauer waren grünliche Glasscherben einbetoniert. Die Stallungen für Pferde, Kühe und Schweine, das Schlachthaus, die Speicher und Scheunen, das Waschhaus mit den Duschen und das Lagerhaus mit dem Kühlraum bildeten mit der Mauer ein geschlossenes Viereck um das Gutshaus, unterbrochen nur durch das Haupttor und eine rückwärtige Pforte auf der gegenüberliegenden Seite, durch die man direkt in den Wald gelangte. Die Gärtnerei mit

grandfather had contacted a cousin in Bavaria because he was hoping to find work and a home there. When he received the offer to take over the state-owned estate Holzwedel, the day of their move to a village in lower Bavaria had already been fixed; nevertheless, he decided at least to have a good look at the estate. After his return my grandmother and his brother-in-law inquired whether he liked the estate and whether he wanted to reconsider the move to Bavaria. Grandfather made no reply and merely shook his head doubtfully, stroking his bald pate.

'So, what now, Wilhelm,' grandmother asked him in bed after she had been waiting all evening for him to say something.

'It's unlikely that we'll get a better offer anywhere else.'

'So it's Holzwedel and not Bavaria?'

'I think I should take the estate on, Klara. The soil is good and fertile, the stables seem reasonable, the house can be repaired and the people, well, I will win the people round.'

When grandmother told me this she looked at me and said, 'That's what he's like, your grandfather, that's what he's always been like. I only said to him, "I thought as much. We can finally go to sleep then."'

Holzwedel consisted of a large manor surrounded by a stone wall. In the middle stood the imposing manor house, in which the manager lived and which also housed the offices and the long farm kitchen with its tiled floor. The front of the farm was closed off by a tall wall with an enormous gate whose posts were decorated with stone balls; fragments of green glass had been cemented on to the top of the wall. The stables for the horses, cows and pigs, the granaries and the barns, the wash house with the showers and the store house with the cold storage room formed a closed square with the wall round the house which was only broken up by the main gate and a back gate on the opposite side through which one could get direct access into the wood. The nursery garden with a

einem Glashaus und dem Bienenwagen befand sich außerhalb des Gehöfts. Auf beiden Seiten der Teerstraße, die zum Gut führte, standen die Häuser der Landarbeiter, niedrige, sich gleichende Lehmkaten mit winzigen Fenstern und einem Stück Gartenland, vier Häuser rechter Hand, fünf links. Hinter der letzten Kate war ein Straßenschild mit der Aufschrift „Staatsgut Holzwedel" zu sehen.

Dorle und ich wurden auch in diesem Jahr im Dachzimmer über der Vorratskammer untergebracht, einem Raum mit einer schrägen Wand, in dem nur zwei Betten und ein Nachtschränkchen standen. Hoch oben über der Tür befand sich ein schwarzer Kunststoffkasten, eine viereckige Box, in der es leise summte. Ich hatte mich im Jahr zuvor bei den Großeltern erkundigt, was das für ein merkwürdiger Kasten sei, und mir wurde erklärt, es sei der elektrische Schaltkasten für die Kühlgeräte. Ich wollte wissen, warum es in dem Kasten immerzu summte. Großmutter war über meine Frage erstaunt. Sie war mit mir ins Zimmer gegangen und hatte sich auf einen Stuhl gestellt, um das Summen zu hören.

„Du hast Recht", sagte sie, als sie mit meiner Hilfe vom Stuhl herunterstieg, „der Kasten summt, das macht die Elektrik. Die Elektrik summt gern, sie summt im ganzen Haus. Aber das ist ungefährlich, man darf da nur nicht anfassen."

Die Erklärung befriedigte mich nicht. Eines Morgens nämlich – ich lag noch im Bett, um mir eine Ausrede auszudenken, weil ich am Tag zuvor die Katze aus dem ersten Stock des Treppenhauses auf die Steinfliesen des Hausflurs hatte fallen lassen, erwischt und in mein Zimmer geschickt worden war, ich hatte feststellen wollen, ob Katzen wirklich jeden Sturz überlebten, ob sie, wie Großvater sagte, tatsächlich sieben Leben hätten, doch das konnte ich nicht gestehen, wenn ich einer weiteren Strafe entgehen wollte –, an jenem Morgen sah ich eine dicke Spinne aus dem schwarzen summenden Kasten kriechen. Ich sah, wie sie sich aus dem schmalen Spalt an der Vorderfront zwängte, zur Decke hinauflief, dort minutenlang bewegungslos verharrte, um danach auf dem gleichen Weg zum Kasten zurückzulaufen und in ihm zu verschwinden. Seit diesem Tag wusste ich, dass es kein

greenhouse and a beehouse were outside the farm buildings. On both sides of the tarmacked road which led to the estate stood the houses of the farm labourers, identical low wattle and daub cottages with tiny windows and a piece of garden, four houses on the right-hand side and five on the left. After the last little cottage there was a street sign which read 'State-owned estate Holzwedel'.

This year Dorle and I were once again put up in the attic above the provisions room, in a room with a sloping wall, in which there were only two beds and a bedside table. High above the door there was a black plastic box, a square box, which made a soft humming sound. I had inquired of my grandparents the previous year what this strange box was, and it was explained to me that it was an electrical junction box for the cooling equipment. I wanted to know why there was a constant humming sound inside the box. Grandmother was surprised at my question. She had gone into the room with me and had stood on a chair in order to hear the humming.

'You are right,' she said, when she got down from the chair with my help. 'The box is humming, this is what electricity does. Electricity likes humming, it hums all over the house. But that's not dangerous, one just mustn't touch it.'

The explanation did not satisfy me. Because one morning – I was still lying in bed in order to think up some excuse: the day before I had dropped the cat from the first-floor landing on to the stone tiles below and had been caught and sent to my room; I had wanted to find out whether cats really survived any fall, whether, as grandfather said, they really had nine lives, but I could not confess that if I wanted to escape further punishment – on that morning I saw a big spider crawl out of the humming black box. I saw how it squeezed out of the small gap in the front, ran up the ceiling, remained there motionless for several minutes, only to take the same way back to the box and disappear back inside it. From that day on I knew that it was not an electric box, for if

Elektrokasten war, denn wenn ich ihn wegen der Elektrizität nicht anfassen durfte, wie sollte da eine fette Spinne eine Berührung mit ihm überleben. Der Kunststoffkasten war ein großes Spinnennest, ich war davon überzeugt, dass unendlich viele dieser widerlichen Tiere mit behaarten Beinen in dem Kasten herumkrabbelten, so wie im Stülpkorb der Imkerei Tausende von Bienen über die Waben kletterten und unablässig übereinander krochen. Das Summen wurde nicht von der Elektrizität verursacht, es kam von den Spinnen. Ich wusste natürlich, dass Spinnen eigentlich keine Geräusche machten, aber in einem großen Nest, wo sie ihre Eier ausbrüteten, wo ständig neue Spinnen ausschlüpften und versorgt wurden, war ein so leises Summen, gleichmäßig und eindringlich, durchaus möglich. Und dass ich nur einmal, nur ein einziges Mal eine dieser Spinnen gesehen hatte, konnte nur bedeuten, dass sie das Tageslicht scheuten und nachts unterwegs waren und durch mein Zimmer spazierten.

Ich hatte keine Angst vor dem Hengst, und ich ging gern in den abgetrennten Verschlag des Kuhstalls, wo der Bulle stand und schnaubend das Stroh mit seinen Hufen in die Luft wirbelte und an der Kette riss, die an seinem Nasenring befestigt war, sobald jemand in seine Nähe kam oder wenn eine der Milchkühe nebenan brünstig war und ihr langes, heiseres Brüllen ausstieß. Vor dem Bullen hatte man mich gewarnt, er hatte sich einmal den Ring aus der Nase gerissen und die Balken und Bretter des Verschlags zerstört. „Ein Bulle ist immer gefährlich", hatte Johannes, der ältere Schweizer, gesagt, „halt dich fern von ihm." Aber ich hatte keine Angst und war sehr stolz, als Großmutter mich einmal im Bullenverschlag entdeckte, mich aufgeregt wegzerrte und beim Mittagessen erzählte, dass sie fast einen Herzschlag bekommen hätte, weil ich allein zu diesem heimtückischen[4] Biest gegangen war.

Und vor den übrigen Tieren hatte ich auch keine Angst. Großvater hatte mir gezeigt, wie man mit dem Ganter umgehen musste und wie man sich der Ziegen erwehren konnte. Die beiden Hofhunde, die tagsüber an der Kette lagen und nur nachts auf dem Hof frei umherlaufen durften, kläfften[5] zwar wütend, wenn ein Huhn oder eine Taube in ihre Nähe kam, um nach Körnern zu suchen,

you were not allowed to touch it because of the electricity how could a fat spider survive contact with it? The plastic box was a big spiders' nest; I was convinced that countless of these repulsive animals with hairy legs were crawling around in the box, just as in a bees' straw hive thousands of bees were climbing over the combs and constantly crawling all over each other. The humming was not caused by electricity, it came from the spiders. I knew, of course, that spiders do not really make any noise, but in such a large nest, where they were hatching eggs, and a constant stream of new spiders had to be looked after, such soft humming, which was constant and penetrating, was quite possible. And that I had only seen one of these spiders once, just one single time, could only mean that they disliked daylight and were walking about at night, wandering all over my room.

I was not afraid of the stallion and I liked going to the special pen in the cowshed where the bull stood snorting and tossing up the straw with his hooves and pulling at the chain which was fixed to the ring through his nose as soon as anybody came near him or whenever one of the milk cows next door was on heat and giving out its long, hoarse low. I had been warned off the bull; he had once torn the ring out of his nose and smashed up the beams and planks of his pen. 'A bull is always dangerous,' John, the older dairyman, had said, 'keep away from him.' But I was not afraid and I was very proud when grandmother discovered me in the bullpen one day, agitatedly pulled me away and told us during lunch that she had nearly suffered a heart attack because I had gone to this treacherous creature on my own.

And I was not afraid of the other animals either. Grandfather had shown me how to deal with the gander and how to fend off the goats. The two watchdogs who were kept on a chain during the day and who were only allowed to roam round the yard freely at night barked viciously if a chicken or a pigeon came near them looking for grain, but I could touch them and stroke

aber ich konnte sie anfassen und streicheln. Sogar wenn sie ihr Futter bekamen und ich mich neben sie stellte, knurrten sie nur leise.

Vor den Bienen hatte ich Respekt, aber keine Angst. Man musste nur ruhig bleiben, man durfte nicht rennen oder mit dem Armen herumwedeln, dann blieben sie friedlich. Wenn sie sich einem auf den Arm setzten oder auf den Kopf, hatte man nur stehen zu bleiben und durfte sich nicht bewegen. Man durfte nicht einmal zucken, sonst stachen sie. Früher, als ich noch kleiner war, war ich schlimm von ihnen gestochen worden, einmal sogar in die Zunge, weil ich mit offenem Mund geschrien hatte. Ich musste zum Arzt gebracht werden, weil die Zunge anschwoll und Gefahr bestand, dass ich erstickte. Aber inzwischen wusste ich, wie man sie behandeln musste, und konnte mit dem Gärtner, der sie betreute, ins Bienenhaus gehen, geschützt von einem Bienenschleier und für den Notfall mit einer Bienenpfeife ausgerüstet.

Vor keinem Tier hatte ich Angst, nur vor den Spinnen ekelte ich mich entsetzlich. Ich erzählte Großmutter von meiner Entdeckung und ich fragte, ob ich nicht in einem anderen Zimmer schlafen könne, aber sie sagte sehr unwillig, dass sie kein anderes Zimmer für mich habe und dass ich mich unterstehen solle, diesen Unsinn noch meiner Schwester einzureden.

„Erzähl das nur deinem Großvater", sagte sie drohend, und damit war das Thema für sie erledigt. Aber ich wusste auch ohne ihre Ermahnung, dass ich Großvater nichts von dem Spinnennest im schwarzen Kasten erzählen durfte. Er würde mir einen kräftigen Stups[6] geben und wieder einmal sagen: „Der Junge liest zu viel, das ist nicht gut für den Kopf." Und in den folgenden Tagen würde er beim gemeinsamen Mittagessen bestimmen, welche Arbeiten ich auf dem Hof zu erledigen hätte, damit ich an die frische Luft käme und kein Stubenhocker würde. „Du musst Muskeln kriegen, Junge." Dann müsste ich aufstehen, zu ihm kommen und eine Faust machen, um ihm meine kümmerlichen Bizeps zu zeigen. Er würde seine Hand um meinen Oberarm legen und ihn drücken, bis ich aufschrie. „Das ist noch nichts. Das ist zu wenig für dein Alter. Das müssen feste Muckis[7] werden. Da musst du ein bisschen zufassen, Junge, und nicht im Zimmer hocken." Nein, von den Spinnen konnte ich

them. Even when they got their food and I stood next to them, they only growled softly.

I respected the bees, but I was not afraid of them. You just had to stay completely calm; if you didn't run or wave your arms about, then they remained quite peaceful. If they landed on your arm or head you just had to stand still and not move. You were not even allowed to twitch, otherwise they stung. In the past, when I was smaller, I had been stung badly by them, once even on my tongue, because I screamed with my mouth open. I had to be taken to the doctor because my tongue had swollen up and there was a danger that I might suffocate. But meanwhile I knew how to handle them and could go into the beehouse with the gardener who looked after them, protected by a beekeeper's veil and, in case of an emergency, equipped with a beekeeper's pipe.

I was not afraid of any animals, but I loathed spiders terribly. I told grandmother about my discovery and asked whether I could sleep in another room but she said very indignantly that she had no other room for me and that I should not dare talk my sister into believing such non-sense.

'Just tell your grandfather,' she said menacingly, and that settled the matter. But I knew even without her reprimand that I should not tell grandfather of the spiders' nest in the black box. He would give me a good thump and say once again, 'The boy reads too much, it's not good for the head.' And during the days that followed he would decide, while we were having lunch together, which work I was to do on the farm so that I would get some fresh air and not turn into a stay-at-home. 'You must develop muscles, boy.' Then I would have to get up and go to him and clench my fist and show him my puny biceps. He would put his hand round my upper arm and squeeze it until I screamed. 'There is still nothing there. That's not enough for your age. They must become hard muscles. You want to get stuck in a bit, boy, and stop sitting around in your room.' No, I could not tell grandfather about

Großvater nichts erzählen. Ich musste mich damit abfinden, in einem Zimmer zu schlafen, in dem nachts lange Kolonnen von fetten Spinnen mit behaarten Beinen über Decke und Wände krochen und wahrscheinlich auch über das Bett und mein Gesicht.

Dorle, meiner kleinen Schwester, konnte ich schon deshalb nichts davon erzählen, weil sie den Mund nicht halten würde und ich wieder eine Kopfnuss[8] von Großvater zu erwarten hätte. Außerdem würde sie abends nicht einschlafen, sondern alle paar Minuten das Licht anknipsen, um den Spinnenkasten zu kontrollieren. Und mich würde sie wecken und, weil sie Angst hätte, in mein Bett kriechen.

Mit Dorle war ich viel zusammen. David, der ältere Bruder, hatte für mich keine Zeit, er hatte seine Freunde, mit denen er zu Hause durch die Stadt zog, und konnte es überhaupt nicht leiden, wenn ich auftauchte und mich ihnen anschließen wollte. Auch wenn ich baden ging und ihn dort zufällig traf, gab er mir gleich zu verstehen, dass ich mich woanders hinlegen sollte und dass ich nicht mit ihm und seinen Freunden in den Wrackteilen im Fluss tauchen dürfe, weil das für mich zu gefährlich sei. Mit Michael und Markus aber konnte man nicht viel anfangen, sie waren noch zu klein und hingen wirklich an Mutters Schürzenzipfel. Außerdem hatte ich wenig Lust, mich mit ihnen abzugeben, weil doch immer ich die Schuld an allem bekam. Sie konnten tun, was sie wollten, sobald sie etwas anstellten, bekam ich eine Standpauke zu hören,[9] weil ich nicht ausreichend auf sie aufgepasst hätte. David galt schon als erwachsen, ihm wurden zu Hause nur die wichtigen Aufgaben übertragen. Mutter rief nach ihm, wenn eine elektrische Leitung kaputt oder ein Gerät zu reparieren war, obwohl ich das auch gekonnt hätte. Er musste auch viel weniger in der Küche helfen als ich.

So blieb mir zu Hause nur Dorle. Sie war das einzige Mädchen in unserer Familie, und Vater liebte sie besonders, jedenfalls zog er sie vor. Sie wurde auch nie so hart bestraft wie ich. Ich glaube, Vater wünschte sich noch ein Mädchen. Als Mutter schwanger war, hörte ich, wie er einmal zu ihr sagte, er hoffe, dass es ein Mädchen werde, denn von der anderen Sorte habe er schon

the spiders. I just had to put up with sleeping in a room where at night long columns of fat spiders with hairy legs were crawling over the ceiling and walls and probably also over the bed and over my face.

I could not say anything to Dorle, my little sister, because she would not keep her mouth shut and I could expect to be clipped round the ears by grandfather again. Besides, she would not go to sleep at night, but would turn on the light every few minutes in order to check the spiders' box. And she would wake me and, because she was afraid, get into my bed.

I was together a lot with Dorle. David, my older brother, had no time for me; he had his own friends with whom he hung around in town, and he could not stand it if I turned up and wanted to join them. Also, when I went swimming and met him there by chance, he quickly gave me to understand that I should go and lie down somewhere else and that I was not allowed to dive with his friends among the remains of the wreck in the river, because it was too dangerous for me. You couldn't do a lot with Michael and Markus; they were too small and still hanging on mother's apron strings. Besides, I did not feel like spending much time with them because I always got the blame for everything. They could do whatever they wanted, but as soon as they did something wrong I would get a telling-off, because I had not kept enough of an eye on them. David was regarded as grown up; he was given only the important tasks at home. Mother called for him if an electric lead had gone wrong, or if a gadget needed to be repaired, although I could have done it. He had to help out far less in the kitchen than I did.

So at home I only had Dorle. She was the only girl in our family, and father was especially fond of her, or at least he favoured her. She was never punished as hard as I. I think father would have liked to have had another girl. When mother was pregnant I once heard him saying to her that he hoped it would be another girl, as he had had enough of the other sort

genug. Aber auch das letzte Baby wurde kein Mädchen, und schließlich waren es sechs Jungen und Dorle.

Für Dorle hatte ich aus Brettern ein Haus gebaut, in das man hineinkriechen konnte, und für ihre Puppen Kleider angefertigt. Einmal habe ich sogar ein richtiges Kleid für Dorle geschneidert nach einer Anleitung aus einem Buch, das ich mir aus der Bücherei geliehen hatte. Ich ließ mir von keinem helfen, nicht von Mutter und auch nicht von Tante Magdalena. Auf dieses Kleid war Dorle sehr stolz, und sie hat es allen Verwandten und ihren Freundinnen gezeigt und ihnen erzählt, dass ich es für sie genäht hatte.

Dorle war ein sehr schönes Mädchen mit schwarzen Haaren und großen schwarzen Augen, und sie hat immer alles geglaubt, was ich ihr sagte. Wenn mir die Eltern etwas nicht geben wollten, hat sie bei Vater oder Mutter so lange gebettelt, bis sie es für mich erhielt. Nur gelogen hat sie nie. Ich konnte sie nie bitten, den Eltern irgendetwas vorzuflunkern,[10] damit ich einer Bestrafung entging. Da war David besser geeignet, der mir dann zwar selber den Kopf wusch, aber den Eltern gegenüber zu mir hielt. Dorle konnte das einfach nicht, sie konnte nicht lügen. Und sie war ängstlich, deshalb brauchte sie nicht zu erfahren, dass in unserem Zimmer in Holzwedel nachts die Spinnen über die Betten krabbelten.

Sobald ich Licht ausgemacht hatte, verkroch ich mich unter dem dicken Federbett. Keinen Zentimeter von mir sollten die Spinnen mit ihren ekelhaften Beinen berühren.

Am Morgen nach unserer Ankunft kam Großmutter in unser Zimmer, zog die Gardinen zur Seite und sagte, wir sollten endlich aufstehen, es sei bald Mittag. Ich sah auf meine Armbanduhr, es war gerade erst halb neun und ich hatte Ferien. Großmutter setzte sich auf Dorles Bett, küsste sie und pustete ihr ins Ohr. Dann kam sie zu mir, zog mir das Deckbett weg und gab mir einen Klaps auf den Hintern. Ich zog rasch mein Nachthemd herunter. Bevor ich aus dem Bett stieg, warf ich einen Blick auf den schwarzen Kunststoffkasten über der Tür.

In der Küche waren Mutter und zwei Mägde mit der Vorbereitung des Mittagessens beschäftigt. Unser Baby war wach und lag in einem großen Wäschekorb. Die beiden jungen Frauen scheuerten

already. But the last baby was not a girl either, and so in the end we were six boys and Dorle.

For Dorle I built a house out of boards which you could crawl into and made clothes for her dolls. Once I even made a proper dress for Dorle following the instructions in a book that I had borrowed from the library. I did not let any-body help me, neither mother nor aunt Magdalena. Dorle was very proud of this dress and she showed it to all our rela-tives and to her girlfriends and told them that I had made it for her.

Dorle was a very pretty girl with long black hair and big black eyes, and she always believed everything I told her. If my parents did not want to give me something she pleaded so hard with father or mother until she got it for me. But she never told a lie. I could never ask her to tell our parents some tale so that I might escape a punishment. For that David was more useful, he would give me a good talking-to himself, but in front of my parents he would stand by me. Dorle simply could not do this. She could not tell lies. And she was nervous and therefore she did not need to know that there were spiders crawling over our beds at night in our room in Holzwedel.

As soon as I had put the light out, I crawled under the heavy eiderdown. The spiders with their repulsive legs wouldn't be able to touch an inch of me.

On the morning after our arrival grandmother came into our room, opened the curtains and said it was about time we got up, it was almost lunchtime. I looked at my watch; it was only half-past eight and I was on holiday. Grandmother sat down on Dorle's bed, kissed her and blew into her ear. Then she came to me, pulled back my bed cover and slapped my bottom. I quickly pulled down my nightshirt. Before I got out of bed I cast a glance at the black plastic box above the door.

In the kitchen my mother and two maids were busy prepar-ing lunch. Our baby was awake and was lying in a big linen basket. The young women were polishing the iron pots in

die eisernen Töpfe, in denen das Mittagessen aufs Feld gebracht wurde, und liefen immer wieder zu dem Wäschekorb, um mit dem Baby zu reden. Großmutter war in der Vorratskammer verschwunden. Die Kammer war stets verschlossen, nur Großmutter besaß einen Schlüssel dafür, der an ihrer Schürze baumelte.

Auf dem langen, blankgescheuerten Holztisch in der Mitte der Küche stand an einer Ecke unser Frühstück, zwei Gläser mit angewärmter Milch, geschnittenes Brot, Butter, grobkörniger Weißkäse und Rübensirup. Mutter nahm das Baby hoch, setzte sich zu uns und fragte, wie wir die erste Nacht auf dem Gut geschlafen hätten. Sie wollte am nächsten Tag zu Vater und den anderen Geschwistern zurückfahren.

„Ihr bleibt doch gern bei Oma und Opa, nicht wahr? In drei Wochen hole ich euch wieder ab. Ich hoffe, ihr vergesst mich bis dahin nicht."

Wir kauten unsere dick beschmierten Brote und nickten nur. Dann setzte sich Großvater neben uns, eine der Mägde stellte ihm einen Teller hin und er zerschnitt mit dem Taschenmesser seine in Fett gebratene Brotscheibe mit dem Spiegelei darauf. Er spießte die Stücke mit der Messerspitze auf und schob sie sich in den Mund. Mir hatte Großmutter verboten, das Brot mit dem Messer zu essen. Es sei eine sehr dumme und gefährliche Angewohnheit, hatte sie gesagt und dabei kopfschüttelnd Großvater angesehen. Nach dem Essen stopfte Großvater seine Pfeife, legte sie neben den Teller, trank seinen Kaffee aus, zündete die Pfeife an und erhob sich. Großvater frühstückte jeden Tag zweimal, und wenn wir zu Besuch waren, aß er sein zweites Frühstück, das tägliche Bratbrot mit Ei, mit uns zusammen. Dann neckte er Dorle,[11] kniff sie in die Wange, und da er harte, mit Hornhaut überzogene Finger hatte, tat das weh, so dass Dorle aufschrie. Mit mir sprach er über die Arbeit, die ich zu erledigen hatte. Ihm missfiel, dass ich mich lieber in mein Zimmer verzog, um Bücher zu lesen, und mich einen ganzen Tag draußen herumtreiben konnte, ohne etwas Vernünftiges zu tun. Er war grob zu uns, auch mit Großmutter ging er sehr schroff um, aber das war seine Art. Wenn er uns seine Zuneigung zeigen wollte und uns in den Arm nahm, war er derb, und wir

which lunch was taken out into the fields, and kept running to the linen basket in order to talk to the baby. Grandmother had disappeared into the store room. The room was always locked, only grandmother had a key, which dangled from her apron.

On the long, shiny, polished wooden table in the middle of the kitchen our breakfast was placed at one corner: two glasses of warmed milk, slices of bread, cottage cheese and sugarbeet syrup. Mother picked the baby up and sat down beside us and asked whether we had slept well during our first night on the estate. She wanted to go back to father and our other siblings the next day.

'You like staying with grandma and grandpa, don't you? I will collect you again in three weeks' time. I hope you won't forget me before then.'

We were chewing our thickly buttered bread and just nodded. Then grandfather sat down next to us, and one of the maids put a plate in front of him and with his pocket knife he cut his piece of bread, which had been fried in fat and had a poached egg on top. He speared the pieces with the tip of his knife and shovelled them into his mouth. Grandmother had forbidden me to eat bread with my knife. It was a stupid and dangerous habit, she had said, looking at grandfather and shaking her head. After he had eaten, grandfather filled his pipe, put it down next to his plate, finished his coffee, lit his pipe and got up. Grandfather had a second breakfast every day, and when we were visiting he had his second breakfast, the daily fried bread with egg, together with us. Then he teased Dorle and pinched her cheek, but as he had hard fingers with horny skin it hurt, causing Dorle to shriek. To me he talked about the work he wanted me to do. He disapproved of the fact that I preferred to disappear to my room to read books or that I could roam around outside all day without doing anything constructive. He was rough with us, and he was also quite abrupt with grandmother, but that was his way. When he wanted to show us affection and took us into his arms, he was heavy-handed and we

versuchten deshalb, seinen Umarmungen zu entgehen. Nach den Sommerferien hatten wir blaue Flecken, wo er uns angefasst hatte. Großvater war eben sehr stark, er konnte, wie er sagte, nur „richtig zufassen". Er war so ein kräftiger Kerl, wie ich einer werden sollte, aber wenn ich so arbeitete, wie er es von mir verlangte, taten mir der Rücken und die Arme weh, ich war völlig zerschlagen[12] und meine Muskeln wuchsen trotz aller Plackerei[13] überhaupt nicht. Doch er lachte mich aus, wenn ich mich beklagte, und sagte nur, ich dürfe nicht so viele Pausen machen und Bücher lesen.

Nach dem Frühstück ging Großvater auf den Hof. Ich stellte unsere Teller und Gläser in die gusseiserne Spüle und sagte, dass ich in den Pferdestall wolle.

Ich rannte hinaus. Vor dem Kuhstall standen die Schweizer und rauchten, sie lehnten an der Wand und unterhielten sich. Ich grüßte sie, aber sie reagierten nicht. Plötzlich hörte ich Großvaters laute Stimme. Die Schweizer traten rasch ihre Zigaretten aus und verschwanden im Kuhstall. Großvater kam vom hinteren Hof, wo der Misthaufen war und die Pforte zum Wald. Mit der rechten Hand hielt er einen sehr dünnen Mann am Kragen und stieß ihn, unablässig schimpfend, vor sich her. Sie gingen in Großvaters Büro, oder vielmehr führte Großvater den dünnen Mann mit einem Rucksack dorthin. Als sie im Haus verschwunden waren, lief ich ihnen hinterher. Ich öffnete die Tür zum Kontor, in dem die Sekretärin, Fräulein Bump, saß. Sie nickte mir zu und beugte sich dann wieder über ihre Schreibmaschine.

Der Raum war durch eine hölzerne Barriere geteilt. Hier wurden Lieferanten und Kunden empfangen, jedenfalls diejenigen, die nicht wichtig genug waren, um direkt in Großvaters Büro geführt zu werden, wo es eine Eckbank und Sessel für die Besucher gab. An der Barriere wurde auch der Lohn an die Landarbeiter ausgezahlt. Hier lagen die Tageszeitung und das Grüne Blatt aus und stapelten sich die Briefe und Postkarten, die nicht für die Groß-eltern oder das Büro bestimmt waren. Hinter der Barriere stand der Schreibtisch von Fräulein Bump, der Registerschrank mit den zwei hölzernen Rolläden, die beim Öffnen über und unter den

therefore tried to avoid his embraces. After the summer
holidays we had bruises where he had taken hold of us. Grandfather was just so strong; he could, as he said, really get stuck in.
He was the strong fellow I wanted to become, but when I
worked as he wanted me to, my back and arms ached, I felt
completely shattered and my muscles did not grow in spite of
all this drudgery. But he just laughed at me when I complained
and just said I should not have so many breaks and not read
books.

After breakfast grandfather went out into the yard. I put our
plates and glasses into the cast-iron sink and said that I wanted
to go to the horses' stable.

I ran out. The dairymen were standing in front of the cow
shed smoking; they were leaning against the wall talking. I
greeted them, but they did not react. Suddenly I heard grandfather's loud voice. The dairymen quickly put their cigarettes
out and disappeared into the cowshed. Grandfather came from
the back part of the yard where the dung-heap and the gate to
the woods were. With his right hand he was holding a very thin
man by his collar, pushing him along and shouting at him the
whole time. They went into grandfather's office, or rather grandfather led the thin man with his rucksack there. When they had
disappeared into the house, I ran after them. I opened the door
to the office where the secretary, Miss Bump, was sitting. She
gave me a nod and then bent over her typewriter again.

The room was divided by a wooden counter. Here trades-
men and customers were received, at least all those who were
not important enough to be taken directly into grandfather's
office, which had a corner bench and an armchair for visitors.
The wages for the farm workers were paid over the counter.
Here lay the daily newspaper and *Das Grüne Blatt*, and a pile of
letters and postcards which were neither for my grandparents
nor the office. Behind the counter were Miss Bump's desk and
the register cupboard with two wooden roller blinds, which slid
over the top and under the bottom of the cupboard when opened;

Schrank geschoben wurden, daneben ein Aktenschrank und der Tresor, ein schwerer grüner Klotz aus Stahl.

Ich öffnete die Klappe der Barriere und ging zu der offen stehenden Tür, hinter der Großvaters Büro lag. Fräulein Bump zischte mir leise zu, dass ich nicht hineindürfe, dass Großvater beschäftigt sei, doch ich tat, als höre ich sie nicht, und lief rasch in das benachbarte Zimmer. Fräulein Bump kam mir hinterher, blieb aber an der Tür stehen, warf einen Blick auf Großvater und kehrte unentschlossen um. Ich stellte mich neben der Tür an die Wand. Der dünne Mann saß auf der Eckbank, blickte auf seine Hände, die seine Mütze zerknautschten, und schwieg. Auf Großvaters Fragen antwortete er nicht und sah ihn nicht an, er blickte unverwandt auf seine Hände nach unten. Doch auf Großvaters Fragen musste er auch nicht antworten, es waren keine Fragen, die man hätte beantworten können. Zwei Knechte hatten den Mann erwischt, als er eine Gans mit dem Taschenmesser getötet hatte und gerade in seinem Rucksack verstauen wollte. Sie hatten ihn gefasst und zu Großvater gebracht, und nun wollte Großvater von ihm wissen, warum er die Gans gestohlen hatte und warum er ein so schlechter Mensch sei und ob er nicht wisse, dass Stehlen eine schlimme Sünde sei.

Großvater fasste ihn am Jackett, mit einer Hand griff er gleichzeitig beide Jackenaufschläge, Großvater nannte das: am Schlafittchen nehmen,[14] und drehte sie zusammen, so dass der Mann verloren darin hing. Dann zog er ihn zu sich heran und stieß ihn überraschend gegen die Rücklehne der Holzbank. Im Rucksack des Mannes, den er noch immer umgeschnallt hatte, knackte es laut. Großvater sah mich an, doch er sagte nichts und verzog auch nicht unzufrieden das Gesicht, wie er es sonst tat, wenn ihm etwas nicht passte. Er nahm den Mann wieder am Revers.

„Was hast du für einen Beruf?" fragte er.

„Lehrer", sagte der Mann heiser, „ich bin Lehrer."

„Was bist du?" rief Großvater. „Lehrer? Was will denn einer wie du den Kindern beibringen. Das Stehlen, du Hund, du verfluchter?"

„Wir sind Aussiedler, Spätaussiedler",[15] flüsterte der Mann eindringlich, „wir haben nichts mehr."

next to it were a filing cabinet and a safe, a huge green block of steel.

I opened the flap of the counter and went towards the open door, behind which lay grandfather's office. Miss Bump hissed at me softly that I wasn't allowed in, that grandfather was busy, but I pretended not to hear and ran quickly into the adjacent room. Miss Bump followed me, but stopped at the door, cast a glance at my grandfather and went back indecisively. I stationed myself next to the door against the wall. The thin man was sitting on the corner bench looking at his hands, which were crumpling up his cap, and saying nothing. He wouldn't answer Grandfather's questions or look at him, but simply stared fixedly down at his hands. But he did not have to answer grandfather's questions, they were questions which couldn't be answered. Two farm hands had caught the man when he had killed a goose with his pocket knife and was just about to stow it away in his rucksack. They had seized him and taken him to grandfather, and now grandfather wanted to know from him why he had stolen the goose and why he was such a bad person and whether he was aware that stealing was a terrible sin.

Grandfather seized him by the jacket, grabbing it by both lapels at the same time – grandfather called this collaring – and squeezing them together so that the man was left dangling helplessly inside it. Then he pulled him towards him and then pushed him unexpectedly against the back rest of the wooden bench. In the man's rucksack, which he still had on his back, there was a loud crackling sound. Grandfather looked at me, but he said nothing, nor did he pull an irritated face, as he normally did if something did not suit him. He took the man again by the lapel.

'What sort of job do you have?' he asked.

'Teacher,' said the man hoarsely, 'I am a teacher.'

'What are you?' shouted grandfather. 'A teacher? What has someone like you got to teach children? Stealing, you damned dog?'

'We are evacuees, late evacuees,' whispered the man imploringly. 'We have nothing left.'

„Ach was, Aussiedler bin ich selber. Da musst du halt von vorne anfangen. Aber mit Arbeit, nicht mit Stehlen."

Mein Großvater nahm ihn wieder am Jackett, zog ihn zu sich und stieß ihn mit all seiner Kraft gegen die Lehne der Bank. Der Lehrer stöhnte leise auf.

„Hast du Arbeit?"

Der Mann nickte.

„Dann hau ab, und lass dich hier nie wieder blicken. Hast du verstanden?"

Der Mann schob sich ängstlich auf der Bank entlang.

„Lehrer willst du sein und weißt nicht einmal, wie man eine Gans schlachtet. Du hast sie massakriert, aber nicht geschlachtet, du Bandit. Du hättest sie ausbluten lassen müssen. Jetzt ist der Vogel aasig, den kannst du wegschmeißen. Hau ab. Na, für einen Lehrer ist er gut genug. Hau ab. Und noch eins, Lehrer, mach das nicht noch einmal: stehlen und sagen, dass du Aussiedler bist. Auch ein Aussiedler muss wie ein Mensch leben."

Der dünne Mann schob sich mit dem Rücken an der Wand entlang und ging, unverwandt auf Großvater blickend, langsam zur Tür, um rasch hinauszuhasten. Großvater setzte sich an seinen Schreibtisch und blätterte in einem Bündel Papiere. Er hatte seine dicke gelbe Hornbrille aufgesetzt, mit der man ihn kaum erkannte, weil er sie selten trug. Den Daumen befeuchtete er fortwährend an seiner Unterlippe.

„Hast du gemerkt, was der alles im Rucksack hatte?" fragte er, ohne aufzublicken. „Das hat ganz schön geklirrt, nicht wahr. Der hat sicher ein paar Eier stibitzt.[16] Na, nun wird er einen schönen Brei nach Hause bringen."

Großvater lächelte zufrieden.

„Und so etwas will Lehrer sein. Habt ihr auch solche Lehrer?"

Ich schüttelte den Kopf. Ich glaubte nicht, dass Fräulein Kaczmarek oder Herr Greschke Gänse oder Eier stahlen. Ich versuchte mir vorzustellen, wie Großvater meinen Geschichtslehrer am Revers nimmt und auf die Bank schmeißt und wie Herr Greschke, den Rucksack mit den gestohlenen Eiern auf dem

'So what? I am an evacuee myself. You just have to start again, but by working, not stealing.'

My grandfather took him again by his jacket, pulled him towards him and pushed him with all his might against the arm-rest of the bench. The teacher moaned quietly.

'Do you have work?'

The man nodded.

'Then push off, and don't ever show up here again. Do you understand?'

The man was sliding timidly along the bench.

'You claim to be a teacher and don't even know how to kill a goose. You massacred it, you did not kill it, you bandit. You should have allowed it to bleed. Now the bird is putrid, you might as well throw it away. Push off. For a teacher it will be good enough. Push off. And one more thing, teacher, don't do that again: steal and say that you are an evacuee. Even an evacuee has to live like a human being.'

The thin man slid with his back along the wall, constantly looking at grandfather, and went slowly towards the door only to rush out quickly. Grandfather sat down at his desk and thumbed through a pile of papers. He had put on his thick yellow horn-rimmed glasses; you hardly recognized him when he had them on, as he wore them so rarely. He wet his thumb constantly on his lower lip.

'Did you notice what a lot of things he had in his rucksack?' he asked without looking up. 'That smashed into nice little pieces, didn't it? He most likely pocketed a few eggs. Well, he will be bringing some nice purée home.'

Grandfather smiled contentedly.

'And something like that claims to be a teacher. Do you have such teachers?'

I shook my head. I did not think that Miss Kaczmarek or Mr Greschke stole geese or eggs. I tried to imagine how grandfather would take my history teacher by the lapel and hurl him on the bench and how Mr Greschke, the rucksack with the stolen eggs on his back, would sit in front of him

Rücken, vor ihm sitzt und demütig und verlegen zu ihm aufsieht, aber es gelang mir nicht. Nein, meine Lehrer stahlen nicht. Ich hatte zu viel Angst vor ihnen, um das glauben zu können.

„Und du?" fragte Großvater. „Was hast du jetzt vor?"

„Ich gehe in den Pferdestall."

„Mach das. Aber geh nicht zu dem Hengst, das ist ein tückischer Belgier. Und mach dich nützlich, du bist alt genug."

Großvater blätterte weiter in den Papieren, und ich ging hinaus. Jetzt war der Hof leer, am Kuhstall war niemand zu sehen. Die Hunde lagen in der Sonne und öffneten nur schläfrig die Augen, als ich an ihnen vorbeilief. Ein paar Hühner kratzten auf dem Misthaufen, sie mussten im Drahtgitter ein Loch gefunden haben. Im Pferdestall lud Alfred, der Knecht mit dem großen roten Muttermal am Hals, den Dung auf eine Holzkarre. Ich sagte ihm Guten Tag, aber er erwiderte nichts. Mit der Schaufel stocherte er im Pferdemist, dann stellte er die Schaufel ab, holte seine Pfeife aus der Schürzentasche und stopfte sie. Nachdem er sie angebrannt hatte, nahm er die Karre auf und schob sie an mir vorbei zum Hof hinaus. Als er an mir vorbeiging, sagte er, die Pfeife zwischen die Zähne geklemmt und ohne mich anzusehen: „Hat mir der Chef einen Aufpasser geschickt?"

Mir war unbehaglich, aber ich blieb dennoch im Pferdestall. Ich fragte Alfred, ob ich ihm helfen könne, aber er meinte nur, ich solle aufpassen, dass ich mich nicht schmutzig mache.

Am nächsten Tag, gleich nach dem Mittagessen, brachte Großmutter Mutter und das Baby mit dem Auto an die Bahn, und Dorle und ich durften mitfahren und winken, bis sich der Zug in Bewegung setzte. Großmutter tröstete Dorle, weil die das Gesicht verzog, als der Zug verschwunden war. „In drei Wochen holen euch Vati und Mutti mit dem Auto ab, und drei Wochen trägt die Katze mit dem Schwanz fort."[17]

Dorle weinte nicht. Sie wollte aber wissen, warum Großmutter so etwas sage und wie die Katze das mache.

Großvater hatte sich bereits am Morgen von Mutter verabschiedet. Er war mit dem Motorrad zum Landratsamt gefahren. Man hatte ihn hinbestellt, weil man, wie er sagte, ihm wohl wieder mal

humble and embarrassed, but I couldn't manage it. No, my teachers did not steal. I was too afraid of them to be able to imagine that.

'And you? What do you want to do now?'

'I am going to the horses' stable.'

'Do that. But don't go to the stallion, he is a treacherous Belgian. And make yourself useful, you are old enough.'

Grandfather went on thumbing through the papers and I went out. Now the yard was empty; at the cow shed there was no one to be seen. The dogs were lying in the sun and only sleepily opened their eyes when I ran past them. A few chickens were scratching around on the dung-heap; they must have found a hole in the wire fence. In the horses' stable Alfred, a farm hand with a big red birthmark on his neck, was loading dung on to a wooden cart. I said hello to him but he did not reply. He was poking the dung about with his shovel, then he put the shovel down, took his pipe from his apron pocket and filled it. After he had lit it he lifted up the cart and pushed it past me out into the yard. When he went past me he said, the pipe clenched between his teeth and without looking at me, 'Has the boss sent me a minder?'

I felt uncomfortable, but in spite of that I stayed in the stable. I asked Alfred whether I could help him, but he only said that I should take care that I did not get dirty.

The next day, straight after lunch, my grandmother took mother and the baby to the station by car and Dorle and I were allowed to go along and wave until the train started moving. Grandmother comforted Dorle, because she was pulling a face when the train had moved off. 'In three weeks daddy and mummy will be coming by car to fetch you, and three weeks is something the cat carries off on her tail.'

Dorle did not cry. But she wanted to know why grandmother was saying something like this and how the cat did this.

Grandfather had already said goodbye to my mother in the morning. He had gone to the district council by motorbike. He had been asked to go there because, as he put it, they wanted to

erklären wolle, wie man eine Kuh melkt. Er hatte es auf dem Hof gesagt, ganz laut, und noch ein paar Ausdrücke drangehängt, dass Großmutter ganz blass geworden war und nur Jessesmaria vor sich hin murmelte. Beim Frühstück hatte er die Arbeit verteilt und angekündigt, dass er erst am Nachmittag zurück sein und alles kontrollieren werde. Und dann hatte er sich die alte Lederkappe, eine Fliegermütze aus dem Weltkrieg, über seine Glatze gezogen, so dass er wie ein alter Uhu aussah, und war auf seiner Zündapp vom Hof gefahren.

Er kam spät zurück. Wir hatten bereits mit den Arbeitern in der Gutsküche Abendbrot gegessen, die Schweizer waren im Kuhstall verschwunden, und nur die Köchin und die beiden Küchenhilfen waren bei Großmutter in der Küche geblieben. Sie wuschen das Geschirr ab und bereiteten die Mahlzeiten für den nächsten Tag vor. Ich war noch einmal auf den Hof gegangen und saß mit Jochen, einem ein Jahr älteren Jungen, dem Sohn eines Gutsarbeiters, auf dem großen Querbalken des Hoftores. Im vergangenen Jahr hatte ich für Jochen gelogen. Er hatte einen Frosch mit einem Strohhalm aufgeblasen und das unförmige, bewegungslose Tier mit einem Stein plattgequetscht. Sein jüngerer Bruder hatte es ihrem Vater gepetzt,[18] und als dieser Jochen zur Rede stellte und ihn ohrfeigen wollte, behauptete ich, dass wir mit einem toten Frosch gespielt hätten, mit einem Frosch, den eine der Katzen zuvor zu Tode getatzelt habe.[19] Mein Einspruch verwirrte Jochens Vater. Er sah mich finster an, und ich wiederholte meine Behauptung. Ich spürte, dass er mir nicht glaubte, aber ich bemerkte auch, dass er nicht wusste, wie er sich verhalten sollte. Schließlich ließ er seinen Sohn los, ohne ihn zu schlagen, und drohte uns beiden fürchterliche Strafen an, falls er uns jemals dabei erwischen sollte, wie wir ein Tier quälten. Als er weggegangen war, fragte mich Jochen, ob ich schon einmal eine Pistole gesehen habe, kein Kinderspielzeug, sondern eine richtige, eine aus dem Krieg. Ich nickte und sagte, dass bei mir zu Hause einige Jungen richtige Pistolen besäßen und Armeedolche und Ledergürtel mit dem verbotenen Hakenkreuz auf dem Koppelschloß. Er fragte mich, ob er mir seine Pistole zeigen solle, und ich nickte. Ich musste schwören, keinem davon zu

explain to him again how to milk a cow. He had said so in the yard very loudly and had added a few more expressions so that my grandmother went quite pale and just murmured 'Holy Mother of God' to herself. At breakfast he had given out the work and had announced that he wouldn't be back until the afternoon and that he would check everything. Then he had put the old leather cap, a pilot's hat from the war, on his bald head, so that he looked like an old owl, and had driven away out of the yard on his Zündapp.

He came back late. We had already had supper with the workers in the farm kitchen, the dairymen had disappeared into the cowshed and only the cook and the two kitchen hands had stayed with grandmother in the kitchen. They were washing the dishes and preparing the meals for the next day. I had gone out into the yard again and was sitting on the cross beam of the farm gate with Jochen, a boy who was a year older than me and the son of one of the estate workers. Last year I had told a lie for Jochen. He had inflated a frog with a straw and had then squashed the enormous immobile animal with a stone. His younger brother had blabbed it out to his father, and when he challenged Jochen and was going to box his ears, I claimed that we had been playing with a dead frog which a cat had killed with her paws. My intervention confused Jochen's father. He looked at me darkly and I repeated my claim. I sensed that he did not believe me but I also noticed that he did not know how he should react. Eventually he let his son go without hitting him and threatened us both with terrible punishment should he ever catch us torturing an animal. When he had gone Jochen asked me whether I had seen a pistol before, not a toy but a real one from the war. I nodded and said that at home several boys had a real pistol and army knives and leather belts with forbidden swastikas on the buckles. He asked me whether he should show me his pistol and I nodded. I had to swear not to tell anyone, especially not his brother. Then he fetched from the

erzählen, vor allem nicht seinem Bruder. Dann holte er die ange-
rostete Wehrmachtspistole, in einen öligen Putzlappen gewickelt,
aus dem Haus und wir gingen damit in den Wald. Er zeigte mir,
wie man sie auseinander nimmt und wieder zusammensetzt, und
ich durfte sie auch halten. Seit diesem Tag waren wir befreundet.

Wir saßen auf dem Torbalken und stießen uns mit dem Fuß ab,
so dass der gesamte Torflügel mit dem Balken sich langsam
bewegte und wir im großen Bogen über der Einfahrt schwebten,
als wir Großvaters Motorrad hörten. Rasch sprangen wir herunter,
um den Torflügel weit zu öffnen. Großvater fuhr direkt in die offen
stehende Garage. Ich rannte hinterher und half ihm, sie zu verschließen. In der Küche setzte sich Großvater an den langen
Holztisch und aß schweigend sein Abendbrot. Großmutter fragte
ihn, was der Landrat gewollt hätte, aber er knurrte nur und antwortete nicht. Als er gegessen hatte, räumte Großmutter das Geschirr
weg und stellte ihm eine Flasche Leichtbier hin. Sie setzte sich ihm
gegenüber und sah ihm zu, wie er seine Pfeife stopfte und
anzündete.

„Was hast du? Warum guckst du so katholisch,[20]
Wilhelm?"

„Es ist wieder mal vorbei", sagte Großvater, ohne seine Frau
anzusehen.

„Was redest du? Kannst du dich etwas deutlicher ausdrücken?"

„Es ist vorbei, Klara. Wir werden unsere Sachen packen müssen."

Großvater sah auf. Mit leicht zusammengekniffenen Augen
schaute er zu seiner Frau. Er schien zu lächeln, aber genau konnte
ich es nicht erkennen. Beide sahen sich an und sagten lange Zeit
kein Wort. Ich saß neben Großvater und wartete darauf, dass er
endlich weiterspräche, doch er deutete nur wortlos mit dem Kopf
zu den beiden Küchenhilfen, und Großmutter sagte: „Nun macht
Schluss. Für heute ist genug. Macht Feierabend, Mädchen."

Die zwei nickten erfreut, verabschiedeten sich und liefen hinaus,
und Großmutter sagte zu mir: „Und für dich ist es auch Zeit.
Dorle liegt schon im Bett. Geh dich waschen. Und lass nicht die
ganze Nacht in deinem Zimmer das Licht brennen. Du wirst dir

house the rusty army pistol, which was wrapped in an oily cleaning rag, and we went out into the wood with it. He showed me how you took it apart and put it together again, and I was also allowed to hold it. From that day onwards we were friends.

We were sitting on the beam of the gate and pushed ourselves off with our feet so that the whole wing of the gate with the beam moved slowly and we were suspended in the arch over the entrance, when we heard grandfather's motorbike. We jumped off quickly in order to open the wing of the gate wide. Grand-father drove straight into the open garage. I ran after him and helped him to close it. In the kitchen grandfather sat down at the long wooden table and ate his supper in silence. Grand-mother asked him what the district administrator had wanted from him, but he only grumbled and did not answer. When he had finished eating, grandmother cleared the dishes away and put a bottle of light beer in front of him. She sat down opposite him and watched him as he filled his pipe and lit it.

'What is the matter with you? Why are you looking so pious, Wilhelm?'

'It is over again,' said grandfather without looking at his wife.

'What are you saying? Could you express yourself a little more clearly?'

'It is over, Klara. We will have to pack our bags.'

Grandfather looked up. Squinting a little, he looked at his wife. He seemed to smile, but I could not really make it out. Both of them looked at each other and did not say a word for a long time. I was sitting next to grandfather and was waiting for him to continue, but he just nodded without a word in the direc-tion of the kitchen hands and grandmother said, 'Finish up now, that's enough for today. Call it a day, girls.'

The two nodded delightedly, said goodbye and rushed out, and grandmother said to me, 'And it's time for you, too. Dorle is already in bed. Go and have a wash. And don't leave the light

die Augen verderben und musst dein ganzes Leben lang eine Brille tragen."

„Es ist noch nicht mal neun. Und vor neun muss ich nicht ins Bett."

„Geh schon, Junge, lass Großvater seinen Feierabend."

Ich schob mich langsam auf der Bank entlang und stand auf. Am Ausguss nahm ich eins der dort abgestellten Gläser und ließ das Wasser lange ablaufen, bevor ich das Glas füllte und trank. Ich tat alles sehr gemächlich,[21] um noch möglichst lange in der Küche bleiben zu können. Ich wollte wissen, was Großvater zu sagen hatte, es musste etwas Wichtiges sein, da er noch immer schwieg und nur ab und zu durch die Nase schnaufte und Großmutter ihre Arbeit unterbrochen hatte.

„Was ist denn nun passiert, Wilhelm?"

„Am 20. August kommt ein neuer Inspektor. Ich wurde abgesetzt. Seiffert sagt, wir können auf dem Gut bleiben. Ich soll mir aussuchen, was ich arbeiten will. Feld oder Stall, aber nicht mehr als Inspektor."

„Jesses.[22] Aber warum?"

„Die alte Geschichte, Klara. Erst hat mich Seiffert eine Stunde warten lassen. Als er endlich Zeit für mich hatte, hat er mir Honig ums Maul geschmiert. Wie sehr er meine Arbeit schätzt, dass im ganzen Kreis nur mein Gut Jahr für Jahr den Plan und die Abgaben erfüllt, dass er mich überall als Vorbild rausstreicht und so. Schließlich fragte er, wie es auf dem Gut steht, und ich habe gesagt, dass noch viel zu tun ist. Dass ich mit den rotweißen Milchkühen erst angefangen habe, dass wir eine zweite Schafherde aufbauen, dass die Stallungen noch nicht fertig sind, na, das weißt du alles selbst."

Großvater sah zu mir, sagte aber nichts, so dass ich mich weiter mit dem Abtrocknen des Glases beschäftigte. Großmutter schüttelte unaufhörlich den Kopf und murmelte etwas, was ich nicht verstand. Dann sprach Großvater weiter. Er sagte, er hatte sich vom Landrat schon verabschiedet und bereits an der Tür gestanden, als Seiffert aufgestanden sei und ihn gefragt habe, wie lange er sich noch gegen die neue Zeit sträuben wolle.[23] Er habe gleich gewusst,

on all night in your room. You will ruin your eyes and then you will have to wear glasses all your life.'

'It's not even nine o'clock. And I never have to go to bed before nine.'

'Off you go, boy, let grandfather have his time off.'

I slowly slid along the bench and got up. At the sink I took one of the glasses which had been put there, and let the water run for a long time before I filled the glass and drank. I did everything very slowly in order to be able to stay in the kitchen as long as possible. I wanted to know what grandfather had to say; it had to be something important, because he was still silent, just breathing heavily through his nose every now and then, and grandmother had interrupted her work.

'So, now what happened, Wilhelm?'

'On 20 August a new inspector is coming. I have been sacked. Seiffert says we can stay on the estate. I should choose what work I want to do. In the fields or in the stable, but no longer as an inspector.'

'Lord alive, but why?'

'The same old story, Klara. First, Seiffert let me wait for an hour. When he finally had time for me, he buttered me up. How much he valued my work, that in the whole district only my estate was meeting the targets and yields every year, that he held me up as a model to everyone, and so on. Finally he asked me how things were on the estate and I told him that there was still a lot to be done. That I had only just started with the red and white dairy cows, that we were building up a second herd of sheep, and that the stables were not ready yet, well, you know all that yourself.'

Grandfather looked at me but did not say anything, so I went on busying myself drying the glass. Grandmother was constantly shaking her head and murmuring something which I did not understand. Then grandfather went on. He said he had already said goodbye to the district administrator and had been standing at the door when Seiffert had got up and asked him how long he intended to resist the new age. He had known straight

worauf der aus sei, aber er habe sich dumm gestellt. Seiffert habe ihn gefragt, was mit ihm und der Partei sei. Da habe er gesagt, er sei in Schlesien in keiner Partei gewesen und habe das Gut ordentlich geführt, und er könne auch jetzt ein Gut leiten, ohne in eine Partei einzutreten. Seiffert habe auf den Tisch geschlagen und ihn gefragt, ob er ein Feind der neuen Ordnung sei.[24] Nein, habe Großvater gesagt, er sei kein Feind, er sei Landwirt, und er brauche Saatgut mit Qualität wie vor dem Krieg und ausreichend Viehfutter, wenn er das Soll schaffen wolle, und mit einem Parteiabzeichen kriege er kein Ferkel groß. Seiffert sei an die Tür gegangen, hinter der seine Sekretärin sitzt, habe sie aufgerissen und gebrüllt, dass sich dann ihre Wege trennen müssten, er werde das Staatsgut keinem erklärten Feind der neuen Ordnung ausliefern, keinem unbelehrbaren Helfershelfer der alten Großgrundbesitzer,[25] die lange genug auf Kosten des Volkes gelebt hätten und nun ganz zu Recht und endlich und endgültig enteignet worden seien. Drohend habe er gefragt, ob er ihn verstanden habe, und daraufhin die Tür zum Vorzimmer zugeschlagen. Dann habe er Großvater ganz freundlich gebeten, sich wieder hinzusetzen. Er habe seinen Stuhl genommen, sich neben ihn gesetzt und ihn ohne seine Brüllerei gefragt, ob er nicht doch daran denken könne, in die Partei einzutreten. Er könne ihn sonst nicht als Inspektor eines Staatsgutes halten, nicht in Holzwedel und nicht sonstwo. Er habe sich lange genug vor ihn gestellt, ihn immer wieder verteidigt, aber nun müsse Großvater ihm mal einen Schritt entgegenkommen. Dabei habe er ihm die Hand auf die Schulter gelegt und ihn plötzlich Wilhelm genannt. Großvater habe entgegnet, er sei Christ[26] und habe mit der Partei nichts zu schaffen, aber der Landrat habe gesagt, wenn er Christ sei, so sei das seine Privatangelegenheit und habe damit überhaupt nichts zu tun. Auch seine eigene Frau sei gläubig, aber wenn man das nicht an die große Glocke hänge, kümmere das niemanden. Er schlage ihm vor, gleich den Aufnahmeantrag für die Partei zu stellen, er selbst würde für ihn bürgen, und er könne sich sogar das Gut aussuchen, das er haben wolle, und wenn es Holzwedel bleibe, habe er nichts dagegen. Großvater hatte nur mit dem Kopf geschüttelt.

away what he was getting at, but he had pretended not to understand. Seiffert had asked him what he felt about the party. Then he had said that he had not been in any party in Silesia and that he had run the estate well and that he could also run the estate now without joining a party. Seiffert had hit the table and asked him whether he was an enemy of the new order. No, grandfather had said, he was not an enemy but a farmer and he needed quality seeds like before the war and enough animal feed if he was to meet his targets, and a party emblem would not help him raise his piglets. Seiffert had then gone to the door behind which his secretary was sitting, had pulled it open and shouted that they would then have to go their separate ways, that he would not hand over a state-owned estate to a declared enemy of the new order, not to an incorrigible collaborator of the old great landowners, who had been living long enough at the expense of the people and who had now quite rightly been finally expropriated. Menacingly he had asked whether he had understood him and then slammed the door to the anteroom shut. Then he had asked grandfather in a quite friendly manner to sit down again. He had taken his chair and sat down next to him and without any shouting asked him whether he might consider joining the party after all. Otherwise he could not support him as an inspector of a state-owned estate, either in Holzwedel or anywhere else. He had protected him long enough, defended him time and again, but now grandfather had to make a concession to him. While saying that he had put his hand on his shoulder and had suddenly started calling him Wilhelm. Grandfather had replied that he was a Christian and would have nothing to do with the party, but the district administrator had replied that if he was a Christian, that was his private business and had nothing to do with it. His own wife was also a believer, but so long as you didn't shout it from the rooftops, no one would be bothered. He suggested that he should apply for membership of the party immediately, he would vouch for him, and he could then even choose the estate he wanted to have, and if that happened to be Holzwedel he had nothing against it. Grandfather had just

Darauf sei der Landrat aufgestanden und habe gesagt, er müsse ihn als Inspektor absetzen, aber er könne mit der Frau in Holzwedel bleiben, er sei ein guter Bauer. Von einem staatlichen Leiter müsse er aber noch mehr verlangen. Ich kann nicht anders, Wilhelm, habe er schließlich gesagt, und damit habe er ihn entlassen. Die Sekretärin im Vorzimmer habe bereits die Papiere fertig gehabt, er musste sie nur noch unterschreiben. Der Name des neuen Inspektors für Holzwedel stand auf dem Papier, ein gewisser Karl Bergmann. Es sei ein verdienstvoller Genosse aus Magdeburg, habe ihm die Sekretärin mitgeteilt, ein Parteisekretär aus einer Maschinenfabrik. Großvater hatte unterschrieben, was ihm die Frau vorlegte. Jetzt ist eine neue Zeit, habe sie zu ihm gesagt, und er habe ihr geantwortet: Eine neue Zeit, gute Frau, beginnt mit jedem Tag, den Gott werden lässt. Daraufhin habe sie ihn mit offenem Maul angestarrt und gemeint, dass manche Leute nicht wissen, was gut für sie sei, und dass man die zu ihrem Glück zwingen müsse. Ja, habe er gesagt und sei noch einmal stehen geblieben, es gebe da richtige Künstler, die könnten sich ins eigene Gesicht spucken und hieltens noch für eine Erfrischung.

„Mach den Mund zu, Daniel", sagte Großvater und lächelte mich an. Ich hatte die ganze Zeit wie erstarrt neben dem Ausguss gestanden, Handtuch und Glas in den Händen, und mich bemüht, kein Geräusch zu verursachen, um die Großeltern nicht auf mich aufmerksam zu machen.

„Bist du denn noch immer nicht im Bett?" sagte Großmutter. Sie blickte nicht auf, und ich hörte ihrer Stimme an, dass sie weinte.

„Und was soll werden?" fragte sie. Sie hatte mich wohl schon wieder vergessen.

„Na, was schon. Arbeiten können wir beide doch."

„Ich will aber nicht hier wegziehen. Ich will nicht schon wieder lostrecken."

„Es geht aber nicht nach dir. Und was kommen soll, kommt."

„Warum musstest du dich mit dem Landrat anlegen. Mit deiner Sturheit bringst du uns noch mal ins Gefängnis. Ist es denn eine Sünde, umgänglich zu sein?"

shaken his head. Then the district administrator had got up and said that he would have to sack him as inspector, but he could stay with his wife in Holzwedel, because he was a good farmer. But he had to expect a little more from a state manager. I have no choice, Wilhelm, he had finally said and had then let him go. The secretary had already got all the papers ready, he only had to sign them. The name of the new inspector for Holzwedel was on one of the papers, a certain Karl Bergmann. He was a worthy party member from Magdeburg, the secretary had told him, a party secretary from a machine factory. Grandfather had signed what the girl put in front of him. 'Now we are entering a new age,' she had said to him, to which he had replied, 'A new age begins with every day God gives us.' In response she had stared at him open-mouthed and said that some people did not know what was good for them and that they had to be forced towards their own good fortune. Yes, he had said, and had paused again, there were real artists in this respect who could spit into their own faces and still regard it as refreshing.

'Close your mouth, Daniel,' said grandfather, smiling at me. I had been standing at the sink all the time as if struck dumb, towel and glass in hand, and had tried not to make a noise so as not to attract my grandparents' attention.

'Have you still not gone to bed?' said grandmother. She did not look up and I could hear in her voice that she was crying.

'And what is to happen?' she asked. She seemed to have forgotten me again.

'Well, what do you think? We're both able to work, aren't we?'

'I don't want to move away. I don't want to start all over again.'

'That's not in our hands. And what is meant to be is meant to be.'

'Why did you have to get into an argument with the leader of the council? You will get us into prison with your stubbornness. Is it really a sin to be a little flexible?'

„Was hab ich denn gesagt? Er hat mich gefragt und ich habe ganz höflich nein gesagt. Das war alles. ‚Wenn du einen besseren Mann für Holzwedel hast', habe ich gesagt, ‚gehen wir eben. Wenn du mich nicht brauchst, ich hab dich nicht nötig.' " Er wandte sich zu mir: „Jetzt hast du alles mitbekommen, nun verschwinde endlich."

Dorle schlief bereits, als ich in unser Zimmer kam. Ich machte die Lampe neben meinem Bett an und suchte das Bettzeug und die Wände nach Spinnen ab, bevor ich mich hinsetzte und auszog. Die Sachen legte ich über den Stuhl. Ich bemühte mich nicht, leise zu sein, ich wollte Dorle wecken.

„Mach das Licht aus."

„Gleich. Soll ich dir etwas erzählen?"

„Morgen. Lass mich schlafen."

„Du darfst es aber keinem weitersagen. Es ist noch geheim."

„Lass mich schlafen."

„Opa geht weg."

„Geht weg? Wohin denn?"

„Er verschwindet von Holzwedel. Wir müssen alle weg. Opa, Oma, und wir beide auch."

„Warum denn?"

„Die Partei sagt das, sagt Opa."

„Die Partei? Was ist denn das?"

„Weißt du das nicht?"

„Nein."

„Dann kann ich dir das auch nicht erklären."

„Weil du es nicht weißt."

„Ich weiß es."

„Sag es doch."

„Das sind die Bestimmer."

„Die Bestimmer? Was bestimmen die denn?"

„Alles."

„So wie die Russen und die Amerikaner?"

„Was haben denn die damit zu tun! Das ist etwas ganz anderes."

„Nein, das sind die Bestimmer. Tante Magdalena hat mir

'What have I said? He asked me and I politely said no. That was all. "If you have a better man for Holzwedel," I said, "we will go. If you don't need me, I don't need you."' He turned to me, 'Now you have heard everything, it is time you were off.'

Dorle was already asleep when I came into our room. I turned on the light next to my bed and searched the bedding and the walls for spiders before I sat down and got undressed. I put my things over the chair. I made no attempt to be quiet, I wanted to wake Dorle.

'Turn the light off.'

'In a minute. Shall I tell you something?'

'Tomorrow. Let me sleep.'

'But you must not tell anyone. It is a secret.'

'Let me sleep.'

'Grandpa is going away.'

'Going away? Where to?'

'He's leaving Holzwedel. We must all leave. Grandpa, grandma and the two of us as well.'

'What for?'

'The party says so, says grandpa.'

'The party, what's that?'

'Don't you know?'

'No.'

'Then I can't explain it to you.'

'Because you don't know.'

'I do know.'

'Then tell me.'

'They are the decision-makers.'

'The decision-makers? What do they decide then?'

'Everything.'

'Like the Russians and the Americans?'

'What have they got to do with it? That's something quite different.'

'No, they are the decision-makers. Aunt Magdalena has told

gesagt, in Deutschland bestimmen jetzt die Russen und die Amerikaner."

„Die bestimmen ganz andere Sachen. Das verstehst du nicht. Du hast ja noch nie einen Russen oder einen Amerikaner gesehen."

„Du vielleicht?"

„Ich habe schon drei Russen gesehen."

„Aber keine richtigen."

„Die waren richtig, allerdings. Die waren sehr richtig, das kannst du mir glauben."

„Und ich habe schon einen Amerikaner gegessen."

„Ooh, bist du blöd. Was du gegessen hast, war doch kein richtiger Amerikaner."

„Ich weiß. Und warum muss Opa weg?"

„Weils die Partei so sagt."

„Ja, aber warum?"

„Warum! Wenn du Bestimmer bist, musst du das nicht erklären. Du bestimmst einfach und fertig."

„Aber was passiert mit Opas Karnickeln und mit den Pferden? Nimmt er die mit, wenn er weggeht?"

„Die kann er nicht mitnehmen. Die gehören ihm doch nicht. Die bleiben natürlich hier."

„Aber dann, dann sehen wir sie nicht mehr."

„Natürlich nicht. Wenn Opa weggeht, dürfen wir auch nicht mehr hierher. Hör auf zu heulen."

Aber Dorle heulte[26] noch lauter und wollte das Licht anmachen, und ich verbot es ihr, weil ich den Kasten nicht mehr sehen wollte und mich bereits unter mein Deckbett verkrochen hatte.

Am nächsten Morgen hat sie gleich der Großmutter erzählt, was ich ihr gesagt hatte, und Großmutter hat sich zu ihr aufs Bett gesetzt und sie in den Arm genommen, und dann haben beide geheult.

Großvater teilte mir nach dem Frühstück keine Arbeiten zu. Er sagte an diesem Morgen überhaupt nichts. Ich hatte erwartet, dass er oder Großmutter mit mir schimpfen würden, weil ich Dorle alles erzählt hatte, aber sie sagten nichts. Sie saßen am Tisch und sahen uns beim Frühstück zu, vor Großvater stand sein Bratei, aber er rührte den Teller nicht an.

me, in Germany the Russians and the Americans make the decisions now.'

'They decide quite different things. You don't understand. You have never seen a Russian or an American.'

'Have you, then?'

'I have seen three Russians.'

'But not real ones.'

'They were real, honest. Believe me, they were very real.'

'And I have eaten an American.'

'Oh, you are stupid. What you have eaten wasn't a real American.'

'I know. But why must grandpa go?'

'Because the party says so.'

'Yes, but why?'

'Why! If you are a decision-maker you don't need to explain that. You simply decide and that's it.'

'But what is going to happen to grandpa's rabbits and to the horses? Will he be taking them with him?'

'He can't take them with him. They don't belong to him. They will stay here, of course.'

'But then, then we won't see them any more.'

'Of course not. When grandpa goes away, we won't be allowed to come here any more either. Stop crying.'

But Dorle cried all the more loudly and wanted to turn the light on. But I forbade it because I did not want to see the box and had already crawled under my bed cover.

The next morning she immediately told grandmother what I had told her and grandmother sat down next to her on the bed and took her in her arms, and then they both wept.

Grandfather gave me no jobs to do after breakfast. He said nothing at all that morning. I had expected he or grandmother would tell me off because I had told Dorle everything. But they said nothing. They sat at the table and watched us having breakfast; grandfather's poached egg was standing in front of him, but he did not touch the plate.

The Suspect

JUREK BECKER

Der Verdächtige

Ich bitte, mir zu glauben, daß ich die Sicherheit des Staates[1] für etwas halte, das wert ist, mit beinah aller Kraft geschützt zu werden. Hinter diesem Geständnis[2] steckt nicht Liebedienerei und nicht die Hoffnung, ein bestimmtes Amt könnte mir daraufhin gewogener sein[3] als heute. Es ist mir nur ein Bedürfnis, das auszusprechen, obschon man mich seit geraumer Zeit für einen hält, der die erwähnte Sicherheit gefährdet.

Daß ich in solchen Ruf gekommen bin, erschüttert mich und ist mir peinlich. Nach meiner Kenntnis habe ich nicht den kleinsten Anlaß gegeben, mich, wessen auch immer, zu verdächtigen. Seit meiner Kindheit bin ich ein überzeugter Bürger, zumindest strebe ich danach. Ich weiß nicht, wann und wo ich eine Ansicht geäußert haben könnte, die sich nicht mit der vom Staat geförderten und damit nicht mit meiner eigenen deckte; und sollte es mir unterlaufen sein, so wäre es nur auf einen Mangel an Konzentration zurückzuführen. Das Auge des Staates ist, hoffe ich, geübt und scharf genug, Gefährdungen als solche zu erkennen, wie über Kleinigkeiten hinwegzusehen, die alles andere als gefährdend sind. Und doch muß etwas um mich herum geschehen sein, das Grund genug war, ein Augenmerk auf mich zu richten. Vielleicht versteht mich jemand, wenn ich sage: Ich bin inzwischen froh, nicht zu wissen, was es war. Wahrscheinlich würde ich, wenn ich es wüßte, versuchen, den ungünstigen Eindruck zu verwischen und alles nur noch schlimmer machen. So aber kann ich mich unbeschwert bewegen, zumindest bin ich auf dem Weg dorthin.

Es wird inzwischen klargeworden sein, daß man mich observiert.[4] Erheblich kompliziert wird meine Lage dadurch, daß ich solch ein Verfahren im Prinzip für nützlich, ja geradezu für

The Suspect

Please believe me that I regard the security of the state as something that is worth protecting with almost all one's might. It is
not sycophancy and the hope that a certain government department might be more kindly disposed towards me that lies
behind this confession. I just have a need to say it, even though I
have been regarded for some time as someone who endangers
the aforementioned security.

That I should have gained such a reputation shocks
and embarrasses me. As far as I know I have not given the
slightest cause to be suspected of anything whatever. Since
my childhood I have been a committed citizen, at least I
have striven to be. I have no idea where and when I might
have expressed an opinion that did not conform to that
promoted by the state and hence did not coincide with my
own; if I did slip up, it could only be due to a lack of con-
centration. The eye of the state, I hope, is experienced and
sharp enough to recognize dangers as such and overlook
trifles that are anything but dangerous. And yet something
must have happened around me which provided sufficient
reason to focus attention on me. Perhaps someone will understand me when I say: now I am glad that I do not know what it
was. If I knew I would probably try to efface the unfavourable
impression and just make everything worse. As it is I can go
about my business in a carefree manner; at least I am getting
there.

In the meantime it will have become clear that I am being
observed. My situation is complicated considerably by the fact
that I regard such a procedure as useful in principle, indeed as

unverzichtbar halte, in meinem Fall jedoch für sinnlos und, wenn ich offen sein darf, auch für kränkend.

Ein Mann namens Bogelin, den ich bis dahin der Regierung gegenüber für loyal gehalten hatte, sagte mir eines Tages, man beobachte mich. Natürlich brach ich den Umgang mit ihm auf der Stelle ab. Ich glaubte ihm kein Wort, ich dachte: Ich und beobachtet! Fast hatte ich die Sache längst vergessen, als mich ein außerordentlicher Brief erreichte. Er schien zunächst von einem Bekannten aus dem Nachbarland[5] zu kommen, mit dem ich in der Schulzeit gut befreundet war. Es war ein Umschlag von der Art, wie er sie seit Jahren benutzte, darauf waren seine Schrift und hinten sein gedruckter Name. Doch nahm ich einen Brief aus dem Kuvert heraus, der nichts mit ihm und nichts mit mir zu tun hatte: er war an einen Oswald Schulte gerichtet und von einer Frau Trude Danzig unterschrieben, zwei Menschen, von deren Existenz ich bis zu jenem Augenblick nichts gewußt hatte. Sofort fiel mir Bogelins Hinweis wieder ein: es mußten im Amt für Überwachung die Briefe nach der Kontrolle verwechselt worden sein. Es läßt sich auch anders sagen: Ich hatte nun den schlüssigen Beweis, daß man mich observierte. Jeder weiß, daß man in Augenblicken der Bestürzung zu Kopflosigkeit neigt, nicht anders ging es mir. Ich nahm, kaum hatte ich den Brief gelesen, das Telefonbuch, fand Oswald Schultes Nummer und rief ihn an. Nachdem er sich gemeldet hatte, fragte ich, ob er Trude Danzig kenne. Es war eine ganz und gar überflüssige Frage, nach dem Brief, doch ich in meiner Panik stellte sie. Herr Schulte sagte, ja, Frau Danzig sei ihm gut bekannt, und er fragte, ob ich eine Nachricht von ihr hätte. Ich war schon drauf und dran, ihm zu erklären, was uns so eigenartig zusammenführte, als ich mit einem Schlag begriff, wie unwahrscheinlich dumm ich mich verhielt. Ich legte auf und saß verzweifelt da; ich sagte mir, nur eben viel zu spät, daß man wohl auch die Telefone derer überwacht, in deren Briefe man hineinsieht. Für das Amt befand sich nun der eine Überwachte zum anderen in Beziehung. Zu allem Unglück hatte ich auch noch das Gespräch abgebrochen, bevor von den vertauschten Briefen die Rede gewesen war. Gewiß, ich hätte Oswald Schulte ein zweitesmal anrufen und ihm

essential, but in my case as pointless and, if I may speak freely, offensive.

A man called Bogelin, whom I had regarded as loyal to the government until then, told me one day that I was being observed. Naturally I broke off all contact with him immediately. I did not believe a word of what he said: me under observation! I had almost put the whole matter well behind me when an extraordinary letter reached me. At first it seemed that it was from an acquaintance from the Neighbouring State with whom I had been good friends at school. It was an envelope of a type that he had been using for years; it had his handwriting on it and on the back his name was printed. But the letter I took out of the envelope had nothing to do with him or me: it was addressed to a certain Oswald Schulte and signed by a certain Mrs Trude Danzig, two people of whose existence I had known nothing until that moment. I immediately remembered Bogelin's hint again: the letters must have got mixed up in the bureau of surveillance after they had been checked. To put it another way: I now had conclusive evidence that I was being watched. We all know that in moments of shock we can be inclined to panic and I did not behave any differently. I had hardly finished reading the letter when I grabbed the telephone book, found Oswald Schulte's number and rang him. When he answered I asked him whether he knew Trude Danzig. It was an altogether superfluous question after the letter, but I in my panic asked it. Mr Schulte replied, yes he knew Mrs Danzig well and he asked whether I had a message from her. I was about to explain to him what strange circumstances had brought us together, when it suddenly hit me how unbelievably foolishly I was behaving. I put the receiver down and sat there in a state of despair. I said to myself, only far too late, that people whose letters are inspected probably have their telephones tapped. As far as the bureau was concerned, one person under surveillance was now in contact with another. And to make things even worse I had broken off the conversation before any reference had been made to the mixed-up letters. Of course I could have rung

die Sache auseinandersetzen können; in den Ohren von Mithör-
enden hätte es wie der Versuch geklungen, meinen Kopf aus
der Schlinge zu ziehen, dazu auf eine Art und Weise, die man
mir leicht als Verleumdung des Amtes hätte auslegen können.[6]
Und abgesehen davon war es mir auch zuwider, diesem Herrn
Schulte, den man ja wohl nicht grundlos überwachte, etwas zu
erklären.

Lange hielt ich still, um nicht noch einmal voreilig zu sein,
dann faßte ich einen Plan. Ich sagte mir, daß sich ein falscher
Ausgangspunkt eine eigene Logik schaffe, daß plötzlich eine
Folgerichtigkeit entstehe, die dem sich Irrenden zwingend
vorkomme. Der Verdacht, unter dem ich stand, war solch ein
falscher Ausgangspunkt, und jede meiner üblichen Hand-
lungen, zu anderer Zeit harmlos und ohne Bedeutung für das
Amt, konnte ihn bestätigen und immer wieder untermauern.
Ich mußte also, wollte ich den Verdacht entkräften, nur lange
genug nichts tun und nichts mehr sagen, dann würde er mangels
Nahrung aufgegeben werden müssen. Diese Prüfung traute ich mir
zu als jemand, der lieber hört als spricht und lieber steht als geht.
Ich sagte mir zum Schluß, ich sollte mit meiner Rettung nicht
lange warten, sie dulde keinen Aufschub, wenn es mir ernst sei mit
mir selbst.

Das Erste war, ich trennte mich von meiner Freundin, die in den
Augen des Amtes für Überwachung womöglich eine schlechte
Freundin für mich war. Kurz ging mir durch den Sinn, sie könnte
mit zum Überwachungspersonal gehören, sie hatte unverhüllten
Einblick in alle meine Dinge; doch fand ich dafür keinen Anhalts-
punkt, und ich verließ sie ohne solchen Argwohn. Ich will nicht
behaupten, die Trennung habe mir nichts ausgemacht, ein Unglück
aber war sie nicht. Ich nahm den erstbesten Vorwand und bauschte
ihn ein wenig auf, zwei Tage später befand sich in meiner Wohnung
nichts mehr, was ihr gehörte. Am ersten Abend nach der Trennung
war ich einsam, die ersten beiden Nächte träumte ich nicht gut, dann
war der Abschiedsschmerz überwunden.

In dem Büro, in dem ich angestellt bin, täuschte ich eine
Stimmbandsache vor, die mir beim Sprechen, das behauptete ich

Oswald Schulte a second time and explained the matter to him; to the ears of those who were listening in it would have sounded like an attempt to wriggle out of it and, more than that, in a way which could easily have been construed as defamatory towards the bureau. And apart from all that I was averse to explaining anything to this Mr Schulte, who might well not be under surveillance without reason.

For a long time I kept quiet to avoid doing anything rash again, then I made a plan. I said to myself that when you start in the wrong place this creates its own logic, then suddenly a logical consistency is generated, which must appear compelling to the person who has made the erroneous assumption. The suspicion under which I was held was just such a wrong starting point and all my normal activities, which would have been harmless and without meaning at other times in the eyes of the bureau, would only confirm and corroborate it. So if I wished to dispel the suspicion I just had to do and say nothing for long enough, and then it would have nothing to feed on and would have to be abandoned. I regarded myself as capable of passing this test, as I am someone who prefers to listen rather than speak, to stand rather than walk. And finally I told myself that I should not delay my salvation, that it would not survive any deferment if I was serious about myself.

First of all I broke off with my girlfriend, who in the eyes of the bureau of surveillance might possibly be regarded as a bad girlfriend for me. It briefly went through my mind that she might be part of the surveillance staff, she had complete insight into all my affairs; but I found no basis for such an assumption and so I left her without any such suspicion in mind. I do not wish to claim that I did not care about the separation, but it was not a disaster. I seized the first available pretext, magnified it a little; two days later there was nothing left in my flat that belonged to her. On the first evening after the separation I was lonely, my dreams were not too good the first two nights, then the pain of separation was overcome.

In the office in which I was employed I pretended that there was something wrong with my vocal cords, which, as I claimed

ein paarmal krächzend, Schmerzen bereite. So fiel es keinem auf, daß ich zu schweigen anfing. Die Gespräche der Kollegen machten einen Bogen um mich herum, der bald so selbstverständlich wurde, daß ich die Stimmbandsache nicht mehr brauchte. Es freute mich zu sehen, daß ich mit der Zeit kaum noch wahrgenommen wurde. Zur Mittagspause ging ich nicht mehr in die Kantine, ich brachte mir belegte Brote und zu trinken mit und blieb an meinem Schreibtisch sitzen. Ich gab mir Mühe, ständig auszusehen wie jemand, der gerade nachdenkt und nicht dabei gestört zu werden wünscht. Ich überlegte auch, ob ich mich von einem guten Angestellten in einen nachlässigen verwandeln sollte. Ich meinte aber, daß gewissenhafte Arbeit, wie sie mir immer selbstverständlich war, unmöglich zu der Verdächtigung hatte führen können; daß eher Schlamperei ein Grund sein könnte, den Blick nicht von mir wegzunehmen. So blieb als einzige von meinen Gewohnheiten unverändert, daß ich die Arbeit pünktlich und genau erledigte.

Ich hörte einmal, auf der Toilette, wie zwei Kollegen sich über mich unterhielten. Es war wie ein letztes Aufflackern von Interesse an meinen Angelegenheiten. Der eine sagte, er glaube, ich müsse wohl Sorgen haben, ich hätte meine alte Munterkeit verloren. Der andere erwiderte: Das gibt es, daß einem dann und wann die Lust auf Geselligkeit vergeht. Der eine sagte, man sollte sich vielleicht ein wenig um mich kümmern, vielleicht sei ich in einer Lebensphase, in der ich Zuspruch brauche. Der andere beendete das Gespräch mit der Frage: Was geht es uns an? – wofür ich ihm von Herzen dankbar war.

Ich war auch schon entschlossen, mein Telefon abzumelden und tat es doch nicht: es hätte den Eindruck erwecken können, als wollte ich eine Überwachungsmöglichkeit beseitigen. Allerdings benutzte ich den Apparat nicht mehr. Ich hatte keinen anzurufen, und wenn es klingelte, ließ ich den Hörer liegen. Nach wenigen Wochen rief niemand mehr an bei mir, ich hatte elegant das Telefonproblem gelöst. Kurz fragte ich mich, ob es nicht verdächtig sei, als Telefonbesitzer niemals zu telefonieren. Ich antwortete mir, ich müsse mich entscheiden zwischen einem Teil und seinem

a few times in a croak, made talking painful. So no one noticed that I started to be silent. The conversations of colleagues gave me a wide berth, which soon became so natural that I no longer needed to resort to the problem with my vocal cords. It pleased me to see that in time I was barely noticed at all. At lunchtime I no longer went to the canteen, I brought sandwiches and something to drink and stayed at my desk. I made an effort to constantly look like someone who is thinking about something and who does not want to be disturbed in his deliberations. I also considered whether I should change from being a good employee to being a sloppy one. I was of the opinion, however, that conscientious work, as I had always taken it for granted, could not possibly have given rise to suspicion; that sloppiness might rather be a reason for them not to take their eyes off me. So of all my habits the only one that remained unchanged was that I performed my work punctually and precisely.

I once overheard two colleagues talking about me while I was on the toilet. It was like the last flicker of interest in my affairs. One of them said he thought I must have worries, I had lost all my cheerfulness. The other one replied: that happens if you lose the desire to be sociable every now and then. The first one said, perhaps they ought to look after me a little, perhaps I was in a phase in my life when I needed a little encouragement. The first one finished the conversation with the question: what's it got to do with us? – for which I was heartily thankful.

I had already made up my mind to have my telephone disconnected, but then I did not go through with it after all: it might have created the impression that I wished to eliminate a means of surveillance. However, I did not use the telephone any more. I had nobody to ring, and if it rang I did not pick up the receiver. After a few weeks nobody rang my number any more; I had smartly solved the telephone problem. For a short time I asked myself whether it was suspicious that, as the owner of a telephone, I never rang anyone. I told myself that I had to decide between that and its opposite, I could not regard both as

Gegenteil; ich könne nicht alles beides für gleich verdächtig halten, ansonsten bliebe mir ja nur, verrückt zu werden.

Ich änderte mein Verhalten überall dort, wo ich Gewohnheiten entdeckte, zu diesem Zweck studierte ich mich mit viel Geduld. Manche der Änderungen schienen mir übertrieben, bei manchen fühlte ich mich albern; ich nahm sie trotzdem vor, weil ich mir sagte: Was weiß man denn, wie ein Verdacht entsteht? Ich kaufte einen grauen Anzug, obwohl ich kräftige und bunte Farben mag. Meine Überzeugung war, daß es jetzt am allerwenigsten darauf ankam, was mir gefiel. Wenn es nicht lebenswichtig war, verließ ich meine Wohnung nicht mehr. Die Miete zahlte ich nicht mehr im voraus und nicht mehr bar dem Hausbesitzer in die Hand, sondern per Postanweisung. Eine Mahnung, wie ich sie nie zuvor erhalten hatte, kam mir recht. Zur Arbeit fuhr ich manchmal mit der Bahn, manchmal ging ich den weiten Weg zu Fuß. An einem Morgen sprach mich ein Schulkind an und fragte nach der Zeit. Ich hielt ihm die Uhr hin, vom nächsten Tag an ließ ich sie zu Hause. Bis zur Erschöpfung dachte ich darüber nach, was Angewohnheit in meinem Verhalten war, was Zufall. Oft konnte ich die Frage nicht entscheiden, in solchen Fällen entschied ich für die Angewohnheit.

Es wäre falsch zu glauben, daß ich mich in meiner Wohnung unbeobachtet fühlte. Auch hierbei dachte ich: Was weiß man denn? Ich schaffte alle Bücher und Journale fort, deren Besitz ein schiefes Licht auf den Besitzer werfen konnte. Ich war mir anfangs sicher, daß sich solche Schriften nicht bei mir befanden, dann war ich aber überrascht, was alles sich eingeschlichen hatte. Das Radio und den Fernsehapparat schaltete ich mitunter ein, natürlich nur zu Sendungen, die ich mir früher niemals angehört und angesehen hatte. Wie man sich denken kann, gefielen sie mir nicht, und damit war auch dies Problem gelöst.

Während der ersten Wochen stand ich oft hinter der Gardine, stundenlang, und sah dem Wenigen zu, das draußen vor sich ging. Bald aber kamen mir Bedenken, weil jemand, der stundenlang am Fenster steht, am Ende noch für einen Beobachter gehalten wird oder für einen, der auf ein Zeichen wartet. Ich ließ die Jalousie

suspicious, otherwise I would only have one option left – to go mad.

I changed my behaviour in all areas where I found I had habits, and in order to do this I studied myself with great patience. Some of the changes seemed to go too far, others made me feel silly: I implemented them nonetheless, because I said to myself: how does one know how a suspicion arises? I bought a grey suit, even though I like strong and bright colours. I was convinced that it was of minimal importance whether I liked something. Unless it was essential I did not leave my flat any more. I no longer paid the rent in advance and no longer in cash directly to the owner of the house, but by postal order. All I wanted was a reminder, as I had never received one before. Sometimes I travelled to work by tram, sometimes I walked all the way. One morning a schoolchild stopped me and asked me the time. I showed him my watch and from the next day onwards I left it at home. To the point of exhaustion I pondered the question of which parts of my behaviour were habit and which were coincidence. Often I could not decide, in which case I opted for habit.

It would be mistaken to believe that I did not feel observed in my flat. On this point I also thought: what do they know? I disposed of all books and journals that might cast a bad light on their owner. Initially I was sure that there were no such publications in my possession, but then I was surprised to find what things had crept in. I occasionally switched on the radio and the television, of course only programmes which I would never have listened to or seen in former times. As you can imagine, they did not appeal to me, and so this problem too was solved.

During the first week I often stood behind the curtain for hours watching the little that went on outside. But soon I had doubts, because someone who stands at the window for hours could be taken for a spy or for someone waiting for a signal. I let the blind down and put up with the fact that

herunter und nahm in Kauf, daß man nun auf den Gedanken kommen konnte, ich wollte etwas oder mich verbergen.

Das Leben in der Wohnung spielte sich bei Lampenlicht ab, ich brauchte aber kaum noch Licht. Wenn ich nach Hause kam aus dem Büro, aß ich ein wenig, dann legte ich mich hin und dachte nach, wenn ich bei Laune war. Wenn nicht, dann döste ich vor mich hin und kam in einen angenehm sanften Zustand, der kaum von Schlaf zu unterscheiden war. Dann schlief ich wirklich, bis mich am Morgen der Wecker weckte, und so weiter. Ich ärgerte mich in jenen Tagen manchmal über meine Träume. Sie waren eigenartig wild und wirr und hatten nichts mit meinem wahren Leben zu tun. Ich schämte mich dafür ein wenig vor mir selbst und dachte, es sei ganz gut, daß man mich nicht auch dort beobachten konnte. Dann aber dachte ich: Was weiß man denn? Ich dachte: Wie schnell entfährt dem Schlafenden ein Wort, das dem Beobachter vielleicht zur Offenbarung wird. Ich hätte es in meiner Lage für leichtsinnig gehalten, mich darauf verlassen zu wollen, daß man mich nicht für meine Träume verantwortlich machte, sofern man sie erfuhr. Also versuchte ich, von ihnen loszukommen, was mir erstaunlich leicht gelang. Ich kann nicht sagen, wie der Erfolg zustandekam; die Stille und Ereignislosigkeit meiner Tage halfen mir sicherlich genauso wie der feste Vorsatz, das Träumen loszuwerden. Jedenfalls glich mein Schlaf bald einem Tod, und wenn das Klingeln mich am Morgen weckte, dann kam ich aus einem schwarzen Loch herauf ins Leben.

Es ließ sich hin und wieder nicht vermeiden, daß ich mit jemandem ein paar Worte wechseln mußte, beim Einkauf oder im Büro. Mir selber kamen diese Worte überflüssig vor, doch mußte ich sie sagen, um nicht beleidigend zu wirken. Ich verhielt mich nach besten Kräften so, daß mir keine Fragen gestellt zu werden brauchten. Wenn ich trotzdem gezwungen war zu sprechen, dann dröhnten mir die eigenen Worte in den Ohren, und meine Zunge sperrte und sträubte sich gegen den Mißbrauch.

Bald hatte ich es mir auch abgewöhnt, die Leute anzusehen. Es blieb mir mancher unschöne Anblick erspart, ich konzentrierte mich auf Dinge, die wirklich wichtig waren. Man weiß, wie leicht ein gerader Blick in anderer Leute Augen mit einer Aufforderung

someone might think that I wanted to hide something or myself.

I led my life in the flat under artificial light, but I hardly needed light any more. When I came home from the office I ate a little and then lay down and lost myself in thought, if I felt in the mood. If not, I dozed, slipping into a comfortable, gentle state which could hardly be distinguished from sleep. Then I really fell asleep until the alarm clock woke me in the morning, and so on. In those days I was sometimes annoyed about my dreams. They were strangely wild and confused and had nothing to do with my real life. They made me feel a little ashamed of myself and I thought that it was a good thing that I could not be observed there as well. But then I thought: what do they know? I thought: how easily does the sleeping person utter a word which may be a revelation to the observer. In my position I would have regarded it as reckless to rely on not being held to account for my dreams, should anyone find out about them. So I tried to rid myself of them, which I managed remarkably easily. I cannot say how this success was achieved; the silence and uneventfulness of my days contributed certainly as much as the resolve to shake them off. In any case my sleep soon resembled a kind of death, and when the ringing woke me in the morning I emerged from a black hole back into life.

Sometimes I could not avoid having to exchange a few words with someone when I was shopping or in the office. To me these words seemed superfluous, but I had to say them so as not to appear offensive. To the best of my ability I behaved in such a way that no questions needed to be addressed to me. Nevertheless, if I was forced to speak, then my own words resounded in my ears and my tongue balked at and struggled against the misuse.

Soon I had got out of the habit of looking at people. I was spared many an unpleasant sight and instead concentrated on things which were of real importance. One knows how easily a glance into the eyes of other people can be mistaken for an

zum Gespräch verwechselt wird, das war bei mir nun ausge-
schlossen. Ich achtete auf meinen Weg, ich achtete darauf, was ich
zu greifen oder abzuwehren hatte, zu Hause brauchte ich die
Augen kaum. Es kam mir vor, als bewegte ich mich sicherer jetzt,
ich stolperte und vergriff mich kaum mehr. Nach dieser Erfahrung
wage ich zu behaupten, daß ein gesenkter Blick der natürliche ist.
Was nützt es, frage ich, wenn einer stolz seinen Blick erhoben hat,
und ständiges Versehen die Folge ist? Es blieb mir auch erspart zu
sehen, wie andere mich ansahen, ob freundlich, tückisch, anteil-
nehmend oder mit Verachtung, ich brauchte mich danach nicht
mehr zu richten. Ich wußte kaum noch, mit wem ich es zu tun
hatte, das trug nicht wenig zu meinem inneren Frieden bei.

So verging ein Jahr. Ich hatte mir für diese Lebensweise keine
Frist gesetzt, doch nun, nach dieser ziemlich langen Zeit, regte sich
in mir der Wunsch, es möge bald genug sein. Ich spürte, daß ich
wie vor einer Weiche stand: daß mir die Fähigkeit, wie früher in
den Tag zu leben, Stück um Stück verlorenging. Wenn ich das
wollte, sagte ich zu mir, dann bitte, dann könnte ich in Zukunft so
weiterexistieren; wenn nicht, dann müßte jetzt ein Ende damit
sein. Dabei kam mir die Sehnsucht, die ich auf einmal nach der
alten Zeit empfand, ganz kindisch und auch unlogisch vor, und
trotzdem war sie kräftig da. Ich hielt es für wahrscheinlich, daß der
Verdacht, der über mich gekommen war, sich in dem Amt für
Überwachung inzwischen verflüchtigt hatte, es gab ja keine vernünftige andere Möglichkeit.

An einem Montagabend beschloß ich auszugehen. Ich stand in
meiner dunklen Stube und hatte weder Lust zu schlafen noch zu
dösen. Ich zog die Jalousie hoch, nicht nur einen Spalt breit, sondern bis zum Anschlag, dann machte ich das Licht an. Dann nahm
ich aus einer Schublade Geld – ich will erwähnen, daß ich auf einmal reichlich Geld besaß, weil ich das Jahr hindurch normal ver-
dient, jedoch sehr wenig ausgegeben hatte. Ich steckte mir also
Geld in die Tasche und wußte noch nicht recht wofür. Ich dachte:
Ein Bier zu trinken wäre vielleicht nicht schlecht.

Als ich auf die Straße trat, klopfte mein Herz wie lange
nicht mehr. Ohne festes Ziel fing ich zu gehen an, mein altes

invitation to a conversation; this was now ruled out in my own case. I concentrated on my route, I concentrated on what I had to take hold of or fend off, at home I hardly needed my eyes. It seemed to me that I was moving with greater assurance, I hardly ever stumbled or made a wrong move. As a result of this experience I hazard to suggest the downward gaze is the most natural. What is the use, I asked myself, of proudly raising your eyes if the consequence is constant slip-ups. I was also spared seeing how other people looked at me, whether kindly, maliciously, compassionately or with contempt; I did not need to take any notice of it any more. I hardly knew who I was dealing with, which contributed greatly to my peace of mind.

So a year went by. I had not set myself a time limit for this lifestyle, but now, after this rather long period of time, the wish was stirring within me that enough might soon be enough. I felt that I was standing at a crossroads, that my former ability to live for the day was being lost bit by bit. If I wanted to, I said to myself, I could continue existing like this in future; if not, there would have to be an end to it now. At the same time this longing which I was suddenly feeling for old times seemed childish or even illogical to me, and yet it was quite strong. I thought it was likely that the suspicion which had fallen on me in the bureau of surveillance had evaporated in the meantime; there was no other sensible alternative.

One Monday evening I decided to go out. I was standing in my dark room and felt like neither sleeping nor dozing. I pulled the blind up, not just a little but right to the top, then I turned the light on. Then I took some money out of a drawer – I would like to mention that I had plenty of money, because I had been earning as normal throughout the year, but spent very little. So I put some money in my pocket without quite knowing what for. I thought: a beer might not be a bad idea.

When I stepped out into the road my heart was beating as it had not done for a long time. Without having a fixed goal I

Stammlokal gab es inzwischen nicht mehr, das wußte ich. Die erste Kneipe, die mir verlockend vorkam, wollte ich betreten; ich dachte, wahrscheinlich würde es die allererste sein, die auf dem Weg lag. Ich nahm mir aber vor, nicht gleich am ersten Abend zu übertreiben: ein Bier zu trinken, ein paar Leute anzusehen, ihnen ein wenig zuzuhören, das sollte mir genügen. Selbst zu sprechen, das wäre mir verfrüht erschienen, in Zukunft würde es Gelegenheiten dafür geben, noch und noch. Doch als ich vor der ersten Kneipe ankam, brachte ich es nicht fertig, die Tür zu öffnen. Ich kam mir kindisch vor und mußte dennoch weitergehen, ich fürchtete auf einmal, alle Gäste würden ihre Augen auf mich richten, sobald ich in der Türe stand. Nach ein paar Schritten versprach ich mir fest, vor der nächsten Kneipe nicht noch einmal einer so törichten Angst nachzugeben. Aus purem Zufall drehte ich mich um und sah einen Mann, der mir folgte.

Daß er mir folgte, konnte ich im ersten Augenblick natürlich nur vermuten. Nach wenigen Minuten aber hatte ich Gewißheit, weil ich die dümmsten Umwege machte, ohne ihn loszuwerden. Er blieb in immer gleichem Abstand hinter mir, sogar als ich ein wenig rannte; es kam mir vor, als interessierte er sich nicht dafür, ob ich ihn bemerkte oder nicht. Ich will nicht behaupten, ich hätte mich bedroht gefühlt, und trotzdem packte mich Entsetzen. Ich dachte: Nichts ist zu Ende nach dem Jahr! Man hält mich nach wie vor für einen Sicherheitsgefährder, wie mache ich das bloß? Dann dachte ich, das Allerschlimmste aber sei ja doch, daß es auf mein Verhalten offenbar gar nicht ankam. Der Verdacht führte ein Eigenleben; er hatte zwar mit mir zu tun, ich aber nichts mit ihm. Das dachte ich, während ich vor dem Mann herging.

Als ich zu Hause ankam, ließ ich die Jalousie wieder herunter. Ich legte mich ins Bett, um über meine Zukunft nachzudenken; ich spürte schon die Entschlossenheit, nicht noch ein zweites Jahr so hinzuleben. Ich sagte mir, gewiß lasse sich die Sicherheit des Staates nur dann aufrechterhalten, wenn die Beschützer es an manchen Stellen mit der Vorsicht übertrieben; nichts anderes sei in meinem Fall geschehen und geschehe immer noch. Schließlich tat es ja nicht weh, beobachtet zu werden. Das letzte Jahr war mir

started walking, my old local did not exist any more, that much I knew. I wanted to go into the first pub which looked inviting; probably it would be the first one I came to. I intended not to overdo things the first evening: just to have a beer and look at a few people, listen to them a bit, that should be enough for me. Actually talking myself would have seemed premature, there would be opportunities for this in the future, plenty of them. But when I came to the first pub I could not bring myself to open the door. I felt childish but nevertheless I had to walk on, I was suddenly afraid that all the guests would turn their eyes on me as soon as I appeared in the door. After a few steps I promised myself not to give in to such foolish fears again in front of the next pub. By sheer chance I turned round and saw a man following me.

That he was following me was of course only something I could assume at first. A few minutes later, however, I had confirmation, because I made the silliest detours without shaking him off. He always stayed at the same distance from me even if I ran a little; it seemed to me that he did not care whether I noticed him or not. I do not want to claim that I felt threatened but nevertheless I was seized with terror. I thought: one year on and it's not over! I am still regarded as a security risk, how do I do it? Then I thought that the worst thing was that my behaviour did not matter at all. The suspicion had a life of its own; it had something to do with me, but I had nothing to do with it. That is what I was thinking while I was walking in front of the man.

When I got home I let down the blind again. I went to bed in order to consider my future; I already felt the resolve not to live for another year like this. I said to myself, surely the security of the state can only be maintained if those guarding it overdo it in some cases; nothing else had happened in my own case and still nothing was happening. After all, it did no harm being observed. The last year had not been forced upon me, I

nicht aufgezwungen worden, dachte ich, ich brauchte nicht nach Schuldigen zu suchen: ich hatte es mir selbst verordnet.

Dann schlief ich voll Ungeduld ein. Ich wachte vor dem Wecker-klingeln auf und konnte es kaum erwarten, dem ersten Menschen, der mich grüßte, in die Augen zu sehen und „Guten Tag" zu antworten, egal was daraus werden würde.

thought, I did not need to look for the guilty party: I had pre-scribed it for myself.

Then I fell asleep impatiently. I woke up before the alarm rang and could hardly wait to look the first person who greeted me in the eye and say, 'Good morning,' no matter what might come of it.

Notes on German Texts

THE LISTENER, or a Description of a Route with a Hidden Motive (*Lenz*)

1. *Laudatio*: A speech delivered to honour someone on a special occasion.

2. *Teofila Reich-Ranicki*: The wife of one of the most eminent literary critics of his generation, Marcel Reich-Ranicki, who did a great deal to promote an interest in contemporary fiction through his discussion programme *Das Literarische Quartett*, which ran for some years on German television. Previously Marcel Reich-Ranicki had been in charge of the Literary Supplement of the *Frankfurter Allgemeine Zeitung*.

3. *musterte die abgegriffene Ledermappe*: 'Mustern' suggests a critical attitude, which the critic's wife demonstrates subtly throughout this story. It is a key word that recurs in the course of the story. 'Abgegriffen', which is applied to the briefcase here, can also be used to refer to expressions or ideas to show that they are overused or outdated and therefore singularly lacking in originality. The worn briefcase foreshadows the unoriginal nature of its content.

4. *verdrossen*: This is an old-fashioned word; nowadays 'frustriert' is used instead.

5. *Wiedergutmachung*: This word is often used in a political context, for example in connection with compensation offered to German Jews for what they suffered in Hitler's Germany. It goes beyond the purely financial and also implies an accompanying fundamental change in attitude.

6. *er habe sich einzigartig gelangweilt*: 'Einzigartig' is usually used as a term of praise; it is therefore particularly ironic when applied to the state of being bored and is thus a withering criticism.

7. *und wie in der Erzählung verschlagen*: The word 'verschlagen' can denote

that someone has got to a particular geographical location by chance; in this instance the unexpected visit and reading have placed the critic's wife in this position in the author's story.

WAITING FOR THE GUESTS (*Wellershoff*)

1. *das Berliner Porzellan*: This refers to KPM (Königlich Preußische Manufaktur), the famous Berlin porcelain manufacturer.
2. *Filet Wellington*: i.e. Beef Wellington, beef in puff pastry.
3. *Er hätte wirklich anrufen müssen*: The use of the subjunctive underlines how acutely the narrator feels her lover's omission.
4. *Wolfgangs Geständnisse*: The word 'Geständnis' usually implies guilt; this is ironic, as his affair with the narrator should be a reason for Wolfgang to feel guilty, not the details he reveals to her about his relationship with his wife.
5. *allerhand Krempel*: 'Krempel' has negative connotations: it suggests that the items are of little value and use.

EATING MUSSELS (*Vanderbeke*)

1. *aufsässig*: This adjective is used to refer to the stubborn or rebellious behaviour of children, as here in this context; it can also refer to a rebellious group in society.
2. *Heidenrespekt*: This term is usually used by children to indicate a high level of respect. The word 'Heiden' is used colloquially to strengthen the emotional impact of the word.
3. *Schöngeist*: This word has derogatory overtones, implying an inability to deal with the practicalities of life.
4. *die ganze Winterreise*: Schubert composed this song-cycle in 1821 using a set of poems by Wilhelm Müller. It is a portrait of a love-sick wanderer. Following rejection in love, he ends up by resigning himself to his alienated state in the last song, 'The Hurdy-gurdy Man'. The parallel with the mother's personal fate is a bitter irony here, of which the children are unaware, but which the mother feels all the more keenly, as her tears indicate.
5. *Katzenmusik*: This derogatory term shows how the mother's musical

talents have been suppressed and how her violin has suffered through the bad conditions in which it has to be kept, culminating in its eventual destruction.

6. *das ist immer eine richtige Beerdigung gewesen*: The comparison with a funeral, which is reinforced by the use of 'beerdigen' as a verb in the next part of the sentence – 'im Schlafzimmerschrank beerdigt' – underlines the extent to which the mother had to abandon her musical talent.

THE GOOD OLD DAYS (*Wohmann*)

1. *die Gernsteins*: The name is a play on words, the couple being like stone, i.e. fossils, as illustrated by their unwavering dedication to habit.

LASCIA (*Hermann*)

1. *Lascia*: (Italian) Let go, give up.
2. *Catania*: A town in Sicily at the foot of Mount Etna, which was founded in 729 BC. Two earthquakes and an eruption of Mount Etna destroyed most of the buildings, though a Greek theatre, for example, has survived. The modern Catania is characterized by the many baroque buildings designed by the architect Vaccarini.
3. *Absteige*: This is a derogatory term, implying that the hotel is small and shabby and that its rooms are mostly rented by the hour.
4. *verschlagen*: The word is synonymous with 'schlau', but it is derogatory.
5. *in Francescos marodem Fiat*: The adjective 'marode' is originally an Austrian word meaning 'slightly ill'; in soldiers' slang during the Thirty Years War it was used to convey the fact that someone was unable to march. The more general meaning of 'exhausted' is now old-fashioned, and the term is now generally used to mean 'morally corrupt'. So it could be regarded as a transferred epithet in this context, as the things Francesco offers David to look at suggest that he is certainly morally corrupt.
6. *Capisci?*: (Italian) Do you understand?
7. *Capito*: (Italian) I have understood.
8. *Andiamo*: (Italian) Let's go.

CHICAGO/SHANTY TOWN (*Klein*)

1. *Es hat seinen eigenen Reiz, es bringt in aparte Verlegenheiten, als bloßer Gatte einer bekannten Musikerin durch die USA zu reisen*: This is a good example of the ironic tone of the story, particularly the phrase 'aparte Verlegenheiten': 'apart' is usually used to describe either the appearance of a woman who is attractive and stylish, but not necessarily beautiful, or a setting which is exquisite and stylish.

2. *stand der junge Mann . . . in Bereitschaft*: This phrase tends to be used to refer either to the police or to the army, when they are in a state of alert, for example before a major demonstration.

3. *der wackere Exil-Franke*: 'Wacker' is a synonym for 'tapfer', but it has the connotation of plucky in a plodding way rather than brave. Nuremberg, the town where the young academic was born, lies in the Bavarian province of Franconia. The term 'Exil-Franke' is ironic, as it plays on the contrast between his choice of working in a foreign environment and his continuing allegiance to the values of his provincial origins.

4. *ein infernalisches, von kurzen Ruhepausen gegliedertes Lärmen*: 'Infernalisch' is a synonym for 'höllisch'; it is frequently used in the compound noun 'Höllenlärm', which is usually used to describe a lot of noise generated by people.

5. *Und es müsste Ihnen einleuchten*: Stylistically this is a more elevated way of saying 'Sie müssten verstehen'; it has the implication that it would be rather difficult not to be convinced. It is used ironically here, as the association between the physical fitness of an avant-garde percussionist and the desire to take a partner on excessively long walks is not obvious.

6. *durch ihr forsches, federndes Ausschreiten*: The adjective 'forsch' creates an almost exaggerated emphasis here as it is already implied in the verb 'ausschreiten'. The verb 'ausschreiten' suggests that someone is taking determined possession of a territory, hence the impression here that the percussionist seems like a native wherever she appears abroad, in contrast to her husband, who radiates weariness and insecurity.

7. *Herr Hartstein*: The translation of 'Hardstone' is another ironic touch, as the promotion of the German language is bordering on the farcical here.

8. *in einem Anfall moralischer Schwäche*: 'Moralisch' is used ironically here as it is not referring to any moral principles but to morale in the sense of fighting spirit.

9. *Braun stehe mir unheimlich gut*: The wife's preference for brown has an ironic implication, as it was the colour of the shirts the SS wore; but her husband is the very opposite of all the SS stood for.

10. *'April April! Hereingelegt!'*: This is a saying in German used by someone who has successfully played a trick on someone or made someone believe in a tall story on April Fools' Day.

11. *Meine Frau, gegen die man jeden Luchs schwerhörig nennen muss*: This is a word play on the phrase 'Augen wie ein Luchs'; it is transferred to the sense of hearing here, as his wife is a musician, but it denotes the same ability, i.e. that of detecting the slightest change in the immediate environment without fail.

12. *Ich habe nach dem Abitur den Kriegsdienst verweigert . . . abgeleistet*: 'Abitur' is roughly equivalent to British A-Levels. Young men in Germany are required to do military service unless they can prove that they are genuine conscientious objectors, in which case they can replace it with a spell of civic duty ('Zivildienst'), doing work in the local community.

13. *deutsche Dienstpistole zweier Weltkriege*: Mr Arno is making use of the fact that these pistols were used during the two world wars to con customers into believing that they are genuine articles of the Nazi period, whereas in reality they were also standard issue to the military in the period of the DDR (Deutsche Demokratische Republik, the former Communist state of East Germany). The name he has given to these pistols – 'The Original Adolf's & Eve's Home Gun' – shows that he is targeting Nazi sympathizers.

14. *'Heißt das, Herr Arno, Sie haben sich auf Nazi-Devotionalien spezialisiert?'*: The use of 'Devotionalien' is ironic here, as it normally refers to religious objects such as rosaries or crosses, objects used in the course of worship.

15. *'Entwurf Albert Speer!'*: Albert Speer (1905–81) became Hitler's chief architect in 1934 and Minister of Armaments in 1942. He was the only member of the Nazi government to admit responsibility at the Nuremberg trials, where he was sentenced to twenty years' imprisonment, which he completed in Spandau jail in Berlin.

16. *Glimmstängel*: This is a derogatory term for cigarette; it denotes the narrator's desire not to fall back into the habit of smoking.

17. *ein aus der Lüneburger Heide ausgewanderter Sektierer*: The Lüneburg Heath is an isolated rural area in Lower Saxony.

18. *dass es sich unbekömmlich echauffiert hatte*: 'Unbekömmlich' is used predominantly in the context of eating to convey that something might not agree with someone; 'sich echauffieren' is an old-fashioned expression for 'sich aufregen'. The combination in the phrase 'sich unbekömmlich echauffieren' is deliberately quaint to illustrate that Arno is living in a cultural and linguistic time-warp.

19. *GUTENBERG*: Gutenberg's invention of the printing press facilitated the spread of Martin Luther's German bible. Arno wishes to spread Hitler's words, rendered in American English, as a warning against fascism.

20. *einen salzigen und einen süßen Ozean*: The North Sea and Baltic Sea on the one hand and Lake Constance on the other – the natural northern and southern boundaries of Germany.

GRANDFATHER AND THE DECISION-MAKERS (*Hein*)

1. *Gutsverwalter*: When the Soviet Zone became the DDR (Deutsche Demokratische Republik, Communist East Germany), the farming estates passed into state ownership and estate managers were appointed to run them.

2. *Landgut*: Before the Second World War there were large farming estates in the Eastern half of Germany in particular, which often belonged to aristocrats, who would employ managers to run them; such estates were often called 'Rittergut'.

3. *auf dem Treck*: As the Russian front moved westwards at the end of the Second World War people fled in large groups to escape from the advancing enemy.

4. *heimtückischen*: 'Heimtückisch' is a synonym for 'bösartig', but it is not as strong, the emphasis is more on the potential danger than on an underlying evil intent.

5. *kläfften*: This is a derogatory word for 'bellen'. It indicates that the barking is irritating.

6. *einen kräftigen Stups*: 'Stups' is a colloquial word for 'Schubs', a slight shove.

7. *feste Muckis*: 'Muckis' is a colloquial expression for 'Muskeln'. It is nowadays used in the colloquial term 'Muckibude', meaning fitness suite.

8. *Kopfnuss*: This means a slight tap with the knuckles against the head.

9. *bekam ich eine Standpauke zu hören*: This is a colloquial expression for to tell someone off.

10. *irgendetwas vorzuflunkern*: This is a colloquial expression, which is similar to 'to tell fibs' in English.

11. *Dann neckte er Dorle*: 'Necken' can be used in the sense of 'reizen', 'to tease', but it is usually more akin to 'scherzen', to have a joke.

12. *zerschlagen*: This is a more emphatic way of saying 'erschöpft' and always denotes distinct symptoms of physical discomfort.

13. *Plackerei*: This is a colloquial word for 'Anstrengungen', but it is stronger; a synonym is 'Schufterei', and both are akin to English 'drudgery'.

14. *am Schlafittchen nehmen*: This may have been adapted from 'Schlag-fittich', i.e. the wing of a goose. It is used in variations of the colloquial expression above in the sense of to challenge someone.

15. *Spätaussiedler*: These were people who left East Prussia after it had become Russian or Silesia after it had become Polish. They were allowed to move to East Germany, as it was part of the Eastern Bloc.

16. *stibitzt*: This was originally student language; it means 'swipe' or 'filch'.

17. *trägt die Katze mit dem Schwanz fort*: This is an idiom, which means that something is unimportant, almost irrelevant.

18. *hatte es ihrem Vater gepetzt*: 'Petzen' is a derogatory word, usually used by schoolchildren; it means to 'snitch' on someone.

19. *zu Tode getatzelt habe*: The verb 'tatzeln' is derived from the noun 'Tatze'; it means to hit with a paw.

20. *Warum guckst du so katholisch*: 'Katholisch' is not used in the literal sense of belonging to the Roman Catholic religion, but in the sense of pious and serious.

21. *gemächlich*: This is another word for 'langsam'; it has the implication that one either wants to relish what one is doing or simply that one wishes to delay the end of the activity as long as possible.

22. *Jesses*: This is used as an exclamation here much in the same way as one might use 'Jesus' in English.

23. *wie lange er sich noch gegen die neue Zeit sträuben wolle*: 'Sich sträuben' is similar in meaning to 'sich wehren'; the difference is that in the case of 'sich sträuben' the resistance is more passive than active.

24. *ob er ein Feind der neuen Ordnung sei*: This refers to the recently established Communist regime in the DDR.

25. *keinem unbelehrbaren Helfershelfer der alten Großgrundbesitzer*: This is Communist Party rhetoric. The former landowners were built up as the enemies of progress, hence the confiscation of all land and transfer into state ownership ('endgültig enteignet').

26. *er sei Christ*: Religion was not acceptable in the newly established Communist regime, at least not publicly ('aber wenn man das nicht an die große Glocke hänge').

27. *Aber Dorle heulte*: 'Heulen' tends to be a louder, more wailing sound than 'weinen'.

THE SUSPECT (*Becker*)

1. *die Sicherheit des Staates*: This is an ironic allusion to the STASI ('der Staatssicherheitsdienst'), the secret police in the former DDR (Deutsche Demokratische Republik, Communist East Germany), which had an elaborate spy network in order to trace any activity that was hostile to the regime.

2. *Hinter diesem Geständnis*: The use of 'Geständnis' is ironic here, as the narrator has stated in the previous sentence that this is not a 'confession' to a misdeed or a crime, but merely the statement of a conviction.

3. *gewogener sein*: The phrase 'jemandem gewogen sein' is an expression of bias or favour. The implication here is that the personal favour of officials is more crucial than any objective criteria.

4. *daß man mich observiert*: The use of the verb 'observieren' rather than 'beobachten' underlines the official nature of the observation.

5. *ein außerordentlicher Brief . . . von einem Bekannten aus dem Nachbarland*: The word 'außerordentlich' implies two things here: the envelope does not contain a letter from his friend in West Germany, but a letter between

two people who are strangers to him; at the same time, it is extraordinary because the regime classes any correspondence with someone in the West as unusual, hence suspicious. The irony of the situation is that this second fact does not occur to the narrator as the reason for why he might be being observed.

6. *die man mir leicht als Verleumdung des Amtes hätte auslegen können*: Imputing any actions by the secret service could be taken as slander, as the organization did not officially exist, but was classified as the Office for State Security.

Acknowledgements

For permission to reprint the German stories in this collection the publisher would like to thank the following.

Frankfurter Allgemeine Zeitung for 'Die Zuhörerin oder Eine absichtsvolle Wegbeschreibung' from *Frankfurter Allgemeine Zeitung* (25 March 2000).
Verlag Kiepenheuer & Witsch for 'In Erwartung der Gäste' from *Die Körper und die Träume* (Kiepenheuer & Witsch, 1993), © 1986, 1993 by Verlag Kiepenheuer & Witsch, Köln.
Sabine Groenewold Verlag from *Das Muschelessen* (Fischer Taschenbuch Verlag, 1997), © 1990 Rotbuch Verlag, Berlin.
Piper Verlag for 'Bessere Zeiten' from *Das Salz, bitte* (Piper Verlag, 1992), © 1992 Piper Verlag GmbH, München.
Judith Hermann for 'Lascia' from *Neue Erzählungen von 37 deutschsprachigen Autorinnen und Autoren*, edited by Katja Lange-Müller (Kiepenheuer & Witsch, 2002), © 2002 by Verlag Kiepenheuer & Witsch, Köln.
Rowohlt Verlag for 'Chicago Baracken', reprinted in *Von Den Deutschen* (Rowohft, 2002)
Suhrkamp Verlag for 'Grossvater und die Bestimmer' from *Von Allem Anfang An* (Suhrkamp Verlag, 2002), © 2002 Suhrkamp Verlag, Frankfurt am Main.
Suhrkamp Verlag for 'Der Verdächtige' from *Nach der ersten Zukunft* (Suhrkamp Verlag, 1980), © 1980 Suhrkamp Verlag, Frankfurt am Main.